THE BROKEN PROMISE

A MARINA COVE NOVEL, BOOK THREE

SOPHIE KENNA

The Broken Promise

A Marina Cove Novel, Book Three

By Sophie Kenna

© Copyright 2023

Cover design by Craig Thomas (coversbycraigthomas@gmail.com)

GET A FREE BOOK!

Sign up for my newsletter, and you'll also receive a free exclusive copy of *Summer Starlight*. This book isn't available anywhere else!

You can join at sophiekenna.com/seaside.

1

TWENTY-FOUR YEARS EARLIER

As a strange floating sensation coiled through Diane Keller's body, she instinctively tensed the muscles of her stomach, and for reasons that currently escaped her, a high-pitched giggle left her throat like a bubble breaking the surface of a pond. Elvis was singing "Blue Suede Shoes" on the crackling radio, and bizarrely, her little sister Charlotte's face popped into her mind. She briefly squeezed her eyes shut, trying to find the source of a melodic tinkling, a sound like a fine mist of snowfall against a frozen windowpane, a hand through wind chimes. Something tugged at her mind, something urgent...but it could wait.

Diane had all the time in the world. She knew it like she knew her own reflection.

Fading tangerine sunlight reached through the windows and splayed against the avocado-green dashboard of Trevor's old Plymouth Duster. The evening was hot, and the skin of Diane's legs stuck to the faded ripples of the vinyl seat. The irritable vibrations of the steering wheel through her fingertips had stopped, sending a brief but peaceful blanket of calm through the car's noisy interior. Mulholland Drive stretched out endlessly before her, and she gazed through the lush treeline to the Los Angeles valley below, the rise of Catalina Island and the infinite blue sea in the distance.

A swell of electric warmth stole across her skin as Trevor's strong but comforting hand tightened against her shoulder. She turned from the road to look at him, grinning. His brows were raised nearly to his hairline, and his mouth hung open.

Diane tilted her head slightly, confused. He looked...upset? More than that. Her stomach somersaulted as she saw the color slowly draining from his ruddy cheeks.

Furrowing her brows, she looked into the rearview mirror. Austin had one arm around Victoria. Oddly, Victoria's eyes were pinched shut, her face buried in Austin's chest. His other hand clutched the top of the front seat back, the skin of his knuckles blanched white. The cords of his neck stood out in harsh relief. Diane shook her head slightly, as if to clear the unexpected image. A cold ringing filled her ears.

As she turned back to face the road, gold and ruby light scattered suddenly around her, a beautiful kaleidoscope. The fragrance of saltwater and night-blooming jasmine carrying over the light breeze through the open windows was interrupted by the sharp, industrial edge of gasoline and exhaust. The floating sensation pulled harder at her core, like those thrilling weightless moments just after cresting the top of a roller coaster. Her heart fluttered like a hummingbird.

She regarded the road before her with a distant curiosity. Then, horror dawning over her, it finally clicked into place, the feeling that had been needling at her.

The horizon was upside down.

Her throat constricted to a pinhole as time stretched and pulled like taffy. A thick white void pooled in her mind before being replaced by a cascade of images, flickering and flashing, a film reel spinning out wildly.

How had she gotten here?

She remembered the sand...and the sea. The breeze through her hair.

Trevor. His wicked grin, his piercing green eyes, his haughty laugh. The hot feel of his mouth pressed hard against hers.

The crunching of gravel under the tires as they pulled up to Dockweiler Beach after work. Diane had intended on staying late at the agency. But Trevor had shown up, and flashed his winning smile.

She hadn't stood a chance.

The doors of the Duster shut behind them, the long stretch of sand opening up ahead. Thursday night. The beach was empty. Everyone else was still at work or stuck in traffic. They had the place to themselves.

"Nice one, Trev," said Austin, grinning. "I thought this place would be packed." He held Victoria's hand as she interlocked her other arm with Diane's. Victoria closed her eyes and inhaled deeply, her long auburn hair whipping in the wind.

"I told you, dude, you've got to trust me." Trevor winked at Diane before rushing out onto the beachfront, tossing the large bundle of firewood he'd been carrying aside. His feet kicked up large plumes of golden sand. He pulled off his T-shirt, exposing tanned skin and the lean ropes of muscle on his back and shoulders. He laughed wildly as he splashed through the water and dove headfirst into a breaking wave.

Victoria let go of Austin's hand and, laughing, chased after Trevor. She unhooked her leather belt and yanked off her blue-and-white striped mini-dress, stumbling as she kicked off her boots, and jumped into the dark blue Pacific in her underwear, fire-red hair flying behind her.

Austin turned to Diane and shrugged. "When in Rome," he said with a grin, pulling off his shirt and running toward the water. "Wait for me!" he called. Diane shook her head and laughed, tossing her purse and sandals into the sand and following after them.

Trevor body-surfed a wave to the shoreline and shook water from his thick blond hair as he stood up. His abs glistened in the sunlight, and a shiver ran up Diane's spine. "Come on in, Di, the water's fine!" he said, flicking water in her direction.

She stuck her tongue out at him. "I thought we were having a bonfire. I didn't bring a bathing suit."

He shrugged. "Suit yourself, kid. Vicky's got no problem showing off her drawers."

Victoria came up behind Trevor and dumped a handful of wet sand over his head. He shrieked. "I hate when you call me that," she said, pinching his arm.

"Ow!" he yelped, and flicked her ear. She shoved him playfully before turning and jumping back into the water.

"Come on, children, behave yourselves," called Austin from the water. He was floating on his back, letting the waves carry him. Trevor swam up behind him and reached his arms around his chest, dunking him into the water as a wave crashed over them both. Diane hesitated for a few moments, then smiled and began pulling off her black slacks.

An hour later, she pulled the blanket tight against her wet skin as the bonfire's red and orange flames licked the dimming sky. The coals popped and cracked as Trevor tossed another log into the fire pit. He sat in the sand behind her and wrapped his arms around her, pulling her close. Austin's fingers ran nimbly across the strings of his acoustic guitar, plinking out a sweet, wistful melody. Victoria's head rested on his shoulder, and she hummed along in a bright, clear vibrato.

As the final note rang out, she and Austin looked at each other with an expression so deep, so expansive, that it sent a prickling across Diane's back. Victoria reached her hands around Austin's face and pressed her mouth firmly against his, locked in an impassioned kiss.

Diane looked away, out toward the sea. The sun descending toward the horizon painted the water with shimmering gold sparkles, and in the distance seagulls cried plaintively. Trevor pulled her closer against him. She leaned back against his bare chest and closed her eyes. The steady rhythm of his heartbeat thrummed against her skin. She felt very far away.

The wind slowed. She heard a horrible grinding sound. Dread pooled in her stomach. She opened her eyes.

Austin began to strum another song as Victoria rose to her feet and walked in front of the roaring fire, brushing her fingertips against Diane's shoulder as she passed. Victoria closed her eyes and raised her arms into the air, swaying her hips to the music.

Diane was unable to tear her eyes away from the glow of the fire, from Victoria's rhythmic silhouette. The dancing slowed to nearly a stop. To her left, the strummed chords stretched into eternity; each individual vibration rang into the air, but instead of notes, each time Austin brought his guitar pick against the strings, she heard the splintering of glass.

She turned to look at Trevor. He tilted her chin

and brought her mouth to his. It seemed suddenly that the ground had been removed from underneath her, like she was in freefall. She shot to her feet, stumbling.

The sound of twisting metal. Cracks and bursts like icicles exploding, frozen fireworks.

She watched Victoria, mesmerized. Sparks rose from the crackling fire into the sky and disappeared like dancing fireflies.

Austin's music was replaced with Elvis singing "Blue Suede Shoes." Another crack, louder this time. The sharp undertone of gasoline. Her sister Charlotte. A terrible flash ripped through her of her father, his twinkling eyes. Her youngest sister Ramona, a paintbrush in her hand. A promise to return home to help her after their father had abandoned them. The sinking pit of guilt knowing it wasn't going to happen.

As Diane shook her head violently to rid herself of the images, she opened her eyes. The Pacific horizon was slowly tilting to the right. The fire reached up like a blazing torch and ignited the sky, consuming it in dark and brilliant flames. She locked eyes with Trevor to hold on to something, anything to stop her from falling off the edge of the world. He looked at her with a dangerous excitement in his eyes as he motioned for her to follow him. Beckoning her.

As the horizon fell over completely, the vibrating hum of the car engine rattling through her body suddenly stopped. She looked out through the Duster's front windshield just in time to see them spinning over the guardrail of Mulholland Drive. The screech of metal tearing against asphalt bore into her eardrums while she watched with a fascinated detachment as the valley below her approached fast.

Everything slipping quietly away now, her vision receding at the edges. An eerie, silent calm.

And before the ground finally reached out and embraced them, before it all went dark, the last thought tearing through Diane's mind was how it had all been her fault.

Ella lifted her face to the sky, letting the waning sunlight wash over her skin. She took a deep breath, filling her lungs with bright seaside air, and smiled. Suddenly, her heel gave out beneath her, sending her toppling forward into the arms of a large, sweaty man in a grease-stained T-shirt holding a soft pretzel.

"Oh, gosh, I'm so sorry," she muttered as he steadied her by the elbow. "Not used to these heels."

The man wiped bits of salt from his shirt and smiled. "No problemo. You all right, miss?"

Ella nodded, heat rising to her cheeks. As he turned to walk away, she cleared her throat. "Actually, ah...do you know where The Blue Trombone is? I can't find it anywhere."

He turned and pulled out his phone. A second later, he said, "It's three blocks over, Elm and Cranbury."

She fixed a smile on her face. "Thanks. Have a good night." He nodded and left, chomping on his soft pretzel. She inhaled slowly and smoothed out the skirt of her cobalt dress. Her heart pounded a little harder, her palms sweaty.

Tonight, Ella had a date.

She hobbled down the sidewalk, her feet already blistered, the small of her back whistling in pain. Heels had been a bad choice. She hadn't considered how far she'd have to walk to make it to Marina Cove's northeast shore. Many years had passed since she'd been up here.

As she turned onto Elm Avenue, her throat seized up. How had she not thought of it? Somewhere around here was Fitzpatrick's, the Irish pub that Ramona had visited a few weeks earlier. The bar her husband used to frequent without her knowledge, lost in alcoholism. The bar Jack had left one night all those years ago, drunk, and hit John Keamy, disabling him for life. The night that had apparently been the straw that broke the camel's back, the final thing that made him abandon them.

Before she realized it, she passed Cranbury

Street. Looking around, she spotted The Blue Trombone. Pressure built behind her eyes.

An instant later, she turned to leave. She wasn't ready. She was just an old woman whose time had passed. It was too soon.

She thought of the last letter Jack had left her. Her throat constricted as she hobbled down Elm as fast as she could.

"Hey! Hey, there! Ella! That you?" a voice called out to her.

Ella groaned softly. For one wild moment she considered pretending she hadn't heard him, then bolting away. Instead, she blew out a shaky breath, plastered a smile on her face, and turned to meet Skip. Her blind date.

"Skip?" she asked as a tall man with thick, windswept gray hair jogged up to her. He had ruddy cheeks, and wore a black-and-brown plaid jacket and dark slacks. Her heart fluttered. Skip was a handsome one.

"That's what they call me," he said in a surprising tenor, taking her hand and lifting it to his mouth for a peck. "Lovely to meet you. Looked like you were about to run away."

Ella laughed nervously. "I suppose I was. I don't know how much Helen told you. It's...uh...been a while since I've dated. A long time, actually. I guess I'm a little nervous."

After she'd returned from her stay with Maura in Ireland, resolved to move on with her life now that they'd learned everything that had happened to Jack, she'd decided to try her hand at dating again. One afternoon, she was in the checkout line at the grocery store, catching up with Helen, the cashier who'd been working there forever and who always had the best gossip. On a whim, she asked if Helen had any friends she might be able to set her up with.

Helen's face had lit up like a Christmas tree. "Oh, Ella, I'm so happy for you!" she said. "I have just the man, he comes here all the time. He's a real looker, always fashionably dressed, and has the most *interesting* stories. I'm ninety percent sure he's single. Ooooh, I'm so excited!" She'd come around the checkout counter to give Ella one of her signature crushing hugs.

And so that was that. Before she knew it, she was going on a blind date. After all these years.

"Well, I promise not to bite," said Skip in a quick voice, flashing a big smile. He held out his elbow, and she laced her arm around it. "I hope you're hungry. This place has great seafood. I give it four, maybe four and a half stars."

They entered The Blue Trombone. The large, dim room was circled by a sea of tables, a smooth wood dancing platform in the center. A group of musicians in white tuxedoes sat in a triple row on the far end of the room, playing saxophones, trumpets, and trombones. They were led by a man holding a microphone and singing Bobby Darin. A dozen or so couples danced in the center, laughing and swinging. Ella suddenly felt very self-conscious.

A waiter led them to their table. Skip sat down without waiting for Ella. "Seltzer with lime, splash of cranberry, three orange slices," he said, pulling out a notepad. Ella frowned, wondering what it was for.

"Um. Just water for me, please," she said to the waiter. "Thank you." He nodded and left the table. Ella sat down quietly, irritation scuttering across her skin.

Skip pulled out a pencil, licked the tip, and then looked up at Ella. "Oh, geez, I'm sorry, Ella. I'm being rude. It's...ah...been a long time for me, too. I'm used to going out alone. Please forgive me."

Ella waved her hand in the air. "Oh, it's all right. We're both a little rusty." She glanced out at the couples dancing. She was overcome with a memory of Jack leaning her back in his strong arms, his eyes dancing, electricity in the air. Shaking her head to clear the thought, she took a drink of water. "Would you like to dance?"

He pulled out a pair of glasses and rested them on his face. "Oh, I can't. Situational vertigo, you see... I'll spin right off the planet. I come here for the music. I hope that's all right?"

Ella smiled and waved her hand again. "Of course. I miss this music. I didn't know this sort of place existed anymore."

He pulled out a menu and scanned it. "I know. It's one of a kind. I give the music four and a half stars. What are you thinking?"

Ella furrowed her brows. "I'm sorry?"

He pointed at her menu. "What are you thinking for dinner? I'd suggest the shrimp scampi. Four stars, at least. Just don't go for the specials. Those are usually two, three stars at best."

She stared at him for a moment, perplexed. Was rating everything some sort of deadpan joke? He licked his finger and thumbed through the menu, humming along to the music.

After they placed their orders, she leaned back and sipped her water. Uncomfortable silence stretched between them. She looked longingly at the dance floor.

"So, I have a surprise for you," Skip said to his notepad. He scribbled something down.

"A surprise?" she asked. He lifted his pencil and idly used it to scratch the back of his head. "Uh-huh. Not now. A little later. You're gonna love it, I promise." He looked up at her, pausing as though seeing her for the first time. "Say. You look really lovely. That's a stunning dress. Four and a half stars."

Implying an elusive fifth star. "Gee, thanks, Skip."

He grinned at her. The waiter brought their dishes around. Ella again found herself regretting her decision to get back out there, but she decided to be patient. First impressions were tough. Skip was just a little...out of practice.

"So, tell me about yourself," Ella said hopefully.

Skip cut into his steak and lifted a large bite to his mouth. "Mmmm," he said. "That's the ticket." She watched him as he chewed, waiting for a response. Finally, after several more bites, he motioned to her plate. "I think you're gonna regret that," he said, pointing at her chicken. "Anyway. I do a lot of traveling these days. I don't like to sit still. I used to be a critic for a big travel magazine. Three decades. I've been all over the world."

So that explained the constant star ratings. "That's interesting," said Ella, determined to course-correct the evening. "What sort of things did you write about?"

That question turned out to be a big mistake. Half an hour later, Skip had chattered relentlessly about his time spent as a magazine critic. His stories followed a familiar pattern that showcased him as the big hero, larger than life, saving the day at the last minute. How he'd once brought peace to a remote village in Myanmar with nothing but his trusty accordion. How he'd single-handedly rescued a baby elephant seal who'd fallen down a well in Tanzania. Saved a father in Russia from a crime he didn't commit by winning an arm-wrestling tournament against a man called Dmitry the Destroyer.

"And so to this day, I'm known only as 'El Jefe' all across Argentina," he said through a mouthful of mashed potatoes. He paused, his expression twisting in confusion, before he nodded thoughtfully and continued jotting something down on his notepad.

"Ah, so, what's that you're working on?" Ella strained to keep the annoyance from her voice.

"Review," he said, scratching the back of his head with his pencil again.

"Oh, you still write for the magazine sometimes?"

He looked at her with a raised eyebrow. "Well, sure. I mean, I submit my stuff to my old editor, anyway. The magazine closed down a long time ago, but I know they'll be back. They just need good *content,* Ella. They'll be back in business, just you see. I wrote a great article last week about this new Japanese restaurant a couple blocks away. Four stars." He looked Ella up and down. "You'd look really great in a kimono."

She stared at him for a moment. What did you say to something like that? "Uh. All right?"

He smiled, satisfied. "How's your chicken?"

She looked down at her untouched plate. "I haven't tried it yet."

He watched her expectantly. She sighed, and cut off a piece. "Mmm. Very good."

He frowned. Something dark was running down the side of his temples. She squinted in the dim light. Hair dye.

"Ah, Skip, you might want to—"

"I knew you weren't gonna like it. I've had the chicken. It's two and a half stars at best. They don't know what they're doing back there. Waiter!" he yelled. Heads turned all around them.

Ella shrank in her seat. "Skip, you don't have to—"

"Nonsense. I forgot to tell you. I'm a world-class chef! I was trained by the great Sven Markopoulos. Nice fella. Well, not to me, but to some people. I taught him everything he knows."

"I thought you just said *he* trained *you*—"

Skip suddenly stood up. "Listen, Ella, I know the chef here. I'm gonna go back there and teach him a thing or two. I'll cook you up the best chicken of your life, just you see!"

"Skip, please, I really just want to go now—"

But he was already gone. She turned her attention to her lap, her cheeks flushed with embarrassment. After a few minutes, her stomach rumbled. She looked toward the kitchen, shrugged, and began to eat. She might as well get a good meal out of this night. The chicken was actually delicious. Five stars. But what did she know?

Shouting in the kitchen made the band stop playing. Everyone in the restaurant turned to look. Ella's heart stopped. Oh, no. The sound of pots and pans slamming against the floor carried across the room. More shouts.

A high-pitched alarm wailed from the kitchen. A moment later, Ella yelped as cold water began spraying from sprinklers all across the ceiling. People shouted and ran toward the exit as the band frantically tried to shield their instruments. A busboy burst through the kitchen double doors and shouted, "Everything's fine, people! Just a little cooking mishap! Please remain calm!" But his shouts were drowned out by angry customers filing outside, Ella following suit.

As she stood shivering in front of The Blue Trombone, her dress plastered to her body, wiping water from her eyes, Skip pushed his way toward her. "Ella, sorry about that," he said, flashing an angry scowl toward the restaurant. "Their equipment back there is terrible. Some people just don't know how to take direction." He checked his watch and looked around. "They should be here by now..."

"*Who?*" demanded Ella, losing all patience. "I don't want to do anything else tonight. I think I'm just going to walk home, Skip." She rubbed her shoulders to warm up.

He shook his head. "Nonsense, I told you I had a surprise—hey, there they are! Benny! Gus! Jim-Boy! Over this way!" Three older men in red-and-white pinstripe jackets pushed their way through the wet, angry customers toward Skip. "Ella, you're gonna love this." He grinned ear-to-ear, then tore off his jacket and dress shirt to reveal an identical pinstripe jacket underneath. He pulled out a little orange pitch pipe and blew into it. Ella's eyes widened.

He began to sing, and the other three harmonized with his reedy tenor. No. Please, no. Not a barbershop quartet.

"*Ooooooooooh,   Ellllaaaaaaaaaaaaaa.....*" they began. Oh, no, it was going to be about her... Ella whipped her head around, frantically looking for an escape, but the customers had cleared space for the performance, and she was trapped in the circle. There was nowhere to run. Her face was on fire, and she wanted nothing more than to drop through the sidewalk and disappear forever.

To Skip's credit, he boldly rhymed *Ella* with *umbrella, stellar*, and *Cinderella*. What felt like several long hours later, Skip warbled out his final note and looked across his impromptu audience expectantly. A lackluster smattering of applause ensued. He looked at Ella with a huge, satisfied grin. A horrible bubbling of giggles swelled within her, and she bit down hard on her tongue to stop them.

Five minutes later, they were walking down the street. She'd relented and accepted his offer to at least walk her to the main road that would take her home.

"So, what did you think?"

Ella blew out a long breath. "Well...that was really something."

He nodded, grinning. "I've been singing with those guys since prep school. I worked hard on that song. We might try to get it recorded, maybe send it out to a few record labels, who knows. If I have time for it." He looked up at the sky. "Nice sunset, huh? I give it three and a half stars."

Ella stopped and turned to him. "I'm sorry. Did you just rate the *sky*?"

He paused. "All right. Four stars. I guess." He looked at her and, to Ella's horror, leaned in for a kiss.

She deftly swung herself backward and inexplicably raised her hand in the air for a high-five instead. Skip looked at it for a moment, shrugged, and gave it a slap. He smiled at her, and turned to leave. "I'll call you," he called back over his shoulder, leaving her there on the street corner, wet and shivering.

She waited for him to turn the corner at the end of the block, then sat down on the sidewalk, letting out a shriek of giggles. She ignored the looks of passersby, her body shaking with laughter, tears streaming down her face.

After a while, she finally got to her feet, slipped

off her heels, and began the long walk home. The night was warm, and she'd finally stopped shivering as her clothes began to dry. With each barefoot step, she replayed the disaster of an evening, shaking her head and bursting into fresh gales of laughter.

But after a while, the laughter inside her dried up, replaced with a sort of sinking feeling. She hadn't expected to meet someone *perfect*...but she remembered how it felt the last time she'd put herself out there. How it would start promising, but inevitably there was something she just couldn't get past. She didn't think she was overly picky or anything...she was just being selective. Why should she waste time with someone who didn't make her feel like Jack had?

She winced as she thought of Jack. Sure, he'd been wonderful. But he'd also hidden *so much* from her. So much of his life she hadn't been remotely aware of, and then he'd abandoned her and their children, thinking he was saving them. Her heart was shattered when she found out what he'd been going through, but it had also left her with the terrible feeling that she couldn't trust anyone again.

Ignoring the pain drilling up from the sidewalk into her bare feet, Ella kept her eyes on the road ahead. Maybe trying to get back out there so soon had been a mistake. She thought of the letter again, the last one Jack had written to her, sitting in the top drawer of the bedroom dresser.

She still hadn't been able to bring herself to read it.

She sighed and shook her head. All at once it was like she was facing an empty abyss, a pooling darkness she couldn't see through. She had no idea what she was doing. The feeling crept through her, weighing her down with each step she took toward the Seaside House, the home she'd once shared with the only true love she'd ever known.

3

Diane woke with a start. The room was still mostly dark. She inhaled sharply to ease her heart drumming against her chest, and winced as spikes of pain shot up from her lower back into her shoulders. She groaned and rolled over to put her arm around Grant. For some reason, her right arm was throbbing. Despite the sweat dripping down the back of her neck, she shivered and pulled him closer, trying to force herself back to sleep.

"*Diane,*" Grant whispered.

"Five more minutes," Diane said into her pillow.

Grant placed an arm on her shoulder and shook gently. "*Diane, are you okay?*"

Diane winced again as she rolled her neck

around. She couldn't remember her bed ever making her this sore. As she rubbed the sleep from her eyes, her throat tightened as the last shadows from some terrible nightmare slowly faded from her mind. She sat up, and a jolt of confusion ran through her as she saw that it was Charlotte next to her, a look of concern on her face.

Heat rushed to Diane's cheeks. "Sorry, thought I was in my bed at home..." she whispered to Charlotte, forcing a smile. Fire pounded through her arm and into her fingertips as she wiped fresh sweat from her forehead. "Didn't mean to wake you."

Charlotte smiled and waved a hand. "It's all good...actually, you were moaning in your sleep before you curled up next to me. Bad dream?"

Diane squeezed her eyes shut and shivered again. "Something like that. I'm fine. Thanks."

She patted Charlotte's shoulder awkwardly before standing up from the bare hardwood floor she'd been sleeping on for the last couple of weeks. Mariah was asleep on her stomach on the other side of the room, a purple knitted blanket twisted around her body. The very first glimmers of daylight were peeking through the shutters on the far wall. The faint sound of the ocean lapping against the shore carried over the breeze.

After her visit to Jack's sister in Ireland, Ella had moved into the Seaside House with Ramona, whose house had been foreclosed on. They were sleeping down the hall in another bedroom they'd just managed to clear out a few days ago.

Diane took a long breath to ease the pounding in her ears and tiptoed over to the bathroom, shutting the door behind her with a soft click. She pushed back the hard lump in her throat and reached for the porcelain sink with trembling hands to steady herself. Her breath was coming in short gasps as she tried to clear the thoughts of that day from her mind, the memories. Suddenly, she ripped her right arm away from the sink as a bolt of lightning shot through it, and bit down on her lip to stop herself from yelping.

Her fingers found the old, faded scar that ran from her middle knuckle all the way to the crook of her arm. The scar she'd gotten from the accident.

She wiped hot tears from her eyes as the familiar pit of guilt pooled in her stomach. While she'd thought about the accident every day for the last twenty-four years, she'd been having more nightmares about it in the last few weeks than usual. But her scar hadn't hurt for ages. Why would it start up again now?

She jumped nearly a foot as her phone buzzed in the front pocket of her jeans. As she scrambled to pull it out, she fumbled it, dropping it on the floor with a terrible *crack*. She swore under her breath as she lifted it up, groaning at the splintered glass of her screen. A ripple of panic surged through her as she saw the eleven missed calls and nine texts, swiping through them frantically.

Closing her eyes and holding her breath to steady her voice, she dialed. After the third ring, a voice dripping with an exaggerated Southern California accent answered.

"Heyoooo, look who it is." The words slinked through the phone. "What's the good word, D-Money?"

Diane pinched the bridge of her nose with her fingers. "Hey, Parker."

She heard a thick slurping sound and twisted her face in disgust. She knew he was undoubtedly drinking his kombucha, snacking on his dried seaweed crisps. "So, how's life on the lesser coast? Havin' fun on your vacation?" he asked.

"It's not a vacation, Parker," she said, straining to keep her voice pleasant. "Remember? I said I needed to deal with a family issue."

He snorted. "Mmm. Right on, right on. Sending

good energy, good vibes. Anywhooo," he said, munching happily on his seaweed, "Danner Post sent us new edits to approve for the Frosty Dee-Lite commercials. I think it needs more of those old dudes we took out after last round. Just not too many, am I right? Maybe we pop a couple of those hot blondes in there to balance it all out. And seriously, no one looks happy enough in the lake dance sequence. They should be holding those popsicles *way up in the air*. Big ol' grins. I know we shot better takes." He paused to slurp his kombucha. "You need to send your notes too, friend-o, like, *yesterday*. It's meant to air next Tuesday. Anyway. You finish the pitch for Larson Brands today? I'm stoked to see how you plan on making those vegan bratwursts appealing." *Slurp*.

Diane stifled a scream and clenched her fists to steady her incredible disdain for Parker. Along with Grant and herself, he was one of the five partners at Nicholls+Kline, the ad agency in Los Angeles's West Side she'd taken over with Grant a few years after they got married. She'd never trusted Parker, but he'd somehow weaseled his way in after years of ingratiating himself with the other two partners. She could picture him now, sitting with his laptop propped up on the legs of his three-hundred-dollar skintight jeans cuffed up to the shins, his trendy orange horn-rimmed glasses, his slicked-back hair with the sides and back shaved to the skin. Slippery as an eel.

She giggled inwardly as she thought of Grant's spot-on imitation of Parker's affected SoCal accent. *Duuuuuude. Sweeeeeeeeeeet.*

Diane glanced at her phone. "Parker, isn't it like three in the morning over there?"

He barked a laugh somehow tinged with both derision and pity for Diane. "Hey, money doesn't sleep, baby. I'll sleep when I'm dead."

It was no wonder Grant often had nightmares about Parker. Diane squeezed her eyes shut and idly pulled the rubber band she always kept around her wrist back, then released it with a loud *crack*.

There was a lot Parker didn't know. A lot the other partners didn't know.

If Diane had any idea what was to come after she and Grant took over the agency...she would have run a thousand miles in the opposite direction.

After the conversation finally ended and Diane's entire day again filled with mind-numbing work tasks, she swiped through the remaining texts from Parker, deleting them with tremendous satisfaction, before she saw a text sent the night before that made her blood run cold.

Hey, Mom...hope all's well. Finished my semester a week early. I thought I'd visit you in Marina Cove for a couple of days. Leaving tomorrow morning. Love you.

Diane's vision narrowed to a tunnel. A thousand thoughts tore through her mind in an instant. Her hand frantically grabbed at the rubber band on her wrist. *Crack.*

No. No, no no no. Kayla knew, she *knew* not to do this. There had to be a *system.* Diane reached into her pocket, running her fingers across the folded pink note she carried everywhere.

No. She could not do this.

Some distant part of her fumbled with her phone, jamming her finger against Kayla's name. *Ring. Ring. Ring. Ring.*

Diane gasped wildly for breath. Cold beads of sweat broke out on her forehead. She cracked the rubber band twice as she dialed again. Nothing.

As quietly as she could, she opened the bathroom door, tiptoed through the bedroom where everyone was still sleeping, and tore down the stairs into the dining room. One hand dialed Kayla's number again while the other ripped her laptop from her satchel that was leaning against the table.

Her mind raced. Would Kayla have left this early in the morning? She was an early riser. She was just finishing her first year in the architecture program at the Rhode Island School of Design, and Diane hadn't expected her to finish her summer semester for another week or two. Kayla was then supposed to visit them in Los Angeles. She hadn't expected this.

Diane's vision swayed as she opened the usual browser tabs with practiced speed: maps, local weather reports, traffic reports, the real-time highway accident reports. The last tab she opened was the geo-tracker app she'd forced Kayla to place on her car that showed Diane her location in real time.

Her fingers trembled as she stared at the pinwheel on the screen. The sites were taking forever to load. She cursed the spotty internet in the Seaside House under her breath and frenetically set up a local hotspot from her phone.

A frozen blast of fire shot across the scar on her arm, making her yelp in pain. The geo-tracker page finally loaded, but the icon showing Kayla's car was nowhere to be seen.

Her throat constricted. She snapped the rubber band. *Crack. Crack.*

Diane reviewed the five most likely routes Kayla

would have taken from her school in the maps tab and began searching through the traffic reports, the accident reports, her eyes running wildly over the lines of data. A quick trip to the weather report along her routes. Rain. Of course. Of course it was going to rain.

Diane sent a text to Kayla. *What time did you leave? Did you leave yet? What route are you taking?*

A burst of images tore through Diane's mind with such force that she splayed her arms across the table to steady herself. The upside-down horizon. Austin's blanched knuckles gripping the seat, Victoria's eyes twisted shut. The look of horror on Trevor's face.

"Diane, everything all right?" a faraway voice asked.

With tremendous effort, Diane tore herself away from that day. "What?" she asked breathlessly.

Ramona was standing at the foot of the stairs, sleep still in her eyes. She furrowed her brows. "I just asked if you were all right. You look..." She took a few steps toward Diane. "What happened?"

Diane blew out a shaky breath and smiled. "Nothing, nothing. It's, ah, just agency stuff again. Never lets up. Someone's gotta help sell those popsicles." She forced out a small laugh and stopped her hand just as it reached for the rubber band.

Ramona watched her for a moment with an unreadable expression. "Want some coffee?"

Diane nodded, ignoring another streak of pain across her scar. "That would be great. Thanks, Ramona."

Ramona went into the kitchen, and Diane used her sleeve to dry the sweat on the back of her neck. As she dialed and re-dialed Kayla's phone, she rolled through all her browser tabs, hitting refresh. She couldn't understand why the geo-tracker wasn't showing Kayla's location. Of all the days, it had to be today.

Diane sent another text to Kayla. *You don't have to do this. I don't want you to change your plans. I can't have you change them on my account. We've talked about this...* Once again she regretted letting her daughter know she was visiting Marina Cove. What had she been thinking?

This never would have happened if she hadn't said anything. It was the reason Diane refused to directly change anyone else's plans, refused to ask anyone to visit her, refused to drive anywhere herself. She wouldn't ever again put herself in a situation where she'd be responsible for something terrible happening. The rational part of her understood the twisted logic, but when push came to shove, she didn't care. As long as she didn't change anything, she wouldn't be responsible.

And now, if something happened to Kayla, it was going to be on Diane.

She would be at fault, again.

She sat back and reviewed her options. Either Kayla was still at school and hadn't left yet, or she was already en route. Unless her car appeared on the geo-tracker site, or she returned Diane's calls, she had no other options but to wait, and suffer. She couldn't drive to meet Kayla en route...she hadn't been behind the wheel of a car in many years, and that wasn't going to change now. She could get a rideshare...but Kayla could have taken any number of routes. No dice.

Kayla *knew* she was supposed to go over the route with Diane in advance. How else was she supposed to know where she was? How long it was supposed to take? What if something had already happened?

A terrible image of her daughter's car smashing into an oncoming eighteen-wheeler ripped at her. A scream rose in Diane's throat before she pushed it back at the last second.

Ramona returned with a large cup of black coffee. "Thanks, Ramona," Diane said, and began chugging the coffee. She didn't feel the hot liquid searing her throat until the cup was drained. Ramona's eyes widened slightly. The sound of water boiling in the kettle carried in from the kitchen.

Ramona sat down at the table as Diane quickly opened another tab, pulling open her agency email. "Diane," Ramona started, then closed her mouth. Diane looked up at her. "You can talk to me, you know."

Diane nodded and forced another smile. "I know. I'm fine, honestly. Just a little harried. I have so much work to do." She hid her browser, and felt her fingers itching to pull the rubber band. She thought again of the small lined sheet of pink paper in her pocket, folded over once. The familiar expanse of guilt widened within her stomach.

"I think...ah, that my daughter might be coming to visit...today, actually," Diane said, carefully keeping the roiling panic from her voice.

Ramona put her hand on Diane's forearm, right against the scar. Prickling heat rushed from her knuckle to her elbow. "Oh, that's great! Now this would be..." A look of embarrassment flashed across her face.

"Kayla. She's studying architecture at the Rhode Island School of Design...I guess she finished her semester early."

"Good for her," Ramona said, cautioning a glance down at Diane's wrist. The skin underneath the rubber band was bright red. "I'm excited to meet her." Ramona paused. "You have a son too, right? I'm sorry, you just never really talk about them."

Heat rushed to Diane's neck. "I know, I'm sorry. I think I'm just still getting used to everything. Seeing you all again. I'm sorry for...uh. Being so closed off. I don't mean to be like this."

Ramona shook her head. "Don't be. We Keller siblings are all like that, aren't we? Charlotte's been here for a long while now, and I still know almost nothing about her family. I basically don't know anything about Gabriel...and when's the last time any of us even knew where Natalie was?" She laughed humorlessly. "It's going to take some time. You know?"

Truth be told, Diane wasn't exactly sure why she was still in Marina Cove. She'd only planned on a few days. But something had kept her around. Perhaps a chance to escape from everything happening at home, if only for a short time.

Diane exhaled a long breath and forced back

tears threatening to form. "My son...he doesn't talk to me anymore, actually. Jamie. It's a long story. I'm not sure where he's living now...last I heard, he was up in Canada somewhere. I haven't seen him in a long time."

She froze as she felt the color drain from her face. Oh, no. The rain. The roads would be slick. A cold fist punched her in the gut. She'd completely forgotten to remind Kayla to put air in her tires as spring turned into summer. She was going to get in an accident...she was—

Suddenly, the room was tilting, the guard rail rolling beneath her as she looked through the windshield, the ground approaching fast.

The tea kettle in the kitchen began whistling. "Oh, I'm sorry to hear that," Ramona said from a thousand miles away. "Ah, how's Grant doing? He planning on visiting here too, then, if Kayla's coming?"

Diane shook her head in a slow daze. "No, he's, uh, really mired with work, too. Our agency, he and I are two of five partners...he's all tied up with that right now. I am too...I think I actually put in more hours since I've been here than I do in LA." She looked up at Ramona, her fingers tapping on the table. The whistle from the tea kettle rose in pitch, drilling painfully into her ears.

Ramona sighed, her eyes flickering back and forth over Diane's. "You never told me what happened, what's going on. After that day on the porch a couple of weeks ago. You told me that you had done something terrible."

Diane looked at her sister. She wanted so badly to open up to her, to let it all out, to let Ramona stroke her hair and tell her it would be all right. But something was blocking her, something impassive, holding her back.

So instead, she waved her hand. "I know. I'm sorry again about that. I was, uh, just all caught up in something with the agency. Work stuff. I missed some deadlines. It just got to me. I shouldn't have said anything. Everything's fine now. Really." She saw that Ramona knew she was lying. Before she'd realized it, her fingers released the rubber band on her wrist with a loud *crack*. "I'm fine. I promise." She paused. "I should get back to work, though. Sorry. I have a very long day ahead of me."

Ramona's shoulders dropped slightly, and she stood up from the table. "All right. Well, if you ever do want to talk, you know where to find me."

The tea kettle continued shrieking from the kitchen. Diane crushed back the pressure behind her eyes. "Thanks, Ramona," she heard herself say. "I'll see you guys later. Maybe we can have dinner tonight?"

Ramona nodded, and left. Diane watched her feet rise up the stairs, and then tore open her laptop. She rotated through all the tabs. Nothing. She went into the kitchen, poured a second cup of coffee, and drank it all in one go by the time she sat back down at the table. Another text. Another re-dial. Her head was pounding, her mouth dry as dust. She shuttled furiously through the local news, looking for anything related to a car accident involving a silver Honda Civic. Hot rays of sunlight slashed through the front windows of the Seaside House as tears fell from Diane's face and splattered against the keyboard.

Diane knew her behavior looked crazy from the outside. She wasn't stupid. But no one else could understand. No one could know what it had been like...they didn't carry with them the burdens that Diane did. The regret. The shame.

The minutes dragged across the face of the clock on the wall like feet through quicksand. The whistling scream from the tea kettle reverberated throughout the house as Diane downed a third cup of coffee with trembling hands. She paced around the table, sweating profusely, and pushed back the old, dread-riddled guilt that always simmered within her and was now boiling over.

She hit refresh on the browser tabs again, and again, and again. Another phone call, another voicemail, another text. Refresh. Refresh. She cracked the rubber band against the red splotches on her wrist, ignoring the stripes of pain.

Refresh. *Crack.* Refresh. Refresh.

She jumped up as her phone screen suddenly illuminated with a text, sending her chair flying behind her and toppling over to the hardwood floor. Coffee spilled all over the tabletop, pooling around her laptop. Her heart lodged in her throat as her fingers clumsily opened the text, tears pouring from her eyes.

Hey, Mom. I hadn't left yet. My phone died. I got your calls...I didn't think...I forgot about everything. I just wanted to visit. Just forget about it. I'll just stick around here for the summer.

Diane squeezed her eyes shut and fell against the wall. A harsh, strange giggle popped up from her throat. She wheezed as she sucked in huge lungfuls of air that suddenly tasted sweet with relief. She wiped tears from her eyes and began a text, but then deleted it. She didn't want Kayla to change her mind. She didn't want to affect what Kayla did at all.

Her limbs felt weak and shaky as she stood against the dining room wall. The relief she'd felt had been swept away by a cold, burrowing shame.

Diane knew she was pushing her daughter away. She'd been doing it for a long time.

Jamie already didn't speak to her...and Kayla was going to be next. Diane was smothering her.

But she didn't see another option. It was like a second Diane took over, a child hiding under the bed, afraid of monsters and ghosts. A child desperately looking for the light but unable to find it. A hollow, tired child.

A growing pool of helplessness sloshed through her, bringing fresh tears to her eyes. She never asked to be this way. She was doing her best. No one understood what she'd been through.

She moaned and buried her face in her hands. Work. At least she had work. A steady, infinite supply of all the work she could ever want, the piping-hot bath to drop herself into and distract from the pain of everything else, for as long as she wanted. She let out a long breath. A moment later she dug a sweater from her satchel, pulled with all her might against the stuck front door of the Seaside

House, and ran out to the beach, where no one would find her.

Diane sat down hard in the sand, tears streaming down her face, her body racked with sobs. She had so much else to contend with at the moment...she didn't need this. The agency, everything with Grant. The man she thought had been following her. Her arm burned dully as she squeezed her eyes shut and reached into her pocket, running her fingers along the pink paper.

At that moment, her phone began ringing. Parker's ringtone. Fire rose in her throat like a coal furnace. She balled up the sweater, brought it to her mouth, and screamed into it until her voice finally gave out completely, the great wide void of her future stretching out endlessly and oppressively before her.

And there was nothing she could do about any of it.

4

"Okay. I mean, come on. I would pay just about anything for this. Like, here's a blank check, put any number down. What did you call these?" asked Sylvie through a mouthful of pastry, crumbs falling down her shirt.

Charlotte laughed. "It's a *religieuse*. Just choux pastry, chocolate cream, and a coffee glaze. It's from the French word for 'nun.' See how it sort of looks like a plump little nun in a habit?"

Sylvie lifted it up, squinted, and grinned. "I see it. Now I feel bad. We have to add these to the menu, Charlotte. We're gonna be millionaires, I tell you. Well, thousandaires, at least."

Charlotte took another bite as the saltwater wind whipped gently at her hair. "It's not quite ready for primetime. I'm still working on it. But now I see I'm on the right track."

They were sitting on a bench in front of the water just down the street from The Windmill, the restaurant Sylvie owned with her husband, Nick. The restaurant where Charlotte had been working hard at her new job as a pastry chef, constantly learning and experimenting and honestly having the time of her life. For the first time she could remember.

Charlotte inhaled a long breath of the crystal-clean Atlantic air before she turned to Sylvie, considering. "Want to talk about it?" she asked after a moment.

Sylvie lowered her pastry into her lap without looking at Charlotte and stared out at the water. A harbor seal barked in the distance.

"Not really." She lifted her mug of coffee and downed half of it, unconsciously twirling her wedding ring in her other hand. "He was supposed to be back yesterday. I just don't understand why he keeps doing this. He *knows*, Charlotte. He *knows* I don't like it. The man can be so freaking selfish sometimes."

Charlotte listened as Sylvie closed her eyes, lifting her face to the sun. "I don't really want to talk about it, though. But he can't keep doing this to me. You know? I'm not that woman. I won't put up with it." She looked up at Charlotte. "But that's it, that's all I want to say about it. This is my happy place." She leaned back against the bench. "I just wish I knew why he does this. Where he is. I'm sick to death of having to be the bad guy. I'm not a worrier...it's just basic respect, isn't it? This isn't me."

Charlotte nodded sympathetically and waited for Sylvie to continue. Nick was a stubborn man, and had a very...casual relationship with time. He would go long stretches without letting Sylvie know where he was, which drove her crazy. He was always traveling all over the place to meet with suppliers for their restaurant; they worked hard to maintain high standards and were always adapting their menu to stay current.

Sylvie sighed. "He's always been like this. But we've been fighting so much lately...and I think he's just staying away longer and longer to, I don't know, get a break from me or something. He's pulling away. I try to talk about it, but he's like a freaking brick wall, honestly. It hurts."

Sylvie's phone rang, sending a yelp from her throat. "It's Nick," she breathed, shooting up from the bench. "Back in a sec." She walked down the sand, her finger in her ear, talking rapidly into the phone and gesturing wildly.

Charlotte watched the waves roll in, thinking about Nick. Seeing Sylvie so upset, afraid...it sent hot waves of anger across Charlotte's chest. A few minutes later, Sylvie plopped back down on the bench next to her, rubbing the bridge of her nose with her fingers.

"I swear, that man." She groaned. "He's fine. After all that, he's like, 'What? I told you it was gonna take a couple days, babe. I emailed you about it,'" she said in her deep Nick voice, shaking her head. "I didn't think to check it. Why would I? Who emails their wife where they're going to be? I feel like an idiot."

"No. It's not your fault, Sylvie. It's his. He shouldn't be acting like this...not when you've asked him to change."

Sylvie sighed and ran her hands over her face, nodding softly. She glanced at her watch and suddenly stood back up. "Shoot, I have to get back in there. Thanks for this, Charlotte. Sorry to talk your ear off again. I'll see you later, okay?"

Charlotte gave her a quick hug. "I'm really sorry about Nick. I can give him a good talking to if you want. Get him in line."

Sylvie groaned. "Maybe I'll just go on a nice vacation and not tell him where I am, see how he likes it. Somewhere tropical. With well-muscled men feeding me grapes and rubbing my feet."

Charlotte laughed as they parted ways. She turned from the sand on the way home. To the Seaside House, anyway, her home for the time being. Smiling at a little girl in pigtails chasing her brother down the sidewalk, Charlotte was suddenly filled with dread.

Tomorrow was an important day. Tomorrow, she was meeting Sebastian in Manhattan so that she could move the divorce process along.

The process Sebastian had been doing his level best to stall.

Charlotte allowed a brief moment of helplessness to wash over her before taking a breath and letting her mind still. There was only so much she could do. Finally, she'd decided to meet him in person, to try to get the ball rolling. With her relationship with Christian finally beginning to blossom, she didn't want to remain stuck in the past with the man who had treated her so poorly. Who had decided to give everything up.

She lifted her phone from her pocket to call him to confirm when she saw a missed call from him.

Heart pounding in her ears, she pressed down on his name.

He answered on the first ring. "Charlotte! Hey. Hi. How are you?"

Charlotte rubbed her temple with her fingers. "Fine. I saw you called. I was just about to call you about tomorrow."

She could hear cars honking in the background, someone swearing at someone else. She didn't miss the big-city life. "Yes. That's why I called. Listen. I know you want to talk. I have it all set up. I reserved us a table at Il Cane Blu. I thought maybe we could grab drinks at Castello beforehand. Catch up."

Charlotte felt heat rising in her throat. "Sebastian, this isn't really—"

"I know you want to talk about the divorce. I understand. I just thought we could do it like old times. I reserved us all a little expedition on Alastair's yacht."

Charlotte felt her stomach twist. "Us all?"

"Yeah. I invited Allie and Liam to join us. I know Mariah's busy working as a waitress or whatever out there, but bring her. It's going to be a blast."

Her chest tightened as she clenched the phone, working hard to steady her voice. "Sebastian, our children should not be part of this—"

"I haven't seen Steph, you know," he interjected, quieter. "I don't ever see her. We, ah, relocated her to another part of the company. I told you I had ended it before you even found out about her. I just wanted you to know."

Charlotte moved her mouth to speak, but found she couldn't. A spike of pain slashed through her heart. "I...I can't—" she stammered.

"I miss you, Charlotte," he said softly. "I miss you, and I love you. Look. I wanted to wait until tomorrow to say this, but I want you to give me another chance. I can't change the past. But I want you back in my life. I want you to come home."

Charlotte shook her head violently. "*Stop it!*" she screamed into the phone. Several people turned to look at her. She ignored them and continued, finding her voice. "Just stop, Sebastian! I can't believe you! I don't care about *Steph* right now! Did you forget about your *six-year* relationship with Brielle? Six *freaking* years! And *then* Steph! And who knows who else! And you have the nerve to tell me you want me back? Are you out of your mind?" She forced back the tears threatening to form.

"All I can keep saying is that I'm sorry, Charlotte. I am. It was a terrible thing to do. I'll do whatever I can to make things work again." He blew out a long breath. "Think about our children, Charlotte," he said softly. "What will we do during holidays? Family get-togethers? Are we really going to do this to them? Without even trying to fix things first?"

"Don't you *dare* use our children against me!" she shrieked. A sob caught in her throat. "*You* did this to us, Sebastian. I didn't ask for this. I'm *never* getting back together with you. Okay? I don't know how else to tell you." She wiped tears from her eyes.

Sebastian sighed. "Is this about that old boyfriend you've been seeing again? Christian, or whatever? Because we can work through that. I don't blame you, after what I did to you."

Charlotte groaned aloud. "*Stop,* Sebastian. What I do now is none of your business. You don't get to control what I do anymore. I know that's going to be an adjustment for you." She squeezed her eyes shut and tried to steady her heartbeat. "I'm ending this call."

"Don't bother coming to Manhattan tomorrow," he said in a low voice.

A shiver ran up her spine. "What?"

Silence on the line. She plugged her other ear and listened. Just the sounds of crawling Manhattan traffic. "*I can't do this,*" she thought she heard him mutter to himself.

"Sebastian, I can't hear you. Why did you just tell me not to come to Manhattan tomorrow? You've already delayed three times, I already took off work—"

"I'm sorry. I completely forgot I'm going to be out of town this week. Meetings and...whatnot. You understand. Let's try next week, okay? We'll go wherever you want."

"*No!*" she yelled. "You can't keep delaying this! I shouldn't even have to come out there in the first place!" Her voice cracked. She sat down on the curb in front of a barber shop and let all the air out of her lungs. "Sebastian, please. I'm asking you. For me. I just want to move on." Tears dropped onto her lap.

Silence filled the other line for a long moment. He sighed. "Well, I'm not ready to move on."

Click.

5

D iane adjusted her sunglasses as she quickly walked down Ocean Avenue, feeling conspicuous. She didn't expect to run into anyone she knew this morning, after all the years she'd been away, but you never knew. She felt guilty enough as it was.

With each step, her resolve weakened. Overnight, she'd made up her mind. But now, in the harsh light of day, she felt like a real coward.

She turned off Ocean Avenue onto a weathered boardwalk, wincing as the wheels of her suitcase made a loud *pop* each time they rolled over a wooden beam. The shore opened up in front of her, the water glimmering with white morning sunlight and dotted with sailboats. Her heart pounded in her ears as she approached the Hightide Port ferry terminal and pulled out her wallet.

They would understand. They'd have to. She had only planned on staying a day or two anyway, not a few weeks. She had to get home, get back to work, everything. And besides, Kayla might change her mind and decide to visit home like she'd originally planned in a couple of weeks.

Diane couldn't quite put her finger on why she'd gathered everything she owned and snuck out of the Seaside House before anyone woke. It probably had something to do with avoidance. Or she was scared. Blah, blah, blah. Something else to add to the endless merry-go-round of things to feel ashamed over. Part of her badly wanted to stay, to try to connect with her sisters. She loved them. But she had problems to deal with, big problems back home that required her attention now. Hop on the ferry, grab a rideshare so she wouldn't have to drive, get back to her real life as soon as possible. She could pick things back up with her family later...once the dust settled. Another time. She had time.

As she paid for her ticket, she sat down on a long wooden bench and pulled the sun hat down to shield her eyes. She couldn't shake the shame, the guilt of leaving them. Charlotte's sweet, lilting voice filled her mind, Ramona's newfound warmth. Her throat constricted as she thought of her mother. How they had made so much progress lately...how they'd been able to be so open with each other.

But not Diane. She listened to them, sure, and she had been supportive...but they didn't know what she was contending with. They didn't know about the agency, about the steady downward spiral of her marriage with Grant, about her failing relationship with her kids.

They didn't know the things she'd done.

She wasn't ready to talk to them. They wouldn't understand, they couldn't help her. No one could. And besides, she hadn't asked for things to change. Just because they'd finally figured out why their father had abandoned them...it didn't just fix everything.

No. She was going to get herself back above water first. Get everything back on track. That was the only way. She'd always found a way to get through things...she'd just stick her head down and *make* it happen.

She pulled out her phone and opened the email she'd received yesterday from Parker. She'd read it at least a dozen times, her anger mounting each time.

Heyo, D-Money! Hope your little vacation's going

great! One thing, though. You need to come back, like, NOW. Larson Brands is having second thoughts. That's on you, champ. They want to meet in person and it isn't looking pretty. Geoff and Lisa are obviously pretty steamed. I wouldn't be surprised if they started thinking about some, er, alternative arrangements ;) LOL. Anyway, I'll send you the meeting details. See ya in a couple of days. Later, alligator!

Clenching her fists, Diane felt a blaze of heat rush up from her chest into her throat. Parker was a freaking snake. After everything that had happened over the last few years, Parker had slowly and systematically poisoned the other two partners, Geoff and Lisa, against her and Grant. As though Diane had been part and parcel to what Grant had been doing.

In a way, she couldn't blame Parker. He saw an opportunity and took advantage. After what Grant had done, a new partnership agreement had been voted on that made him and Diane minority partners, with plenty of provisions that would allow them to be pushed out of the business. They hadn't really had a choice but to sign.

But Diane had no intention of going down easy. She'd overcome more difficult things than *Parker*. All the more reason to get back home as soon as possible.

Diane felt the hairs on the back of her neck stand up. She had a sudden strong sensation of being watched. She snapped her head up, scanning the boardwalk, her eyes darting across the ferry, the stretch of sand down the shore, the storefronts on Ocean Avenue behind her.

There he was, standing in front of a small coffee shop. The man she'd sworn she spotted several times, but he always disappeared before she could register his face. He wore a red baseball cap and vintage black sunglasses, a gray T-shirt and blue jeans with worn-down boots.

She stood up from the bench and turned right into an older woman walking a Miniature Schnauzer, knocking her purse to the ground. "Oh, my gosh, I'm so sorry," Diane stammered, helping her lift her purse.

The woman smiled and waved a hand. "No harm done. Thanks for keeping me and Gerald on our toes, anyway!" She laughed to herself and continued down the boardwalk.

Diane looked back toward the coffee shop, but of course, the man was gone. He was a ghost.

She frowned. She was probably seeing things...

being paranoid. The last couple of years could do that to a person.

Except...Ramona had seen him around the Seaside House that one afternoon, hadn't she?

Diane sat back down on the bench and pulled her sun hat tighter around her head. She stared at the ground, watching the feet of the ferry passengers who'd just arrived shuffle past her.

"Listen, Teddy, it ain't gonna happen," she heard someone say. Her chest tightened. The voice was familiar, but she couldn't quite place it. "Ask Stuart to figure it out. We're still going live next week. It's up to you guys now. I'll call you later tonight."

Diane's head whipped around to the source of the voice. She saw a man with thick, dirty-blond hair and a white button-down shirt and black slacks walking down the boardwalk in her direction. He was handsome. Stunning, actually. She was mesmerized. He pressed a button on his phone, put it in his pocket, and raised his face in her direction, his eyes locking on hers.

Diane's mouth went dry as the whole world seemed to slow to a crawl around her. Suddenly, she was back in the old Plymouth Duster, the gold and ruby kaleidoscope of sunlight through the shattering windshield, the horizon flipping over and the guardrail of Mulholland Drive passing beneath them. The sound of frozen snowflakes against a window, the sharp bite of exhaust. The last look at his face, his mouth twisted in horror, his skin drained of all color. Guilt tearing through her body before it all went dark.

She splayed her hands against the bench to stop the world from falling over and clenched her eyes shut. Someone had ripped the ground from beneath her. Hot tears sprang to her eyes as her lungs cried for oxygen. She gritted her teeth and pressed her feet into the ground, something solid, an anchor. Looking down at her hand, she saw at some point she'd pulled back the rubber band, and she released it with a piercing *crack*. After a moment, the roller-coaster sensation passed, and she was back at the ferry terminal, the sounds of splintering glass replaced with the peaceful lapping of water against the shore.

She looked back up to the gorgeous man, but he was gone. Before she knew what she was doing, she bolted up from the bench and forced her limbs to move as fast as they could. She had to get out of here. Two steps away from the bench and her shin slammed against her suitcase, sending her sprawling out toward the wooden beams of the boardwalk. She barely had time to break her fall with her arms as she collapsed to the ground, skin scraping away from her knees.

Diane groaned, clutching her knees as fire rushed to her face in embarrassment. She scrambled to her feet, and as she stood up, a voice called out behind her.

"Diane?"

She froze. In a matter of seconds, she could be on the ferry, if she ran hard enough. Frantically scanning her route, she just caught Leo pulling off his captain's hat and stepping off the ferry, shaking hands with another operator who was taking his place. He looked in her direction and waved. The world still had a strange, dream-like quality to it, like she hadn't quite woken up all the way just yet.

But in the end, she couldn't bring herself to do it. She took a long breath, and turned to face the man. The man she hadn't expected to see ever again.

Trevor Cullen. The man she had once been certain she was going to marry, to spend the rest of her life with. He still looked so much like his little sister, Victoria.

Victoria, whose untimely death Diane was responsible for.

Diane felt her limbs trembling as she slowly

approached him, tilting her head slightly, unsure if this was really happening. It was like she was seeing him as he was then, so many years ago, and couldn't quite square it with the man before her.

She stood before him and removed her sunglasses, angry with herself for being unable to bring words to her mouth. His bright green eyes scanned her face, those piercing, all-knowing eyes that always made her feel he could read her mind. The years had changed him, but not much. The angles of his jaw were now lined with salt-and-pepper stubble, and his hair was no longer long and free-flowing. But it was him. The man she'd once loved.

"Diane," he said, his rumbling baritone seeming to course through her. "Wow. It's been a long, long time." His eyes bored into hers, making her heart flutter. "You look beautiful." One corner of his mouth turned upward as his face softened.

Diane's mouth lifted upward of its own accord. She'd never been able to resist his smile. "Trevor," she finally managed to say. Her cheeks felt like they were on fire. "Uh. I, ah, didn't recognize you for a second. I mean I did, it's just, ah...been a long time. Hi." She flushed again, irritated by her stammering.

His face broke into a grin. That winning smile.

Her legs felt like jelly. "I never thought I'd see you back in Marina Cove," he said, looking at her suitcase.

She cleared her throat. Her palms were sweating. "I was just here visiting my family...Did you move back here?"

Trevor shook his head. "I live in Chicago now, actually. I run a software development company there. But I bought a little summer home here. I guess part of me never really left this place." He looked around, smiling. "I still think of it as home."

Diane swept her hair behind her head and nodded. "I miss it here too, sometimes. I don't make it back as much as I'd like to." That didn't quite capture it, though, did it? She'd avoided coming home like the plague. Too much pain, too much regret. "Complicated family issues," she added lamely.

He nodded. "How long are you staying? I'm surprised I didn't see you on the ferry."

Her brows twisted in confusion for a second before she understood. "Oh, I'm, uh..." Her mind went strangely blank. "I'm not sure yet." She wasn't sure why she'd lied about leaving, but some part of her wasn't ready to go at the moment.

His green eyes sparkled. Electricity cracked and

popped across her skin. She forced her eyes not to wander across the tightness of his shirt across his chest, the hard ridges of his arm muscles. Guilt pinched at her as she thought of Grant.

As if reading her mind, he glanced down to her left hand before his eyes locked back onto hers. "So, you're married then?" His expression was unreadable.

She forced the tight muscles of her mouth to move, like the rusted gears of some old machinery. "Yeah. His name is Grant. We, ah, met in LA."

His expression remained even, but if Diane wasn't mistaken, there was an ever-so-subtle down-turn of his mouth. He nodded slowly. "Well, that's great. I'm happy for you." He shifted his weight to his other foot, still watching her. "Listen, I'm having a little get-together at my place tomorrow night. Super casual. You should come. For old times' sake."

She felt like a deer in headlights. "Well, I—"

"I'll invite Austin, too. Haven't talked to him in a few years, but I'm sure he'd love to see you, get the old gang back together again..." He trailed off slightly.

Diane's mouth went dry as cotton again. He'd left the rest of the sentence unspoken. The old gang... minus one member.

"*Austin*?" Her mind was working slowly, her thoughts moving through molasses. "He's back home too?" A fresh punch of guilt hit her in the back of the throat.

Trevor grinned. "Yeah, it's funny. When we all moved to LA, we always swore we'd never come back. Bigger and better things, and all that. I guess it's a siren song." He ran a hand through his hair. "He moved back a long, long time ago. Lives up on the north shore now. Owns a restaurant. I'd love to see him again, actually. What do you say?"

She forced back tears as she thought of everything she'd taken away from Austin. There was no way he wanted to see her again. Trevor was being kind. Sweat broke out on her brow. Grant's face swam in her mind. "I don't know, Trevor..."

He moved a step closer. She could smell his aftershave: leather, dark, rich oak, vetiver. "How about this." He reached into his pocket and pulled out a business card and pen, then scribbled something on the back and handed it to her. "Here's the address. People are showing up around seven. If you want to catch up, I'll be there. Hope to see you then." He motioned as though he was going to give her a hug before standing back to give her one last smile. "It was really good to see you, Diane. Take care." He turned to leave before she could say anything.

Diane took the business card and held it in her palm for a moment before sliding it into her pocket. Her fingers brushed against the folded pink note, and she shuddered. She felt suddenly nauseous as she looked up at Trevor walking away.

She could do her work remotely. Larson Brands wasn't going anywhere, it was all empty threats. She wasn't about to let Parker, of all people, pressure her into returning...she and Grant had bought the agency in the first place, after all. They wouldn't be anywhere without them. She could do whatever she wanted.

Besides, she owed her sisters and mother a proper goodbye. They deserved a lot better. Staying an extra few days...it was the right thing to do, regardless. She could plan a little get-together, just the girls. Try a little harder.

Diane spun her wedding ring around her finger as she watched passengers boarding the ferry back to the mainland, debating. After a long moment, she squared her shoulders, reached down for her suitcase, and turned back toward Ocean Avenue, toward the Seaside House, toward everything she'd thought she left behind for good.

6

R amona pulled off her striped socks and rolled up the hem of her jeans to her shins. Wincing slightly, she dipped her feet into the cold rush of the stream, pressing them against the smooth surface of the rocks below. Sunlight danced across the surface of the water, bending and twisting against the wakes formed around the large rocks scattered about Sunflower Run Creek.

A handsome man in jeans and a dark T-shirt splashed past her, laughing, as a little girl of about nine followed, hair streaming behind her. She reached down and splashed water at the man, giggling hysterically, before he suddenly turned around, his eyes wild. The little girl shrieked gleefully as he bounded clumsily after her, sending up huge splashes of water behind him.

"I'm gonna getcha, sparky," he hollered after her. The girl shrieked again, bolting past Ramona and spraying her with water.

Ramona laughed as she watched Danny chase after Lily, arching her back and letting the warm sunshine wash over her skin. It had been a perfect Friday morning, a surprise respite from the spreadsheet-filled madness of the past few days. Danny had been managing his store remotely more and more often, which afforded them opportunities to spend weekdays doing things like splashing around in the creek at the park. Ramona had caught up on most of her work for the week, and welcomed the break. After she'd lost her home, she'd worked harder than ever to fill her bookkeeping client load, desperate to turn her financial situation around.

She looked back down at Danny, smiling fondly. He was such a good father to Lily...she couldn't imagine how hard it must have been to do it all himself. Everything he did was aimed at making her life better in some way. Lily was a terribly lucky little girl.

Ramona's chest tightened as she thought of her

own father, how wonderful he'd been. At least before he'd left them.

Danny stopped for a moment, the water rushing past him, and their eyes met. His face pulled up into a broad grin as he suddenly clambered through the stream toward her, his eyes dancing with amusement. He reached out a dripping hand and touched her arm before running away. "Tag. You're it!" he called behind his shoulder.

Ramona grinned and splashed after them. Lily squealed with delight. This was exactly what she needed, a wonderful distraction from the drudgery of the rest of her life.

She lost herself with Danny and Lily, the glow of the sunlight, the birds singing in the trees lining the stream, the smell of the fresh-cut grass of the expansive park behind them. She reached down and cupped her hands, filling them with cold water and tossing it over Danny's head as he yelped. Out of nowhere, a pang of anxiety hit her in the throat.

At any moment, this could all be taken away from her. It was all so fleeting.

She thought of the lawsuit. Of her alcohol-fueled mistake that had spiraled out of control. Of her tenuous grasp on her early sobriety, her first painful meetings with her new counselor. The upcoming meeting with her lawyer on Monday.

Diane and Charlotte had helped her to find the lawyer. As much as she'd tried to bury her head in the sand, the lawsuit was progressing with or without her. She'd finally come around to the sickening realization that she had to do something about it, that it wasn't going away.

Danny had stopped splashing, his eyebrows furrowed. "Lily, why don't we take a snack break? I brought your favorite cheese crackers." As Lily splashed to the shore and reached into the canvas bag Danny had brought, he approached Ramona and pulled her into a hug.

"You're upset," he said, stroking her hair softly.

Ramona's body tensed. The words "No, I'm fine" were cued up and ready to be released. Every old instinct pressed her to pull away from Danny, from anyone trying to get close.

But times were changing. After they finally found out what had really happened to her father, she'd resolved to stop following in his footsteps, to stop pushing everyone away and trying to do everything herself all the time.

She took a breath and looked up at Danny. "Yes,

actually. I'm having a hard time relaxing...with everything else going on right now."

He nodded, guiding her toward the bench where they'd set their things. His phone rang, and he quickly reached into his pocket to silence it. Lily had taken her snack and was exploring the length of the stream, following a group of bright orange butterflies. Ramona drank some ice water, savoring it. She felt a sudden powerful desire for a drink that hit her like a punch.

But as she'd just learned in her early counseling sessions, part of her desire to drink was being cued by painful feelings she was trying to avoid. She could ride out that craving for a moment, just let it be, and it would eventually wither on its own, like a plant without water. She took a few more breaths, waiting for the feeling to pass. Danny sat next to her and put his hand around hers, giving it a soft squeeze.

As the moment slowly passed, tears formed in her eyes. She was exhausted. But she was doing it, really doing it. One day at a time.

"Thanks, Danny," she said, putting her head on his shoulder. "I'm in a tight spot right now. My old answer was to avoid my problems. But they're not going away." She lifted her head and faced him. "We need to get the Seaside House up and running. That's the only real answer here. I've lost pretty much everything...I'm in so much debt I feel like I'm never going to get out from under it. I have the lawsuit. We still have my Uncle Patrick and everything he did hanging over our heads...his son, Samuel, keeps calling us over and over. God only knows why, after everything. I just feel lost, Danny. I really don't—"

Danny's phone rang loudly from his pocket again. "I'm so sorry, Ramona," he said, silencing the call without looking at the screen. "You were saying."

Ramona sighed and shook her head. "I just don't know what to do."

He took her hands in his. "I wish I could do more here. You know I'm happy to help out financially. I don't have much, but—"

"No, Danny, you're doing *more* than enough already. Your store is giving us all our materials at cost. You've been helping Christian with the restoration in your off time. We already don't deserve everything you're doing. Everything's just an uphill battle. I—"

His phone rang again. He cursed under his breath, took it out, and pressed a button to turn it off before setting it on the table behind him. "I'm really sorry. Why don't you come to stay with Lily and me?"

She glanced at his phone for a second before looking back up at him. "Ah. No. Thank you. That's really sweet, Danny. But I want to take things slow, you know? I'm fine at the Seaside House for now."

He smiled. "Of course. I want to take it slow too. At least let me set you guys up with some real beds? You can't camp out on the hardwood floors forever."

She laughed. "It's actually fine. It's a reminder of what we need to do, how far we need to go. Discomfort's a powerful motivator." She smiled, before the email she'd received this morning swam in her mind against her will. Another client mysteriously "no longer required her services." The word about her lawsuit was apparently getting out. How long until no one would hire her? How long until—

Danny's phone buzzed on the table. He closed his eyes. "I thought I turned it off, I'm sorry."

"Uh. Do you need to get that?" Ramona asked, brushing aside her irritation.

He looked at her and winced. "It's, ah...Caitlyn. She's been calling all morning."

"Oh." Ramona's heart dropped into her stomach.

Danny ran his hand through his hair. "She has the night off work, I guess. She wants us to come up to Providence. She wants to see Lily. I already told her no, though. Several times. I don't know why she keeps calling."

Ramona blew out a breath. His second wife had a knack for choosing the wrong times to suddenly be available. She would go days or even weeks without saying anything, falling off the grid, before reappearing, asking Danny and Lily to drop everything. Poor Lily didn't really understand her mother's instability...her young age and her loyalty to her mother made it impossible for her to see the negative effects it had on her. After Caitlyn's difficult past that involved stints in prison and drug-related issues, Danny had been the only stable presence in Lily's life.

Ramona didn't even know if Lily knew that Danny wasn't her biological father, that her real father was the result of a years-long affair between Caitlyn and some unknown man who dropped them when he found out about her. Ramona's love for Lily had bloomed, and she desperately didn't want to see her get hurt after how much she'd been let down in the past.

"You should go," Ramona said, carefully keeping her voice even. It was upsetting...but she meant it. It wasn't her place to judge Caitlyn. Lily wanted to see her mother too, and Ramona was going to have to navigate the complicated dynamic if she wanted to try to make things work with Danny.

"No." He shook his head resolutely. "Today is about us." He glanced over at Lily to make sure she couldn't hear what he was saying. "She can't expect us to be at her beck and call, when most of Lily's life she's had no interest in being a mother. It isn't fair to Lily, or to me." He moved closer to Ramona. "Or to you." He lifted her chin up, and she slowly touched her mouth to his. A glow of warmth cascaded over her. "Let me go deal with this. It'll only take a second. Then let's forget all about it." He gave her a reassuring smile before heading into the grassy field behind them to call her back.

Ramona watched Lily skipping rocks across the stream, becoming slowly hypnotized. The water gently rushing past her, the buzzing cicadas, the streaks of sunlight through the trees, the gentle bird-songs. A long time passed. She furrowed her brows and looked back at Danny only to find him pacing the field, gesticulating wildly and shouting into the phone.

Ramona's stomach tightened. She turned back to Lily only to find her walking tentatively toward Danny. He put his hand over the phone as she came up next to him, and got on one knee, putting a reassuring hand on her back. Ramona wanted to give them their privacy, but just as Lily was finished talking to him, Danny looked up at her, his mouth slightly open and his eyebrows furrowed.

Ramona felt a twisting sensation in her chest. She knew without being told that Lily wanted to see Caitlyn and that their day together was coming to an unexpected end. Lily skipped over to her, saying, "Guess what? We're going to see my mommy, Ramona!"

Ramona forced a smile on her face. She knew Danny was still looking at her but was unable to meet his gaze. "That's great, honey! Sounds like it'll be a fun day." Lily grinned at her and began gathering her things. Ramona's heart ached for the little girl.

Caitlyn was an unpredictable presence, and there wasn't anything Ramona could do about it. She had no right to be angry, not really, and she wasn't mad, exactly. She was hurt. Today had been about them, or so she'd thought. Caitlyn was part of the package, though, whether she liked it or not.

Ramona knew she would do anything for Danny, and for Lily too. She was getting so much closer to Lily, and felt that she needed a strong, stable female presence in her life, even if Ramona felt like an imposter. But Caitlyn was her mother.

Danny hung up the phone and sat down quietly next to Ramona, poking the ground with a stick he'd found. "I'm sorry," he said.

She nodded and looked up at him, unsure of what to say, what she was supposed to do.

7

Diane tugged at the hem of her skirt as she scanned the expansive living room again, looking for Trevor among the crowd of people milling around. A man dressed in a tuxedo appeared in front of her, holding a tray of cucumber canapés and bacon-wrapped prunes. "No, thank you," she said, before reconsidering and grabbing a handful of everything. Heat rose to her cheeks as the man smiled at her. She stuffed a canapé into her mouth without thinking, and crossed the room over to the bar, trying her best to be inconspicuous.

Trevor's "little summer home" was a mansion perched over the northwest shore. She'd arrived at what she thought was a fashionably late time, only to find that she was one of only a few guests who'd arrived so far. One awkward house tour later, she and Trevor had a brief conversation that she could barely remember. Her heart had been pounding so hard she was surprised he couldn't hear it. She was beginning to have second thoughts about coming.

Trevor had been a polite host, introducing her to other guests, but he had just disappeared with an apology as more people arrived. Diane didn't know anyone else, so she'd been doing her best to keep moving around, nodding and smiling but feeling utterly invisible. As she approached the bartender, she felt her phone buzz in her purse, and pulled it out.

Ice water plunged through her stomach. Parker. Somehow, in the last day, she'd completely forgotten about the Larson Brands pitch. Her mind raced as she struggled to remember what she'd even been doing since she left the ferry terminal after running into Trevor. It was completely unlike her.

She would have to call them and explain. Geoff and Lisa would be more understanding. Hopefully. It was time to get going anyway. Hopefully before Austin arrived.

What had she been thinking anyway, coming

here? Trevor was in her past. She had no business meeting up with him.

Diane asked the bartender for a glass of water, then stuffed her last canapé into her mouth. She turned around, and standing right in front of her, in jeans and a plaid sport jacket, was Austin.

She coughed and spluttered, feeling the color drain from her cheeks. She felt like she couldn't breathe. After a terrifying moment, she realized she was choking. Panic rose like lightning in her chest as her eyes widened.

Austin's eyebrows drew up in surprise as he saw her struggling for air. Diane closed her hands around her throat and shook her head frantically. Several people turned to look, gasping in surprise but doing nothing.

"*Stand back*," Austin shouted at them. "Give us some space." He stood beside Diane, bending her over slightly at the waist. Diane's heartbeat was a jackhammer against her skull. She felt the heel of Austin's hand come down between her shoulder blades once, twice. Her vision beginning to recede at the edges. Austin brought his hand down again, and then she began to cough hysterically. She wheezed as she inhaled huge lungfuls of air, tears burning her eyes.

Austin guided her to the ground, and then Trevor appeared next to him, handing her a glass of water from the bar. "Are you all right, Diane?" Trevor asked, his face tight. After another coughing fit, she nodded, her cheeks on fire. "I'm sorry, Diane, I was out on the deck, I ran in here as fast as I could—" he said, rubbing her back.

"No, I'm fine, it's my fault," she said, shaking her head and then gulping down the entire glass of water. Her vision was pulsating. She glanced up at Austin. "Good to see you again, Austin," she said, and began laughing hysterically. The air in her lungs felt absolutely magical. After a few moments, Austin began to laugh too. He and Trevor helped her to her feet, and guided her out onto the patio.

"AND REMEMBER that dance Austin used to do? It was like..." Trevor stood up and began to wiggle his hips, pumping his fists in the air. Austin and Diane burst out laughing. "It was all that champagne, man. No one else was even on the dance floor yet. I think it was around that time they began to catch onto us." He took a swig from the bottle of wine he'd brought out to the deck.

"No, dude." Austin shook his head. "You kept switching up the names. You started telling them we were Aunt Ethel's kids, but then you started saying Aunt Edna."

Diane giggled and nodded. "That was it. It probably didn't help that I couldn't keep a straight face every time Trevor introduced us to someone. You also told the bride that we were good friends of the groom, but he was standing right next to her." She paused. "It was like you were *hoping* we'd get caught."

Trevor grinned. "What's life without a little adventure? It probably made for a great story on their wedding day." He handed the bottle to Diane, who paused before taking a long drink. It felt great to cut loose for a while.

They'd been sitting on the deck for at least an hour, the sun slowly inching down toward the horizon, casting a warm orange glow all around them. Cool ocean air swept up from the shoreline below, bringing goosebumps to Diane's skin. She had been so relieved to be breathing again that she'd nearly forgotten how terrified she'd been to see Austin, after everything.

But to her profound relief, it had been totally fine. The three of them slipped right back into their old rhythm, right back into how it had been all the way back to when they'd been friends in high school. Back when Diane had started dating Trevor, back to those whirlwind days.

After they graduated, it had been Trevor's idea to make their way out west to California. "Marina Cove will always be here," he'd told them one summer night after some crazy exploit of his making. "We need to explore. See what else the world has to offer." They'd been so young, feeling immortal, wild. The four of them had driven across the country in Trevor's old Plymouth Duster with nothing to their names. Trevor was the ringleader, always able to talk them into another thrilling adventure.

After a few minutes, Trevor broke the comfortable silence, turning to Austin. "It's really good to see you, man. It's been way too long. How's the restaurant? How's the wife?"

Austin leaned back, running a hand through his dark hair. "Kate's good. We're busy. Really busy. The restaurant..." He shrugged. "It's doing okay. We're both putting in a lot of hours. It's tough. You have a few years of success, but then the tides can change, just like *that*," he said, snapping his fingers. "So I guess no, the restaurant's not okay, is what I'm saying. But we're trying to get things going again."

Diane felt a loosening between her shoulder blades as waves of relief cascaded through her. Austin had found someone. He'd been able to move on after Victoria, then. She'd always wondered, but had never been able to bring herself to check on him over social media, or to reach out. Each time she thought of what she'd done over the long years since she'd last seen Austin, a sickening lurch of guilt would twist through her. But it seemed that he'd come out okay in the end. Diane blew out a long breath.

She watched Trevor as he and Austin caught up, unable to tear her eyes away from him. It was like magnetism. The silky rumble of his voice, the way the lock of hair kept falling over his eyes, his infectious laugh. That smile that had always seemed to hypnotize her. She began to scold herself, but stopped. She wasn't doing anything wrong. It was only natural that she'd remember how things had been with Trevor after so long. She'd never cross a line with him now.

Trevor stood up, arched his back in a stretch, and looked right into Diane's eyes, sending a shiver running up her spine. "I'll be back in a sec, I want to show you guys something," he said, a glimmer in his eyes. Diane only nodded as he winked and left them.

"I can't believe the three of us are back here," said Austin. "I never expected to see you again."

Diane tore her eyes away from Trevor's back. "I know. I was actually supposed to leave a few weeks ago, but I'm glad I stayed." She turned toward him, debating for a moment. "So, um," she said, taking a deep breath. "You're...doing okay, then?"

He looked at her, holding her gaze. A moment stretched between them that made Diane's heart leap into her throat. They both knew what she was asking.

His face finally broke into a small smile. "Yeah. Yes. I've been okay. I wish work was going a little better, but I suppose I really can't complain." He looked out over the water.

A long moment passed. Diane cleared her throat. "Thank you again," she said, her voice quiet. "For, uh, saving my life and all back there. No more canapés for this girl."

He turned to her, and then laughed. "It was no problem. I'm sorry all those people just stared at you while you choked. Tough crowd."

Diane shook her head and snorted. A moment of awkward silence passed before Austin rubbed the back of his head with his hand and looked over at

Diane. "So what about you? How are things back home?"

Way too complicated to get into during this conversation. "Things are great," she lied. "You know. Living the LA life. Whatever that means. My husband and I bought an ad agency a while back, so that's been keeping me busy." She quickly took another swig from the wine bottle, ignoring the spikes of pain drilling up the faded scar on her arm.

He nodded. "That's great to hear. I'm happy for you."

Diane smiled just as Trevor reappeared, holding something behind his back. A wicked grin crossed his face. "What's that you've got there?" she asked, raising her eyebrows playfully.

He shrugged, then slowly presented what he'd been hiding. It was a large pair of black bolt cutters. Austin laughed and groaned as Diane rolled her eyes. "Very funny," she said, laughing and taking another drink.

Trevor pulled an innocent expression. "What? I thought maybe we could get out of here...go on a little adventure. For old times' sake."

Austin stood and pulled the bolt cutters from his hands, running his fingers over the smooth handles.

"I can't believe you still have them. You got us into a lot of trouble over the years with these bad boys."

Trevor scoffed as though wounded, still grinning. "Sure, but we also had a lot of great times. Remember when we broke into the Science Center? You were the one who got the projector working in the planetarium. Remember all those stars? Now, stand there and tell me that wasn't one of the greatest nights ever."

Austin returned his grin. "Well, we were already there. I couldn't help myself. I always wanted to see one of those shows. You're a bad influence."

Diane's heart beat harder. Trevor had a wild streak in him, that was for sure. It was one of the things she'd been most attracted to. She'd never been with someone like him. Not before...or since.

Trevor looked at Diane. "What do you say, kid?"

She glanced at Austin. He shrugged. "I've got nowhere to be tonight." He narrowed his eyes at Trevor. "But nothing stupid. Or dangerous. Or, ah, illegal. I'm too old for all that noise."

Trevor put a hand to his chest. "I would never," he said, his eyes sparkling with danger. Diane's stomach fluttered, and she felt a weight pulling on her third finger. Squeezing her eyes shut, she rolled her wedding band around, forcing back the guilt simmering in her stomach. There was nothing wrong with a little fun, a little distraction from the grind.

Her phone buzzed in her pocket. "Sorry," she muttered. Time to turn it off. She glanced at the cracked screen and did a double-take. Her skin went cold.

Her notifications showed a new voicemail, only it wasn't from Parker.

It was from Geoff.

Diane's mind raced. Geoff never called. Never. In all the time she'd been working at the agency, she'd never even seen him pull out his phone.

Parker she could handle. He was a spineless eel. But Geoff...

It wasn't looking good.

She looked up at Trevor, her eyes locking on his. He dangled the bolt cutters in front of him and gave her a beckoning look. All at once, a realization tore through her like a wrecking ball.

When she was around Trevor, it was like all the parts of her that suffered turned off. The *constant* mental grinding about the agency, about her kids, about Grant, about Victoria and the accident...the folded pink paper in her pocket, the rubber band on her wrist...the man who'd been following her...

everything she'd done, all of it...the pure internal torture of it all, the feeling that it was never going to end...gone. Just gone, like flicking off a light switch. Any time she'd ever experience a moment of peace, her thoughts would creep in like slithering snakes, and she was compelled to ruminate over and over and *over* again about everything, the fear of influencing anyone else's outcomes, the guilt, the panic, the shame that roiled within her at all times.

But not with Trevor. After she'd seen him yesterday, she'd been in a pleasant haze, so much so that she'd forgotten about her pitch entirely. It was... relieving. And Diane was sick and freaking tired of being so miserable all the time.

She was unable to break the eye contact with Trevor. His green eyes were like infinite pools of excitement, of danger. It was what had made him so utterly intoxicating back when they'd dated all those years ago. It was the feeling of being *alive*. Of casting away the shackles of the grinding reality of everyday life. Of being free.

At that moment, Diane thought she would do anything to make that feeling last.

She felt the corners of her mouth turn up of their own accord. "What about your party? Won't your guests be upset?"

He grinned at her. "Who cares about them? I barely know any of them. They're mostly work acquaintances. They don't care about me either, they just want free food and booze, to see and be seen. I have more important things to do tonight." His eyes glimmered in the waning sunlight.

Diane stood up and approached Trevor, not breaking eye contact. One of his eyebrows rose slightly as she stopped just inches from him. Without glancing down, she pulled the bolt cutters from Trevor's hands. He laughed.

Diane felt electricity sparking all across her skin. She hefted the bolt cutters over her shoulder and took one last swig from the nearly empty wine bottle.

"All right, then," she asked. "Where are we going?"

lla pulled open the brass doorknob and stepped onto the creaky polished floorboards whose every line and groove she knew by heart. The smell of aged paper and percolating coffee filled the air. She breathed in deeply, sighed, and headed toward the rows of dark chestnut shelves, back to her old stomping grounds. She reached the classics section, running her fingers along the ancient spines, warmth filling her to the core.

Beachcomber Books had long been her sanctuary, her secret place to escape. She scanned the rows of dusty books, that feeling of excitement awakening in her again as she saw her old favorites. Dickens.

Austen. Brontë. There was nothing in the world better than escaping for a while into a great book.

She pulled *Wuthering Heights* from the shelf, sat down on the floor, and opened the book in her lap. Waning golden sunlight cascaded through the large bay windows at the front of the bookstore, and dust motes sparkled and glittered in the air. That musty, earthy smell of old paper and ink brought a flurry of memories to her mind.

Jack used to come here with her. Ella smiled as she remembered the first time they'd come here together, all those years ago. It was one of their first dates.

She'd been nervous...but as always, after a few minutes with him, she felt like she was home. They'd sat in front of the fireplace in the back of the bookstore, on that ancient blue leather couch with the torn seams, talking for hours about books, about their families, about life. Gosh, she'd been so young. She'd had her whole life spread out in front of her.

The bookstore belonged to Martha Sutherland, an incredibly sweet girl whose husband Leo had been a long-time friend of Jack's. The four of them became fast friends, and used to while away Sunday afternoons hanging out in front of the fire together, reading and talking and laughing.

Her stomach filled with acid as she glanced over to the blue couch, and for a second she could swear she heard his big, booming laugh. Jack, always larger than life.

It seemed like a lifetime ago. It practically was.

Now here she was, alone on the floor of the same bookstore, old and withering and sad. After the disaster of a date with Skip, she'd met up with a couple of other men she just didn't hit it off with. That old feeling kept creeping up that had followed her ever since Jack had gone and she'd put herself out there. She was pulled in two directions... believing that she would never find someone again, a good man she could spend the rest of her life with, and believing that even if she did, she wouldn't be able to trust him, and he would inevitably lie to her or abandon her, just like Jack had. Perhaps if she'd been someone else, someone better or more worthwhile or more helpful, Jack would have felt he could be honest about the horrible things he'd been going through, instead of leaving her to try to shield her and their family from his problems.

She shook her head. There it was again, that old voice that always whispered in her ear. *You weren't enough, Ella.*

Jack had loved her. He had. She knew that, knew

it in her bones. Despite his problems, despite what he'd done...Jack had been a good man.

Ella's shoulders slumped, and she swallowed against the lump in her throat. She'd already had her chance, and he was long, long gone.

She took *Wuthering Heights* and a few other books and walked through the empty bookstore to the reading area in the corner. Her heart sank a little as she noticed that she was the only customer. Way back when, the bookstore had been like a beehive; it was a Marina Cove institution. Martha had practically needed to kick customers out at the end of the day. It was a little corner of paradise.

She looked around. Now the place was always empty, falling apart at the seams. The ceiling leaked, windowpanes were cracked, the paint was peeling everywhere. The bookstore looked how Ella felt.

She supposed the store's decline began after Martha passed away. Leo hadn't quite been able to keep things going. It hadn't been easy for him, trying to run the business on top of his job as a ferry captain.

"Hi, Roald!" she called over to the man at the register. He'd been working here for a few months, and she hadn't been able to crack his cold exterior. He glanced up, frowned through his thick horn-rimmed glasses, and looked back down at his phone. Ella sighed and set her books on one of the little round tables in the corner, then went to the carafe against the wall and poured herself a large, steaming cup of black coffee.

Ten minutes later, she was still trying to relax. Things weren't so bad, if you really stopped to think it over. So she wasn't ready to date again. She knew how to be alone.

And besides, she wasn't really alone. Two of her children had found their way back to Marina Cove, and that was something. Charlotte had even decided to move here, to Ella's delight. Diane...well, Diane was always hard to read. Maybe not as tough as Ramona, but there was something there...something wrong that Ella couldn't put her finger on.

All in due time. Diane had said she would only be here a couple of days, and weeks later she still hadn't left. It seemed like she was waiting for something.

The bell above the front door rang, and a man bustled in, hunched over like he was fighting an invisible storm. "Get off your telephone machine, please," he barked as he passed Roald, who raised his eyebrows as though personally affronted.

Leo pushed his windswept salt-and-pepper hair

from his eyes as he scanned the bookstore, scratching his beard and muttering to himself. He had just begun to unbutton his captain's uniform when his eyes landed on Ella. His expression immediately softened, his bright blue eyes dancing with laughter. "Ella!" He laughed. "Didn't mean to start undressing in the presence of a lady! A thousand apologies." He laughed again before his face fell slightly. "Thought the place was empty again. I guess you're going to keep it afloat for me, though, huh?" He walked over to her as she stood up and gave her a hug. "Haven't seen you since your trip to Ireland. How're you holding up?"

She motioned for him to join her, and he poured himself a cup of coffee before sitting at the table. Ella took a slow drink from her cup, inhaling the aroma of the coffee and letting it warm her. "Well, I won't lie and say it was easy," she said, staring at the table. "I went to his gravestone. His sister, Maura... she took me there."

Leo scratched his beard and looked at her thoughtfully. Sadness crossed his expression. She took a long breath, and continued. "I was able to say goodbye, though. I felt like I got a little closure. And Maura, she's a great lady. We actually ended up having a good time. She took me on a little road trip around Ireland. It was beautiful. I could've stayed there for ages, but..." She ran her hands over the table idly. "I have a lot to deal with here, with the Seaside House and all."

Leo nodded and cleared his throat. "I'm real sorry about everything with Jack. Can't imagine what that'd be like...you're a tough one, though, Ella. I wish I was more like you."

Ella laughed ruefully. "I'm not as tough as you think, trust me. Besides, you're doing okay, aren't you? You've been through quite a bit yourself."

Leo opened his mouth, reconsidered, and downed a few gulps of coffee, wincing. His eyes drifted over to Roald, to the place where Martha had spent years handling her customers. A distant expression crossed his face as he unconsciously rolled his wedding band around his fingers.

Ella's stomach lurched unexpectedly as she remembered Martha's face, the way her eyes crinkled when she smiled, the melodic tinkling of her voice. After Jack left, Ella came to the bookstore less and less often, holed up in her bedroom when she wasn't racing around trying to manage the Seaside House as the business slowly collapsed around her. They'd kept in touch over the years, the three of them, but Ella had withdrawn almost completely from the outside world. And then when Martha died, Leo had withdrawn too.

Years ago, when Ella had one of her bouts of failed attempts to start dating again, Ramona had suggested asking Leo to dinner. But he hadn't taken Martha's death well at all, and was very clearly not over her. Ella would never enter into a relationship with someone who was so stuck on someone else. And really, who was she to talk? She knew she'd probably never get over Jack. And Martha had been so wonderful, a true gem. It had all happened so quickly, she didn't blame him at all.

At any rate, Leo had always been a good friend, a good man, if not a little rough around the edges. In the last few weeks she'd made an effort to try to rekindle that friendship, in the interest of not wasting any more of her life away.

Ella rested her hand on his, and he jumped a little. "Are you all right, Leo?" she asked softly.

He leaned back in his chair, scratching his beard. "Oh, you know. I'm all right. I just...have a lot on my mind." He looked off into the distance and said nothing more.

Ella decided not to press any further. He'd open up if and when he was ready. "Well. I have something to take your mind off everything. A little story about a man named Skip."

Ten minutes later, they were both still guffawing as she finished her story with some of the more memorable lines from Skip's barbershop quartet performance. Leo was bright red and wiping tears from his eyes. "Oh, Ella, geez, I'm sorry," he said, laughing again as he ran a hand through his hair. "Hey, at least you got a good story out of it. I know you'll find someone. It's just a matter of time. You're a great catch."

Ella laughed and tucked a strand of hair behind her ear, heat rising to her cheeks. "I sure don't feel like it, Leo. Sometimes I feel like a wrinkly old woman whose time has passed. For good."

He leaned toward her. "No, no, you'll find someone. Maybe it'll take some time, but it'll be worth it. It's hard to be alone. Especially when everything else around you seems to be falling into the gutter." He glanced around the empty bookstore and sighed. "I'm glad you're here. It's good to have someone to talk to when the going's rough."

Ella's stomach clenched as she saw tears rimming Leo's eyes. "Oh, Leo, I'm so sorry," she said, handing him a tissue from her purse. She watched him for a moment. "Is it Martha?"

He shrugged, then shook his head. "I don't know. It's...everything. I never planned for any of this, you know? I thought I had it all figured out. And now here I am, trying to keep Martha's dream alive, her beautiful bookstore, and I'm *ruining* it. Everything she worked for all those years. This place was her life, Ella. It was her baby. She loved it like a child." He cleared his throat and dried his eyes. "I'm sorry. It's...there's a lot happening right now."

Ella rested her hand on his forearm. "What's going on, Leo?"

His face crumpled as he put his hands over it. "I don't know how I got here, Ella. It's..." He breathed into his hands, his shoulders dropping. "Never mind. It doesn't matter how I got here."

Leo looked up at her, his eyes bloodshot and tired. "I can't keep up with the rent here. Business has been on the downslide for years, and it's only getting worse. Things are bad, Ella. I think...I think I'm going to have to sell the bookstore."

The words settled around them heavily. The ticking of the clock on the wall sounded like wooden beams snapping in two, cutting through the otherwise deafening silence.

Ella thought of Leo's sister, Ruth. She'd been sick for a long time. Leo had been beside himself, and had once confided in her that Ruth hadn't been able to afford the treatments, that he was helping her out. He was terrified that it wouldn't be enough, that it would eventually bankrupt him.

Ruth had thankfully gotten better after the treatments faster than the doctors thought she would. Leo had been over the moon. But Ella had noticed him taking on more and more ferry shifts after that.

Ella's mouth was dry. She swallowed hard against the lump in her throat. "You're selling this place?" Her eyes darted over to the old blue leather couch by the fireplace.

Leo squeezed his eyes shut and shook his head. "It's the last thing I want. I don't know what else to do. I can't keep it afloat much longer. It breaks my heart, Ella...this bookstore *was* Martha. I let her down. I did her memory a terrible disservice. I tried, but I couldn't keep it going." He rubbed his temples as he stared at the ground. "This place is all I have left of her...and I wasn't enough."

Ella looked around, speechless. Tears pricked the corners of her eyes. After everything, this how it ended. Her place, her happy place. She supposed she hadn't really noticed how far gone it was.

Her throat constricted as she thought of Jack.

This place was one of her last ties to him. And now, it too would be gone. Like it had never existed in the first place. Her mind went unbidden to the last letter he'd left her.

A terrible memory crashed through her. Pushing through the old front door of the bookstore, her cheeks flushed, a skip in her step. Jack by the fireplace reading *Walden* for the thousandth time, looking like he was about to nod off. Pulling the book from his hands and sitting on his lap, whispering in his ear. She'd just gotten back from the doctor. Another little one would be coming soon. The tears in his eyes as he clutched her close, running his hands through her hair, breathing her in like she was oxygen. Her heart fluttering as she kissed him hard, so much promise and joy ahead of them.

There was nothing she could do, of course. She was massively in debt herself, and was currently sleeping on the hardwood floor of the half-burned-out husk of the Seaside House after Ramona had lost the bungalow she'd been living in for years. There was no end in sight for the restoration, and they were in a terrible spot after Jack's brother Patrick had conned them into signing over a percentage of their future earnings to his fraudulent charity in exchange for work that he'd promised he was only doing to help them. Ramona had signed on the dotted line, so they had no choice but to pay. What were they going to do, prove his charity was fake? He had an endless team of lawyers and powerful people to fix his problems. It was going to send them further into the debt spiral that seemed to go on and on without end.

He'd also told Ramona he planned on billing them for the work he'd done, for God only knew how much. They had no intention of paying that, of course. But Patrick was powerful. He had a long history of getting what he wanted, one way or another.

She thought of where she was supposed to be before she ended up at the bookstore tonight. She'd gotten to talking to a very sweet man at the deli counter a few days earlier, and they'd made plans tonight. She spent more than an hour getting ready, a brand-new dress that still did nothing to help her self-consciousness, but she was determined.

He called her ten minutes before they were supposed to meet, apologetic; apparently, his wife had found out, and he was "in the doghouse." Real nice guy.

It was all a hopeless pursuit.

Ella had known before he'd even called her that something would happen. Because it always did. It was inevitable. And when he'd told her about his wife, all she could think about was how much Jack had hidden from her. How she never could have seen it coming.

There was a heavy pit somewhere inside her, some dark, shapeless thing she couldn't quite make sense of. Each time she tentatively reached out to touch it, to try to sense its shape, she went cold and retreated. It was too much. She couldn't bear to be betrayed again. She was just one of those people whose time had come and gone, who'd already found her person. It hadn't worked out, and there was nothing written into the laws of the universe that said she was meant to find love again.

Some people just didn't get a second chance. And that would have to be okay.

Maybe she'd been looking at everything all wrong, though. There was more to life, wasn't there? She had plenty of things to be happy about. Her children...the ones who spoke to her anyway. Her health, her friendship with Leo. The inn, if they ever got that up and running again.

Something tiny flared within her, a glimmer, a spark. Finding love was off the table, but so what?

There was plenty she could occupy herself with... plenty to distract herself with.

It was easier to distract sometimes.

Ella leaned in, took Leo's rough hands in hers, and squeezed, looking up into his eyes. He returned her gaze before his eyes skittered away.

There was something else, something he wasn't telling her. It was in those big, blue eyes of his. Ella sensed it in him, *knew* it as though he'd said it aloud.

But that didn't matter right now. That could wait.

"Leo," she said, her heart beating hard in her ears, "I think I might have an idea."

9

"I don't know, Trev," said Austin, pulling off his sport coat and wiping his brow. "It's, like, actual breaking and entering. We could be arrested."

Trevor was ahead of them by a few paces. They'd been walking in the sand for what seemed like hours. Diane reached for her phone to check the time, but an invisible force stopped her hand. Right now, she didn't want anything else to exist.

Right now, it was just them. The old gang.

Well, almost all of them.

For a split second, she felt like hands were pressing on her windpipe, closing around it, but as she shook her head and looked up at Trevor, the feeling disappeared.

Trevor looked over his shoulder at them, his blond hair whipping in the wind. "You're over-thinking it, Austin," he said, a casual expression on his face. He could be on the way to the grocery store rather than leading them into who knew what sort of craziness. "No one's ever here this late. I mean, look around. Who's gonna find us? We'll be fine." He glanced at Diane and lifted one corner of his mouth. A thrill stole across Diane's skin.

Austin looked at her and rolled his eyes. She laughed. "We'll just be careful," she said, rubbing his back as they trudged through the sand. The tension in his face dissipated, and he grudgingly returned her smile.

"Besides," Trevor said, lifting a small, flat rock from the sand and skipping it across the waves, "when have I ever steered you wrong?"

Austin stopped in the sand. "Are you serious? All the *time*, man. We *always* got caught."

Trevor laughed, still walking ahead. "No. Maybe someone found us out a few times, but we never got in trouble."

"You almost got me *expelled* senior year, are you forgetting? They never did find all those rubber duckies."

He waved his hand as Diane suppressed a giggle.

"They weren't gonna expel you." He stopped, turning back to them to let them catch up. "Well. Maybe that one was a little dicey. But you got off scot-free, right? And now you have a great story."

Austin shook his head, but a corner of his mouth was turned up. Trevor clapped him hard on the back. "Now. We're almost there. Phones off, voices down." He lifted his bolt cutters in a toast. "To a great night."

Diane and Austin raised invisible glasses and clinked them against the bolt cutters. The waves crashed against the shore next to them, and the wind rolled smoothly across Diane's skin, breaking it into goosebumps. Trevor grinned, and with a graceful motion that belied his age, he hoisted himself over the half-wall that divided the sand from the stairs leading up to Shannon Pier.

The sky was pitch-black as they climbed up to the boardwalk leading out onto the pier. She peered into the darkness. Not a soul around. It must've been after midnight. They quietly passed several vendor carts, stands for cotton candy, funnel cakes, ice cream cones. They were closed up, locks and chains wrapped around them. After a few moments, they arrived at a long chain-link fence that was rolled out from each side of the pier, blocking their way. At the point where the fences met was a short rusty chain and an ancient padlock.

"It looks spooky in there." Diane rubbed her shoulders. Austin came up next to her and offered her his sport coat. "I'm all right, thanks," she said. "I think I'm just nervous."

Trevor paused in front of the gate and turned to them. "Here we go," he said, lifting the bolt cutters to the chain and squeezing down. The chain snapped like a twig.

Diane's heart pounded as they quietly closed the gate behind them. They tiptoed through the darkness until they came upon a large wooden sign, and Diane stopped to look at it. "Shannon Pier Amusement Park." Waves crashed against the tall pillars holding up the boardwalk below them.

It was like walking through a ghost town at this hour. They passed the arcade, the tilt-a-whirl, the old merry-go-round with the painted horses that used to scare Diane as a child. The pale moonlight illuminated the pier, giving everything a sparkling luster. She remembered how she used to come here with her brother Gabriel, when the other Keller siblings were still too young to be out on their own. They'd pool their loose change and spend the afternoon on the rides, eating snow cones, getting their faces painted, and listening to the live music, feeling like the summer would last forever.

What was Gabriel up to now? She hadn't seen him in years...they barely spoke anymore. She ached to see him. After they'd found out what happened to their father, she'd called him several times, but he wasn't interested. He was angry. Gabriel had always been stubborn.

And Natalie...well. Natalie, the wild middle child. She could be anywhere in the world right now. Diane's heart sank as she realized she could barely remember her sister's face.

"What are you doing?" asked Austin, tearing Diane from her thoughts.

She looked around for Trevor. He was next to the side door of a small, long building painted bright green and pink on the far left edge of the pier boardwalk. Pipin' Pete's Burgers, The Marina Cove Taffy Extravaganza, Alicia's Ice Cream Parlor, the Shannon Pier gift shop, all in a row. The door on the side said *Maintenance*. A sign below that read *Do Not Enter*.

Trevor was shimmying a credit card between the door and the frame, frowning in concentration. "Just checking on something," he said just as the door opened with a soft *click*. "Don't mind me." He turned inside, closing the door behind him.

Diane blew out a long breath as she looked up at Austin, unable to keep the smile from her face. Austin was running a hand through his hair and glancing around, looking back toward the street in front of the boardwalk. He shrugged and looked at Diane. "Ah, well. No one's around, I guess. May as well have some fun—"

At that moment, a series of loud bangs reverberated across the pier from behind them. Diane jumped and whipped around to find the source. Section by section, colorful lights popped on all across the amusement park. A tremor ran across her spine. Last, the giant spokes and circular outline of the Ferris wheel illuminated with a final *bam*, followed by the nostalgic melody of old-fashioned calliope music, the kind you'd hear at a carnival.

A thrill of laughter left Diane's throat as Austin whooped and hollered. "You're crazy!" he called to Trevor, just as he pulled up next to them. "You can see these lights for miles!"

Trevor wrapped an arm around Austin's shoulder, then Diane's. Her skin tingled with excitement. "I think we'll be fine. How often do you get to have a whole amusement park to yourselves?" He let go and began jogging toward the bungee trampolines. He turned, beckoning them, a mischievous smile playing on his lips.

They flipped and bounced on the huge trampolines, rode down the steep winding slides that ended in the ball pit, and shot Skee-Ball in the arcade, winning roll after roll of red tickets they'd never cash in. They strolled through the Tunnel Aquarium, staring in awe at the pink fluorescent jellyfish, seahorses dancing around each other, the graceful turtles gliding behind the glass dome above their heads. They played a competitive round of mini-golf, ending in Austin sinking a hole-in-one right into the pirate's mouth. "That's five bucks each, people." He grinned at them, holding out his hand as they crossed the boardwalk to the bumper cars. "Pay up."

"No chance, you cheated!" shouted Diane, running ahead of them. "You can't throw the ball in with your hands!"

Trevor jogged ahead and pulled a large keyring from his pocket, approaching a small stand next to the bumper car arena. He sank the key into a slot, glanced up at them, and, with a wink, turned it. Colored lights popped on each car with a little crack and a static hum. Diane gleefully hopped into one of the cars and stamped her foot hard onto the gas pedal.

Everything was moving slowly, as if they were in a beautiful, hazy dream. The red, gold, and orange lights flickered and flashed all around them, her hair flying behind her as she cackled with delight each time she slammed into one of the guys. The music drifted over the warm salty breeze, and she could swear she smelled the sweet, aromatic whisper of cinnamon churros in the air. She watched Austin lean forward and barrel into Trevor, pumping a fist in the air, clearly having the time of his life. It was such a relief to see him happy.

The thought crossed her mind that they had somehow completely avoided bringing up Victoria. Trevor's sister, Austin's soulmate, Diane's best friend. How could they even stand to be around Diane, after what she'd done? A flash of that long red hair, that crooked smile tore through her mind as the old dead weight of guilt pooled in her stomach.

Time was pulling and stretching around her. She whipped the car around the bend, and across the floor was Austin, heading for her. His face was a stone. Something was wrong. His mouth curled into a snarl as he slammed his foot on the gas and headed toward her. She felt that old feeling of the ground being pulled from underneath her, the horizon tipping over. The shimmering tangerine light through the shattered glass falling like tiny snowflakes.

Diane squeezed her eyes shut and tried to reach for her rubber band, but her limbs weren't responding. The world was tipping over. Nausea sloshed through her. Her eyes popped back open, searching for something, anything to be an anchor, and landed on Trevor's face. His soft expression, the hint of excitement in his eyes. He pushed a lock of hair out of his eyes and smiled at her, sending a flood of warmth through her skin, like she'd just slid gently into a hot tub after a long, hard day. All at once, the vertigo disappeared. She was back in the bumper car. The terrible, crushing guilt that had been tearing through her was just...gone.

Diane looked over at Austin, who was doing a lap around the far edge, a huge smile splayed across his face. She felt the tightness across her chest give way, and tried to recall what she'd been so upset about. Her mind was strangely blank. Something was still there...but it could wait. She had all the time in the world.

She breathed in deeply and pressed her foot into

the pedal, her stomach fluttering with excitement, with relief.

"So," Diane said, tearing her eyes away from the ocean far below them and looking up at Trevor. She shivered as she saw he was already watching her. "What's life in Chicago like? When are you going back?"

Trevor shrugged. "It's good. You know. Busy. I like it. I can work pretty much anywhere, though. I don't know when I'm leaving."

He stretched his arms out across the edge of the Ferris wheel car and leaned back, sighing. "Not too bad," he said almost to himself, his eyes flickering across the dark sky, the starlight.

Diane looked out over the sea as they slowly rose above the ground. She could just barely make out the distant light of ships passing in the night. The faint sparkle of moonlight reflecting against the long stretch of sand looked like a sea of diamonds.

Her heart was in her throat. She hadn't expected to be alone with Trevor up here. Austin had gotten a phone call from his wife, and was down on the boardwalk talking to her. Trevor had tried several keys until the large Ferris wheel began to rotate. "Come on," he'd said with a grin, taking her by the hand and rushing to jump on one of the cars just as it left the ground.

Diane looked across the car at Trevor, her eyes landing on his left hand. She squinted in the dim light, unable to stop herself from seeking out his ring finger. There was no harm in peeking, was there?

Nothing. A distant part of her was surprised she hadn't thought to check earlier. She wasn't exactly in the habit of looking once she'd gotten married. A curious warmth spread across her skin, a flicker of danger. It was...intoxicating. Unlike her.

"So, are you married?" Diane asked, immediately regretting it. Grant's face flashed across her mind. She pushed it away with some effort. There wasn't anything to feel guilty over. She would never let anything happen.

Trevor looked over at her, meeting her eyes. After a moment that seemed to stretch on and on, he shook his head. "Nope. Never got married. Never found the right person, I guess." He looked at her, unblinking, his expression unreadable. Diane averted her eyes, looking out over the water as they dipped back toward the ground. Sometimes looking at Trevor was like staring at the sun.

A memory came to her, unbidden. The last time she saw him, all those years ago. Must've been... what, twenty years? More? It was a little...hazy. She tried to remember exactly what had happened that led to their breakup. A heavy soreness rippled through her, like the dull pain from an old scar.

Whatever had happened that led to them breaking up...it had been her fault. That much she remembered.

She looked back up at Trevor as the Ferris wheel approached the ground and swept back up into the sky. He was watching the sea, his expression distant. He closed his eyes, the wind sweeping his hair all around him like wildfire.

"I wish Victoria was here," he said. He ran a hand through his hair and sighed.

Tears forced their way into Diane's eyes, and her heart skipped a beat, making her cough hard. She wanted to say something, anything, but the words were strangled in her throat. She reached for her rubber band and cracked it against her wrist, hard, as that old sick feeling bubbled in her stomach, twisting and roiling. A bright, scalding pain drove up through the scar on her right arm like a rusty spike, making her bite her tongue to avoid yelping.

Trevor turned to look at her, his eyes like two

deep, dark pools. Diane quickly swiped away the tears streaming down her cheeks. "I miss her too," she managed, her voice shaking.

He opened his mouth to speak, but a call from Austin below them interrupted him. "Hey guys! I have to leave!"

As the Ferris wheel car approached the bottom, Diane and Trevor hopped off, taking a few stumbling steps to avoid falling over. Austin was pacing, a frustrated expression on his face. "Sorry, guys, I have to run."

"What for?" asked Trevor. Some of the spark was gone from his voice. Diane felt weak, stretched too thin.

The line between Austin's brows deepened. He muttered something about the restaurant, shaking his head. "I just have to get home."

Trevor shrugged. "Suit yourself." He rolled his head around on his shoulders and let out a long breath. As he opened his eyes, the sparkle was back, that glimmer of mischief. "Just one more thing before you leave." A slow smile spread across his face as he turned his head up, looking behind them. Diane wheeled around to see what he was looking at.

Towering above them was the outermost track of

The Rocket, the old wooden rollercoaster that terrified Diane as a child.

"No. No freaking way, Trevor." Austin shook his head. "I'm not riding that."

Diane looked from Austin to Trevor. "I think he's right, Trevor," she said, smoothing her hair back. "We've pushed our luck already, haven't we?"

But as Trevor watched her, one eyebrow raised, she felt that buzzing, winding excitement rise through her chest, like strands of shimmering, spooling light.

Diane was so tired of being the good girl all the time. Always on time, always prepared, always working harder than everyone else. Always thinking of everyone else, never thinking about what she wanted, only how everyone else would be affected. Always feeling *guilty*.

It was exhausting.

She needed an escape from it all. If only for one night.

Trevor's eyes were ablaze as Diane's face pulled into a smile. She looked at Austin, who shook his head. "Go for it. I'll be down here, hand over the emergency stop button."

Trevor took her hand, and they hopped into the front of the roller coaster. "Let 'er rip!" Trevor called to Austin. He flicked the switch on the little operating board, and the safety bar in front of them lowered with a *click*. They began to roll down the first slope of the track. Butterflies exploded inside Diane's stomach in a colorful flurry.

As the chain pulled them slowly up the big rise, rusty gears clanking away beneath them, the ground got smaller and smaller, and that terrible weakness that had settled into her bones after Trevor had brought up Victoria leached out of her like a poison. She felt a hundred pounds lighter, like she could float away if she wanted to, whirling and twirling like the fluffy seeds of a dandelion in the summer breeze. As they approached and crested the very top, Trevor reached for her hand and raised it in the air, whooping into the night sky. Electric heat snapped and cracked across her skin.

And then they were plummeting down, down into the darkness, and Diane was screaming with glee. She buried her face in Trevor's chest as she clutched the safety bar. They slammed down and then lifted clear up off their seats as the track rose and twisted again, only to plummet a second time, shooting toward the boardwalk like a rocket before shifting wildly around the outside track right over the crashing waves below. Time had ceased to mean anything as she felt herself whipped around the writhing track, holding onto Trevor's strong and steady frame for support.

Diane's heart pranced around in her chest like a jackrabbit as the car finally rolled to a stop in front of Austin, who was grinning despite himself. "You guys are crazy," he said, shaking his head.

Trevor pulled his hand away from Diane's, hopped out of the car, and clapped Austin's shoulders. "Austin, my boy, you just missed the thrill of a lifetime." He turned to look at Diane, that wild glimmer in his eyes, before his face slowly fell.

"Uh, guys, I think we need to go—" he started, just as a white beam of light splashed against his face.

Diane whipped around. "*Hey! What the*—" an angry voice called from behind the beam of light. "*Are you kidding me?*" A large uniformed man was rushing toward them from the open chain-link fencing down the boardwalk, the harsh jangling of keys from his belt reverberating across the pier.

Austin was staring at him, his mouth slack like he was in a trance. "*Run!*" screamed Trevor, grabbing Diane's hand and reaching for Austin's shoulder, giving it a hard shake. Austin woke from his stupor, his eyes widening. "*Go, go, go!*" Trevor yelled, guiding them beyond the roller coaster to the far end of the pier.

Diane's pulse throbbed in her temples as they frantically wheeled around the back edge of the pier and ran behind the arcade. The digital melodies from the machines carried into the darkness ahead of them. "*Stop! Shhhh,*" said Trevor, taking them behind the darkened merry-go-round. They boarded the platform and ducked behind one of the seats next to a brightly painted unicorn.

Diane's chest heaved as she tried to catch her breath. She could hear the approaching footsteps of the security guard and looked up at Trevor crouched next to her. He put a finger over his mouth, and Diane suppressed a giggle.

The guard's flashlight shone wildly all around them. As he approached the carousel, his walkie-talkie crackled with a voice saying something inaudible. He raised it to his face. "Three of them, at least. Whole pier's lit up like the Fourth of July. Get over here, quick. I already called the cops."

Austin swore under his breath. "We need to get out of here," he whispered. Diane's skin felt hot and cold all at the same time. She could feel Trevor's heat next to her, burning like a furnace. She shivered as her leg brushed against his. They looked at each other in the dark, and Trevor snorted as he suppressed a laugh.

A tiny giggle escaped Diane's throat like a balloon popping before she clamped her hands over her mouth. Trevor's eyebrows rose into his hairline. The beam of the flashlight that had been skittering across the boardwalk suddenly froze on the carousel. The edge of Austin's face was illuminated in the bright flood of light.

"*Run!*" Trevor said, and the three of them bolted across the platform and leaped onto the boardwalk.

"*Hey! Stop!*" called the guard behind them. Diane cautioned a glance behind her shoulder. He was sprinting toward them, yelling into his walkie-talkie. Gaining on them fast.

They burst through the opening of the chain-link fence at the pier's entrance and barreled down the long stairs and onto the sand. "*Stoooooop!*" screamed the security guard as they fled across the shoreline, kicking up huge plumes of sand behind them. Diane's lungs were burning as she pushed her legs harder, harder toward the distant copse of trees. Austin was leading them, both arms pumping as he ran like he was competing in the hundred-yard dash.

Diane was grinning, gripping Trevor's hand, her hair trailing behind her like a banner in the wild wind. She gazed around at the sky, at the treeline, a thrill cascading through her, hot and electrifying. The dark horizon stretched into eternity, and billions of stars sparked in the gossamer sky, a spectral ocean of fireworks. She laughed aloud and ran, ran like nothing mattered anymore, like she was young and free, finally free, wanting, *needing* the feeling to last forever.

10

"Okay, just remember what you've been practicing. Put your feet on the ground. And breathe," said Charlotte, taking a deep breath.

Moments ago, she and Christian had been sitting on the front porch of the Seaside House, scratching Ollie's ears, rocking gently on the swing and looking for shapes in the clouds, laughing like children. It was the perfect end to the day spent working on her pastries at the restaurant and then helping Ramona to continue scrubbing and sanding away at the fire damage to the upstairs bedrooms. A comfortable silence had stolen over them as they listened to the waves lapping at the shore in front of them, watching the sailboats drifting by, when she felt

Christian's hand tighten almost imperceptibly in hers. A moment later, he began holding his breath, and as she looked up at him, she saw that his eyes were pressed shut. Beads of sweat broke out on his brow.

A tremor ran across Charlotte's spine. After the first few therapy sessions Christian had attended to begin treatment for PTSD, he'd learned to recognize the signs of an oncoming flashback, and as he began to institute what he'd been learning, Charlotte had been helping support him. The therapist had told him that it was common for things to get worse before they got better. Which was just terrible. But Charlotte admired Christian for putting in the work.

"Okay. Name five things you see," she said. It was the start of a simple grounding technique he'd been taught, but he wasn't always able to remember what to do when he felt a flashback coming on. She squeezed his hand. "Christian."

He took a long, trembling breath. Charlotte winced as she saw how pale he'd become. Christian forced his eyes open; they were rimmed with tears. "I see the ocean. The sand. Ollie's tail wagging." He pushed his feet into the ground and clenched his fists until his knuckles were white. "The wood of the porch. The chain link on the swing."

Charlotte took a breath herself. "Good. Now name four things you can touch."

A tear fell down his cheek, making Charlotte's heart fold in two. His hands ran over his jeans, over Ollie's fur, over the hair on his head that was now damp with sweat. He clenched her hand. "Your hands," he finished. Some of the color had returned to his face.

After Charlotte guided him through three things he could hear, two things he could smell, and one thing he could taste (the sweet tea she'd made them earlier), he was breathing normally again. He wiped the tears from his face and leaned back against the chair. "Thanks, Charlotte. Thank you."

Charlotte put her head on his shoulder, and they sat there for a while. It was going to take time, but he'd already been able to manage his flashbacks better than he said he'd ever been able to. So it was promising. Even though it broke her heart to see how much he'd been suffering in silence, Charlotte knew she would do whatever she could to help him get better.

Christian wrapped his arm around Charlotte's shoulder and drew her in close. She listened to the steady rhythm of his heartbeat, the in and out of his breathing, and marveled at just how right it all felt.

Things weren't perfect, that was for sure. And she and Christian were still navigating their new relationship. But still...she couldn't remember ever feeling so peaceful, like some missing thing inside her had finally clicked into place.

Christian tapped her shoulder, and she sat up. He motioned with his head out toward the sand. Charlotte squinted, and saw Mariah walking backward across the shoreline, camera against her face, following in front of an older woman in a skimpy red-and-white striped bathing suit, snapping away.

"Mariah!" Charlotte called out to her. She turned to them and grinned.

"Hey, guys!" She exchanged words with the older woman, who jotted something down on a piece of paper and handed it to her. After the woman gave Mariah a hug, she jogged toward Charlotte and Christian.

"Who was that?" Charlotte asked, pouring Mariah a glass of sweet tea.

Mariah leaned down to plant a smooch atop Ollie's head and sat down in a wicker chair across from them. "Oh, that's Opal. She saw me taking pictures earlier and asked if I would take some photos of her for her online dating profile." She laughed. "She told me to go wild, the more risqué the better. More power to her. I wanted to get better at photographing people anyway. It's a whole different ballgame than landscape stuff. What are you guys up to?"

"Oh, just hanging out," said Charlotte. "Want to have some dinner with us tonight? I talked Christian into cooking his famous stir fry."

Mariah looked at him and raised an eyebrow. "Only if he's got his umbrella on deck," she said. She and Christian burst into laughter.

Charlotte frowned in confusion. "Huh?"

Christian shook his head. "Inside joke," he said, still laughing.

Mariah grinned, and handed him her camera. "Go back before all the spicy profile pics. I've got a bunch of 'after' photos from when you finished rebuilding the railing on the stairs. What a difference. Whenever we get a profile up for the Seaside House, someday, I think one of these could go up. It's really beautiful."

He frowned as he flipped through them. "Not bad. My carpentry, that is. Your photos are terrible." She scoffed and kicked him in the shin playfully. "Ow!" he yelped. "Kidding! I love these. You've got a real talent. I love the detail in the close-ups."

"How's the restoration going, anyway?" Mariah

asked, inhaling the salty breeze wafting over from the sea.

Christian grunted. "Slow, but steady. Keiran's been a big help." He looked up at Mariah. "He asked about you, you know."

Mariah didn't look at him. "Hmm," she said, with an air of nonchalance.

Christian smiled. "He's a hard worker. Smart. Pretty handsome too, I'd say."

Mariah shrugged. "I hadn't noticed." If Charlotte wasn't mistaken, a subtle red flush had bloomed in her cheeks. She smiled inwardly.

Charlotte watched the two of them banter in a sort of silent wonder. It hadn't been all that long, and Mariah and Christian were really growing closer. Charlotte hadn't been at all sure what was going to happen when she decided to finally reveal the truth to Mariah about Christian being her biological father. It was an incredible relief. They were actually a lot alike.

"Well, I'm going to go process Opal's profile photos before dinner and email them to her." Mariah stood and arched her back in a long stretch. "She seemed like she was in a real rush. 'Got to get out there while the gettin's good,' I think is how she put it," she said, grinning.

Charlotte laughed. "You could have yourself a little side hustle. At least while you're still here."

The smile slowly fell from Mariah's face. "Right. While I'm still here." She forced the smile back. "Maybe I will. I'll see you guys in a bit," she said, pushing through the front door of the Seaside House before Charlotte could say anything else.

"What was that about?" asked Christian, a line creased between his eyebrows.

Charlotte looked at him, her stomach tightening. "I shouldn't have said anything. She hasn't made up her mind about when to return to her med school program." She frowned, rubbing her temples. "Mariah's so tight-lipped about it...I still don't know what happened, exactly. She turned up here, dark rings under her eyes and way too skinny, like she hadn't been eating enough. It was getting to be too much, I think. She's always been a workaholic. She was having panic attacks, just like I used to get..."

Charlotte shivered and stared at the ground. Some of those panic attacks had been the most terrifying moments of her life. Cold nausea rippled through her as she thought about her daughter having to go through that. "She really seems like she's doing a lot better out here on her break. I've told her time and again that she's under no obligation to continue if she doesn't think it's the right thing...but I'm her mother, so I think she thinks I'm just being supportive." She looked up at Christian. "I'm afraid she's going to label herself a failure if she ends it. Especially after all it took to get where she is now. It would be like..."

"Like starting over," Christian finished.

Charlotte nodded. "This place..." She gestured around her. "It's like...vacationland. Like a year-round summertime dream. I think it would be hard for anyone to leave. And she doesn't have to. You see how much she loves her photography...couldn't she just do something like that for work?" She sighed and leaned back on the swing. "I don't know. I don't want her to go back and be miserable just because she doesn't want to stop doing something she started, even if she knows in her heart it's not the right thing. If that's even what's happening."

Christian furrowed his brows and looked out at the waves sweeping over the shoreline. After a few moments, he looked back to Charlotte. "Maybe I could talk to her about it sometime. If you think that's okay. I've done my fair share of debating about my own future in my life. At the very least, I want her to know she can talk to me."

Charlotte met his eyes. "Christian, that would be

wonderful. She'll open up to you. You two are...two peas in a pod. Smart, driven...stubborn as mules," she said, smiling.

He laughed. "Stubborn? No way. You mean principled."

As Charlotte reached for his hand, her phone buzzed in her pocket. "Sorry, one sec, Sylvie was supposed to call me about something for tomorrow," she said, pulling it out to answer. The screen showed a new voicemail.

Sebastian.

"Oh, no," she said under her breath. "I didn't feel it ring..."

"What is it?"

She looked up at him. "It's Sebastian. He better not be canceling on me again. I took off work again and everything, when am I going to learn..." She pressed her eyes shut. "I'm really sorry, can I just see what he said?"

Christian nodded and gave her an encouraging look. "Maybe it isn't what you think."

As she listened to the terse voicemail, her shoulders sagged. Then she hung up and tossed her phone onto the side table, her eyes brimming with tears. Christian took her hand and squeezed.

They sat in silence for a few moments as Charlotte sniffled quietly, too angry to move. She felt a throbbing in her hand and realized she'd been crushing Christian's fingers in her grasp. "I'm sorry," she said, her voice breaking. "He canceled again. Wants to move it to next week. This divorce is going to go on forever."

Charlotte felt rather than saw Christian stiffen slightly in the wooden swing. She looked up. An unreadable expression crossed his face. She felt a little stab of fear in her chest.

"Christian?" she asked after the silence stretched into uncomfortable territory.

He spoke without looking at her, watching the sea. "Are we doing the right thing here, Charlotte?"

Her stomach tensed. "What do you mean?"

He turned to look at her, letting out a long breath. "I mean...you and Sebastian...your divorce isn't even finalized...." He held her gaze. "Are we moving too fast?"

Charlotte felt her throat constrict. "Do you think we're moving too fast?"

He stared at her, unblinking. "I mean...a lot has happened to you in a short span. How do I know this isn't..." He shook his head. "That's not what I mean. I—"

"How do you know this isn't a rebound, is what

you were going to ask," Charlotte said, working to keep her voice even.

It was a fair question. What seemed like all at once she was back in Marina Cove, an entirely different life. In short order, she'd found out about Steph, about Brielle, about the false job with Carter Enterprises. Sebastian's business partner Alastair's underhanded plans to con Ramona into selling the Seaside House property so he could build a commercial retail center in its place. She was still navigating things with her kids...Mariah wouldn't talk to Sebastian anymore, and Liam and Allie were so hard to read. Everything was a mess.

Yes, she had moved on from Sebastian quickly. But she'd realized her marriage had been over for a long, long time. Sebastian represented comfort and stability.

When he'd taken that away from her...there'd been nothing left.

Charlotte moved closer to Christian and put both hands on his cheeks. "We were in love for a long time when we were younger. I was going to propose to you the night you left. Things only ended because your brother died in battle, and you went to take his place. I never really stopped loving you, even if I didn't think about it. And I think you never stopped loving me. It isn't like we're starting from scratch here, you know? And really, could we be taking things any slower?" She laughed. "I don't want to rush into anything any more than you do. This is too important."

His expression softened. "I know, but that doesn't mean I don't worry a little sometimes." He paused, his mouth turning slightly downward. "I just don't want to do the wrong thing here, that's all. I mean... Sebastian doesn't exactly sound like a trustworthy guy. What if he uses this against you somehow?"

Charlotte released her hands from his face. "He cheated on *me*. I have every right to be with you. We aren't doing anything wrong."

"I know. But..." His eyebrows pinched together. "He's already drawing everything out. If he wants you back so badly, he could try to use this against you, couldn't he?" He shook his head and looked at his hands. "I can't do that."

Charlotte's back straightened against the porch swing. "What are you saying?"

He ran his hands over his face and let out a long breath. "I'm not saying anything. I just don't know. I don't know what to think. This is complicated, and I don't want to do the wrong thing. We need to tread lightly. He obviously still loves you, and I don't want to complicate your life any further. I don't want us to make things worse."

Christian moved to stand up from the swing. Charlotte felt like everything was moving in slow motion as her mind raced. He looked at her and fixed a smile on his face that didn't reach his eyes. "I guess I should get dinner started, huh?" He gave her a peck on the cheek and turned to head inside.

Charlotte squeezed her eyes shut and stood on the porch behind him, watching him turn into the Seaside House. Her mouth felt dry.

She couldn't blame him. At all. It was complicated. When she'd decided to be honest with Sebastian and tell him about Christian, it hadn't even occurred to her that he might use it against her. They were technically still married, after all. And even though she and Christian were...well, dating maybe wasn't the right word just yet, but seeing each other...it could complicate the divorce proceedings if Sebastian wanted it to. Which was crazy. Didn't the fact that he cheated on her make a difference?

Her heart dropped into her stomach as she thought of the connections he had. Access to the best lawyers in the country. Sebastian's billions might have dried up, but he was still so powerful, so well-connected...there was a lot he could do.

Charlotte wrapped her arms around herself, shivering despite the warm summer air. He could hold things up for months, maybe even longer. She took a few breaths, feeling like the steady ground she thought she'd finally been standing on was shifting and cracking beneath her feet.

nock-knock-knock-knock.

Diane jumped and shook her head, her eyes still closed. Someone was knocking at the front door. Way too early. She groaned and stretched, yelping as blades of hot fire sliced across the scar on her arm. Her neck was stiff, and her lower back felt like someone had taken a sledgehammer to it.

Knock-knock-KNOCK-KNOCK.

She squeezed her eyes shut. Maybe they would just go away. For some reason, her mouth was dry, her heart was throbbing in her throat. Something was tight around her chest, like a rubber band squeezing. She winced as a bright beam of light shone across her face and slowly opened her eyes.

Diane couldn't understand what she was seeing. The front door was open in front of her, and a man in a police uniform was shining a light on her face. "You're going to be okay," he said to her in a strange, faraway voice.

She struggled to move, but something was holding her in place. She felt around her chest, pulling against a tight belt running diagonally across her frame. Whipping her head around, she saw the ground a few feet from her face. What she'd taken for the front door was something else...something filled with shattered glass.

The windshield. Oh, no. No, no no.

"*Trevor!*" she screamed at the top of her lungs. "*Trevor, help me!*" She was surrounded by darkness, but for a moment the policeman's flashlight shone a bright beam right into her eyes, filling her mind with white-hot lightning.

"Trevor!" Diane screamed, and shot to her feet. She took three steps before tripping on something and falling against hardwood flooring. She was drenched in sweat, and the thin blanket she'd been sleeping under was now tangled up in her feet.

Her eyes darted across the floor. Sleeping bags, pillows, phone chargers. The bedroom door swung open. "Diane...what's wrong?" asked Charlotte, her face etched with concern.

Diane put a hand against her heaving chest. Hot tears were in her eyes. "I...I thought—"

Knock-knock-knock.

Charlotte turned. "Is someone knocking on the front door?"

Diane wiped her eyes with the sleeve of her T-shirt. "I'll get it," she said, her voice wavering. The long tendrils of the nightmare were still reaching plaintively through her body, desperate for purchase. She needed to get out of the room. The feeling would pass.

She ran down the stairs and yanked open the heavy front door. Standing there on the porch was Austin.

"Hey, Diane, I'm sorry to turn up so early..." he started, then tilted his head slightly. "Are you all right?"

Diane ran a hand through her sweaty hair and pulled the front door closed behind her. "Austin, hey," she said. "Yeah, I'm okay, just a, uh, nightmare." She glanced down at herself, embarrassed. Stained T-shirt with holes in the armpits, sweatpants that were way too big, one purple sock and one pink sock. Nice one. "Sorry I look so scruffy...I wasn't expecting anyone."

He smiled and rubbed the back of his neck with his hand. "No, I'm sorry, I, ah, thought maybe you'd be up." Diane glanced up at the sky and grimaced. It was probably almost noon. She couldn't remember the last time she'd actually slept that long.

"I'm usually up a lot earlier," she said, wishing she'd taken a quick look in the mirror before she'd opened the door. "Late night, I guess. So what can I do for you?"

He grinned and held up his hands. Her black-and-white canvas tennis shoes were dangling from his fingertips. "I brought you a present."

She laughed and reached for her shoes. "How—"

"You took them off when we were jumping on the trampolines last night, remember? I grabbed them when we were getting ready to leave, but then when we got chased away..." He shook his head, still smiling. "I didn't realize I was still holding them until I got all the way home."

"Well, thank you, Austin," she said. "These are the only shoes I brought here. I really appreciate it." She looked up at him. "Can I buy you a cup of coffee? A proper thanks?"

He ran a hand through his dark hair. "Ah, wish I

could, Di," he said, glancing down at his watch. "Have to get to the restaurant...I'm supposed to switch off with Victoria, she'll kill me if I'm late."

Diane's blood ran cold. "Uh...Victoria?" Her voice was hoarse. A hard spike formed in her throat.

Austin's face slackened, his eyes widening. "Oh, God. Kate. I mean Kate. Kate will kill me if I'm late..." He rubbed his eyes with the palms of his hands. "I don't know why I said that. I guess it's just... seeing you and Trevor again, and all..."

Diane opened her mouth to speak, but the words wouldn't come out. She wanted to tell him how sorry she was. But anything she could ever say just wouldn't quite cut it, now would it? She'd robbed the man of the love of his life. Saying *I'm sorry*...it was so utterly inadequate it was obscene.

Austin reached out a hand and squeezed her shoulder. "I'm all right, Di," he said. His face was pale, but he lifted the corners of his mouth into a smile. "I'm fine. Really. I really gotta run, though. I'll see you soon, okay? I'll take you up on that offer for coffee sometime before you leave."

Diane blew out a breath. "Okay. Thanks again for the shoes, Austin." She gave him a quick hug before he turned to leave. Then she sat down hard on the front porch, watching him walk down the sand until he disappeared.

Her phone buzzed in her pocket. All at once, the light feeling she'd had since yesterday disappeared, like a balloon bursting in her chest.

The Larson pitch she'd forgotten about. Parker. Geoff...and his voicemail from last night. She hadn't listened to it, had completely forgotten about it after their late-night escapades.

What had she been thinking lately? She wasn't herself. For years and years she'd been so buttoned-up, a perfectionist. A workaholic. She'd never missed anything before.

Diane looked out over the water. Giant white towers of cumulus clouds shot up into the crystal blue sky, and the horizon was dappled with sailboats.

It was this place. It was being here...seeing Trevor again. It was like a dream...like a drug. A memory spun through her mind, one late night at a high school party, the house of some random girl she didn't know well. The red plastic cups every-where, the steady booming bass of the stereo, the air thick with cheap cologne and perfume and hormones. She'd never been drunk before, never liked the feeling of losing control that came after too many drinks.

But that night, for whatever reason, she'd been sick of always being the good girl, and kept drinking and drinking. It was a thrilling rollercoaster, a wild ride that she could barely remember, a hazy cross-cutting of laughing, dancing, diving into the pool out back. She was having the time of her life. But the next morning, her throat was thick, dry, her head pounding to the relentless drum of her heartbeat. Wincing at every loud sound, the sun far too bright.

That's what she felt like now. It was like a hangover in the light of day after a night of wild partying. She should stop now, get back on track. She could explain everything to the other partners. She was under stress, after all, wasn't she? A lot of stress after everything she'd discovered about her father...She could get out from under this. She'd earned some leeway.

Diane lifted her phone and found Geoff's number. She paused with her finger over the screen for a moment, thinking of Grant. Right now, on a normal workday, he'd be in some meeting, some pitch, maybe stuck in traffic, heading to lunch with a prospective client...good old Grant, head to the grindstone...at least after everything he'd done.

What a mess he'd gotten them all into. Diane took a long breath and pressed the number to call Geoff.

DIANE SAT DOWN HARD on the porch steps, her skin flushed. It could've been worse. She still had her job. For the time being, anyway. Geoff had always been very stoic, very hard to read, but she knew he was angry. Confused, too. She did her best to explain everything, ignoring the derisive snorts of his little henchman Parker sitting in front of him in Geoff's office.

She had one more chance with Larson Brands. Since it was Diane's pitch, the agency hadn't been prepared with a backup, and the execs at Larson were ready to pull the plug. Parker had apparently swooped in and appeased them for the time being, the weasel. But it was up to Diane to salvage the deal, which was...significant. It would float the agency for the next two years. What an industry...a company that made vegan bratwursts and nothing else was somehow now the key to the agency's success.

The only problem was, it was getting harder and

harder to care about work anymore. Her heart just wasn't in it since she'd been here. Since she'd been seeing Trevor. The more time she spent with him, the less everything else bothered her. The constant agonizing mental grind about the accident, about her kids, about Grant, about the agency...it just stopped when he was around.

It was...spectacular.

And right now, she had no plans to quit doing whatever made the pain go away. No matter the cost. She'd suffered enough.

Diane leaned back on her hands and watched the waves rolling in. Things hadn't always been like this. She and Grant had been the agency powerhouses back in the beginning, with everyone else taking their lead, along for the ride.

But then everything had changed in one night.

Grant had surprised her with a trip. A week in Las Vegas, pulling out all the stops. She'd been thrilled, jumping into his arms and kissing him hard on the mouth. With two young kids and hundred-hour weeks at the agency, they hadn't taken time off in several years. It was a sweet gesture; they'd gone to Vegas on their honeymoon and had the time of their lives. It was a chance to get back to where they'd come from, get back on track. Not that their marriage needed fixing...but things had been strained with life pulling them in so many directions.

Diane was having an incredible time. It was so good to just *exist* for a bit with her husband, with the man she loved. To have him all to herself. They'd left the kids with a good friend of Diane's, and they made it clear to the agency that they were to be reached for emergencies only. They held hands walking down the strip, eating the most delicious food at the upscale restaurants they'd only recently been able to afford, seeing the shows. Kissing in the dark as the massive fountains in front of the Bellagio burst into the sky in a glittering shower of water and light. "I've missed you so much, babe," he whispered into her neck. As she pressed her mouth against his, running a hand through his silver hair, she felt a surge of love and affection that she never wanted to end.

A few hours later, she was sitting in the massive jacuzzi tub in their hotel suite, her hair up in a bun and a glass of champagne in her hand. Grant was downstairs in the casino playing poker, giving her a little Diane time. She reached over to the plate and lifted a chocolate-covered strawberry, taking a slow bite and savoring it, pleasure and relaxation sliding over her body like a warm blanket. The bubbles from the jets against her skin, the water sloshing around her, the peaceful piano music flowing from the stereo in the living room...it was heaven. She arched her back and rested her head against the edge, feeling a gorgeous drowsiness taking over.

She snapped to, dropping the glass of champagne against the hard tiles of the bathroom floor, shattering it into a thousand pieces. The front door had burst open. "Grant?" she asked, hastily jumping out of the jacuzzi and wrapping a towel around herself. "Ow!" she yelped as a splinter of glass embedded itself in her left foot. She hobbled into the living room.

Immediately she knew something was wrong. Grant was sitting on the edge of the couch, his face in his hands. The top buttons of his dress shirt were loosened, and his silver hair was standing on end.

"Grant? What's wrong, honey?" she asked, approaching him slowly.

He blew out a long breath into his hands, and then looked up at her. Diane's chest tightened. His eyes were bloodshot and rimmed with tears. She knelt down in front of him, taking his hands, ignoring the throbbing spike of pain from the broken glass in her foot.

"Talk to me, Grant! What is it?"

He looked down at the ground and shook his head. "Diane," he said, his voice trembling. Diane clutched his hands harder. "Diane..." he whispered.

Her blood ran cold. "What happened, Grant?"

He took his hands away from hers and sat back on the couch. He wiped his eyes with his sleeve and scratched the coarse stubble on his face. She hadn't noticed until just now the dark rings under his eyes. Her heart was racing.

"This was supposed to fix it..." he said to the ceiling. "I was supposed to fix it..."

"*What does that mean?*" she yelled at him. "You need to *talk* to me, Grant!"

He dropped his gaze and looked into her eyes. Diane's heart broke as she saw something there, an expanse of pain pooling, something she couldn't understand.

"I have a problem," he said slowly. "A serious problem."

And then he started to cry.

12

Diane was huffing and puffing as she walked up the long road away from the Seaside House, taking turns at random, just trying to clear her head. She wiped the sweat from her brow as she turned left on Oakdale Street, now heading further uphill. Far down a rocky embankment, the waves crashed hard against the shore in a soothing, predictable rhythm that was calming, almost hypnotic.

Out of the corner of her eye, she thought she spotted a red baseball cap, the one worn by the man who'd been following her. Her heart slammed against her chest as her head whipped toward the storefronts where she thought she'd seen him, but he was nowhere to be found. Cursing under her breath, she breathed in slowly and closed her eyes, inhaling the fresh smell of the wildflowers growing in long stretches next to the sidewalk.

She was seeing things, that was all. There was no one who had any reason to follow her. She shook her head, and thought of Grant. Of that horrible trip to Vegas.

The months after that night had passed in a nightmarish blur. The romantic trip Grant had planned...well, it hadn't exactly been what she'd thought it was for. Unbeknownst to her, he had taken the last of the money from the agency coffers... and put it all down on the highest-stakes poker game of his life.

The problem extended back so far that it made Diane's head spin. It had started before they were even married, apparently. A few bets on a football game here, a few horse races there. Always making *just* enough back to keep him going, to keep lighting up those little dopamine pathways in his brain. When Diane met him, he'd already been wealthy. She thought he got his money from his years of work at competing ad agencies. Diane had certainly done well enough for herself. But she didn't know that he was moonlighting as a professional gambler, and doing *spectacularly*. Mostly online betting, but sometimes trips to Vegas, trips he'd always told her were for business.

He'd become especially adept at a poker game called Texas Hold'em. The combination of simplicity and reliance on bluffing, something Grant was naturally gifted at, and the high stakes of going all in appealed to the part of him that needed risk, needed that high that doing something a little dangerous gave him.

It went on for years without Diane's knowledge. They met, they bought Nicholls+Kline, they partnered with Geoff and Lisa to revamp it from a bloated mess into a lean and mean agency, a scrappy outfit that brought clients to the bleeding edge of creativity, style, and substance. It had been a wild ride. They had shot right out of the gates with early success. They poured any money they made right back into the agency, even taking out a second mortgage on their home. Things got tight, financially speaking, but the agency flourished. Diane got pregnant, they had Jamie, and then got pregnant again with Kayla. Life was great.

It was around that time that Grant's luck began to change.

Naturally gifted with numbers, Grant was the obvious choice to manage the agency finances. In retrospect, it would've been far wiser to have someone else in the role, a third party, someone with experience in accounting...but hindsight, and all that. One night, some random Tuesday, when the kids were all snug in their beds, when Diane was fast asleep after another long but rewarding day, Grant was downstairs on the basement computer playing poker. He'd felt the tides of luck shifting in his favor...and went all in on a hand he *knew* he would win. A straight flush, a hand so good that any reasonable poker player would have gone all in as well. A winning hand.

Except that night, someone with the username *pokergod54* also had a straight flush.

One number higher than Grant.

And he saw Grant's bet.

Just like that, Grant had a real problem on his hands. A colossal sum of money, gone in an instant, smoke through the fingertips. He panicked, and panicked some more, and then decided that the agency would never notice if he borrowed some money to pay down the debt.

And so the story goes. His luck continued to falter, and he kept "borrowing" more and more from the agency. He'd known he was playing fast and loose, but had that same spark of hope, of sad, terrible hope that all gamblers did, that the next hand would be *the one*, the next hand would deliver him from his sins.

He dug himself deeper, and deeper, until he could see the bottom of the agency well. So he planned their trip to Las Vegas, where he knew, *knew*, he'd be able to make it back. He had *that* feeling. He withdrew the last remaining money from the agency's accounts and put it all down on another winning hand.

And history repeated itself, as it so often did.

Diane was paralyzed with fear. She'd had no idea what to do. They left Vegas that night. She was determined to figure this out with him.

But then the other partners discovered the missing money, of course. Two days later.

Lisa saw something was awry when she'd posted a small down payment for less than three hundred dollars to a post-production house after landing a huge client, and it had been rejected.

What hurt worst of all was how well Grant had hidden everything from Diane. She knew he had a problem. That he was an addict. That he needed help. But she couldn't for the life of her understand why he hadn't come to her, why he had hidden his problem from her for so long. As he'd explained everything to her, her heart had broken.

She would have helped him. He was a man in pain, her husband, and she loved him. She would have done anything for him.

But it was far too late.

Diane had always tried hard to forget the looks on Geoff's and Lisa's faces when they met to discuss the next steps. She felt...naked, exposed. Small.

In other circumstances, Grant might've gone to prison. He would've had a hard time getting a job anywhere for the rest of his life. But Grant had opened up to them, let his heart pour out about his problem...and they voted down Parker, who'd been quietly ingratiating himself with Geoff and Lisa for years, deciding to handle it internally. Thank God. She and Grant had bought and revamped the agency, and had done so much amazing work together, which they recognized. It was Diane and Grant's saving grace.

But as Grant's spouse, they viewed Diane as complicit in the problem, and so she and Grant signed a new agreement, on the record. An agreement that made them minority partners, partners they could easily push out, if it came to that. It was only fair.

The off-the-record agreement was that Grant and Diane were responsible for paying back every single penny Grant had stolen.

Diane thought it would take them the rest of their lives.

Grant got help, professional help. He attended meetings with fellow gambling addicts every week. He lost some weight, got in great shape, woke up before Diane and went to sleep after her, working constantly. He was a new man.

But something had splintered between them, something important. A line had been crossed. It filled her with guilt, with shame, because he had a problem she couldn't understand, but she no longer trusted him. Things weren't so simple. There were repercussions to his problem, ones that affected others besides Grant.

At first, things hadn't seemed so bad. They celebrated with relief that at least for the time being, they had a plan to get themselves out. They worked sixteen hours a day, sometimes seven days a week, for years. They commiserated over their workaholism, the last two people in the office every night, eating Chinese food under the glare of the fluorescent lights, wondering what their children were up to.

Jamie's first tooth, his first bicycle ride, his first broken bone. Kayla's first soccer game, her first day at kindergarten, her first fight with a good friend. All experienced secondhand, retold to them by a rotating carousel of babysitters and nannies. Time flashed by Diane, like she was watching the world sweep past her from a speeding train.

She and Grant were missing everything.

They didn't really have any other options. There was no one else to turn to. Grant hadn't spoken to his brother or his parents in years, and so there would be no financial help there. And Diane knew she certainly couldn't ask her own family for help. She barely knew her siblings, and judging by the state of the inn the last time she'd visited, Ella was already in financial trouble of her own.

Her life had become about one thing, and one thing only. Work. Resentment pooled and roiled within Diane with every missed baseball game, every missed recital.

The splintering between them deepened, became a fracture.

One spring, Kayla was set to star in her school's musical. She was going to be Dorothy in *The Wizard of Oz*, and she'd been practicing her songs day and night. Diane would drive home as fast as she could in the evenings to practice her lines with her, and then when the kids were back in bed she'd drive back to work, making up the lost time by staying even later.

Several times she'd woken up at her desk, neck screaming in pain and eyes dry and burning. For weeks it went on, Diane determined to be there for her daughter, at least in some small way. She spoke with the other partners about having the night off for the big performance. It was a glimmer of light in the darkness.

She was sitting on the 405 freeway headed home, singing the songs in the car, a broad smile on her face, when naturally, she got the phone call. Grant broke the news to her. They needed her back at the office...no exceptions.

Diane surprised even herself at how devastated she was. This wasn't the life she wanted. This wasn't how it was supposed to be. Her children mattered more to her than anything else in the world, and she wasn't able to be there for them.

She paced around the living room that night, waiting for Grant to come home, sipping red wine too fast and trying to calm down. When he finally opened the door a little after three in the morning, she was at a breaking point.

"Grant, I can't do this anymore," she began, tears already in her eyes. She finished her glass and approached Grant, her fists clenched. "Kayla's been practicing for *months!* I can't believe you didn't stick up for me! *I needed to be there for her tonight!*"

Grant's mouth was a thin line. He rubbed his bloodshot eyes. "What do you want from me, Diane? I have *no leverage.* I don't know what you wanted me to say. I'm sorry, okay?"

"I'm missing my children's lives!" she screamed at him, her face inches from him. She'd never felt so angry in her life. There was something intoxicating about finally letting it all out. "And this is *your fault!*"

"Don't you think I know that?" he yelled back at her, his eyes wide. Diane took a step back. "How many times can I freaking apologize? I *know*, Diane. I know I'm the bad guy, okay? I can only be so sorry. I don't know what else you want from me. I've gotten help—"

"You should have gotten help sooner!" Diane's throat was constricted down to a pinhole. "You should have *trusted me*, and then we wouldn't be in this mess!"

His eyes were wild, his hair sticking out on end. "I should've gotten help sooner? I had a gambling problem, Diane, an addiction. You have no idea what you're talking about."

"I don't have any idea because *you never talked to me about it!*" she seethed. A strangled sob left her throat. "You completely left me out, like I haven't been by your side all these years. And now *I* have to pay the price for *your* problems!"

He stared at her. Diane's chest was heaving up and down. She knew she was being unfair to him. She knew he had a real problem, and that he'd come so far with all the work he'd done. But she was sick and tired of sitting on the edge of her seat every time he left the house, wondering if he was going to the casino, going to the horse track. Tired of scanning over their bank statements, credit card statements, her heart in her throat, looking for telltale evidence. Tired of wondering what he was doing on his phone. She was worn down, exhausted, at the end of her rope, and she couldn't stop the vitriol from coming. If she kept talking, she'd have even more to regret tomorrow.

She looked up at him, physically feeling the expanse between them widening.

"No one's keeping you here, Diane," he said, as if reading her mind. His face was slack, tears welling in his eyes. "I can only say again that I'm sorry. I'll do what I can to take on more work to lessen your burden. I'll talk to Geoff and Lisa tomorrow."

He let out a long breath and started toward the stairs to their bedroom. She stopped him with her arm and twisted him to face her, and then she kissed him. He buried his face in her hair, clenching her hard against his body.

"We'll figure it out," Diane whispered softly, stroking his hair. "We'll figure it out. I love you."

Grant wasn't the problem. It was the fallout from what he'd done that was the problem. Diane had been nothing but supportive through everything. But the repercussions were just too great, and she had absolutely no idea what to do. How to dig herself out of the canyon they were in.

But eventually, they did just that. Years of worka-holism, and they'd finally made up for the losses Grant had caused. Geoff and Lisa didn't know that Grant had borrowed large sums of money to help things along, from some less-than-reputable lenders. They needed to push things along, and their combined work wasn't quite enough.

Once the money was restored, they asked Grant to leave. It was fair. They let Diane stay on, which was something. Grant would just have to find work elsewhere.

Except for some reason, no one would hire Grant. They knew then that someone had let slip what had happened. Diane knew in her heart it had been Parker. He'd denied it, of course, when she confronted him, but there had been a tiny gleam in his eyes that told her all she needed to know.

So Diane became the family breadwinner, toiling day after day after day to pay back Grant's lenders. More missed time with her children. Her resentment grew. The gulf between her and Grant widened.

Eventually she'd paid back all the debt, to the agency and to every lender they'd dealt with. They had no savings, no retirement, nothing. But Diane was still employed, and it looked like they were going to be okay. She and Grant breathed a collective sigh of relief. They'd made it through the worst.

She'd had no idea then that her real problems were still to come.

Diane glanced up, shaking off the dark pool of thoughts she'd been wading through, and did a double take.

She'd been walking across Marina Cove for hours, taking turns at random, and her feet had unconsciously taken her somewhere she never expected.

Straight ahead of her, perched high above the stretch of crystal water, was Trevor's house.

Her stomach somersaulted, and she turned on her heel to leave. She got ten yards down the street when a voice called down to her.

"Hey! Diane! What're you doing here?"

She stopped, grimacing, then turned to face him.

Trevor stood on the edge of his balcony, leaning over the railing, holding a glass bottle of Coke. He wore swimming trunks and nothing else. Diane kept her eyes fixed on his face. He looked down toward her through his sunglasses, a grin on his face. "You want to come up for a quick drink?" he asked, shaking the bottle back and forth in his hand.

Diane shifted uncomfortably on one foot, squinting up at him. She was parched after all the walking...there was no harm in one drink with a friend, was there? A pit formed in her stomach, but she ignored the sensation. It was just her overactive sense of guilt. She was a grown woman and could do whatever she wanted. She would never let anything happen.

Squaring her shoulders, Diane stepped toward Trevor's house. With each step, she felt the burden of everything she'd gone through with Grant lightening, the terrible decline of their relationship, the drudgery of work and the toll it had taken on her, all the problems with her kids. The insomnia, the burning of her scar, the nightmares of the crash. Victoria, sweet Victoria, Trevor's sister and Austin's true love, gone from this world because of what she'd done. The constant checking, the constant worry that she'd somehow be responsible, again, for something terrible happening to someone she loved.

Each step Diane took toward Trevor, she felt lighter, more free, and she smiled.

13

E lla shifted her legs underneath her and pressed a hand to her lower back, groaning. She rolled her head around on her shoulders and lifted the putty knife back up to the long wall, scraping away. Her shoulder ached, her neck ached, her legs ached. Somehow even her face seemed to ache. Getting older was a real bear sometimes.

A long pile of chipped paint and dust trailed alongside her on the hardwood floor. Ella wiped her forehead, covered in a thin sheen of sweat, and ground the putty knife into the ancient, peeling paint. The color used to be a beautiful lavender, but was mostly yellow now, and downright brown and black in other places. Dirt and mold were encrusted into the paint itself. It was, in a word, disgusting.

The front door opened, letting in the sounds of people milling around on the street, the ringing of bicycle bells, the hard drops of rain falling against the sidewalk. Ella winced and got to her feet, quickly winding through the rows of bookshelves to the front of the store.

"Hello there, welcome to Beachcomber Books!" she said effusively to the man who had come in.

He stood at the entrance and closed his umbrella, smiling at Ella. "Hi there," he said, before taking a look around the bookstore. "I was hoping to, uh...to..." He trailed off and frowned. Ella felt her stomach tighten as she followed his gaze, seeing the bookstore through his eyes.

The place was a real mess. Ella had come to realize she'd been blind to it, coasting on her memories of the bookstore, her nostalgia. Everything was cluttered, old, dusty. Falling apart. Mismatched light bulbs flickered overhead. Paint and wallpaper was peeling everywhere. Not another customer in sight. And there was a certain...smell. Ella had been so fixated on that wonderful old book smell that she hadn't noticed how musty it was. Probably the ancient threadbare carpet that had been here since Martha herself had opened the place...

"Can I help you find something?" Ella asked. Perhaps too bubbly, too...pleading. He looked back at her, taking a step backward.

"I, ah..." he said, grabbing his umbrella from the stand. "Actually, I've got to run, forgot I have to be somewhere...have a good night, thank you." He turned to leave through the front door, back out into the thunderstorm.

Well. There you had it. It was no surprise the bookstore was failing. Ella sighed and looked around the empty space, remembering how she used to feel coming in here. It had been warm, inviting. There was something almost magical about a good old bookstore.

Things weren't going to change overnight. She'd learned that lesson well with the Seaside House restoration. Ella sighed again and walked back to the far wall, back to chipping away the old paint.

She and Leo had talked well into the night about her plan, her idea. She couldn't bear to let him sell the bookstore, not when she knew what it meant to her, what it had meant to Marina Cove in years past.

And most importantly, it was Leo's last tie to Martha. His late wife had made this bookstore her own, had loved it with her whole heart, and it showed. Without her...it was never the same.

It wasn't Leo's fault. He had enough on his plate as it was. And he was clearly dealing with something else, something he wasn't telling Ella.

Ideas had poured from her that night. She'd been truly inspired. Leo insisted the bookstore was failing due to online competition. And Ella understood that they couldn't compete with them on a pure sales front, maybe that was true. But they didn't have to. There was nothing wrong with the online stores...anything that got people reading more was great. They just offered something different than Beachcomber Books did.

People used to come here for the experience. It was one of the places where both locals and tourists would gather, to talk, to browse, to drink coffee and people-watch through the windows. A place to just *stop* for a while. She reminded Leo about how she and Jack would spend hours here, just reading by the fire or sipping coffee. Ella was overcome with her memories of the old couch, the beautiful aroma of cracking open a brand-new book, the warmth of the fire and of good conversation. It was something an online retailer couldn't offer.

They needed to revitalize Beachcomber Books.

To declutter it, repaint it, change the layout to make it flow better. Some new furniture, get the fireplace working again. Make it more inviting.

Ella had more ideas to increase revenue that she pitched to Leo. They could pair up with local schools to start a reading program. They could advertise a little, remind Marina Cove residents that there even *was* a local bookstore. Ella also knew there was a small group of authors who resided here, authors whom they could pair up with for book launches, events, book signings. The possibilities were endless.

If they could only get people *in* the bookstore, and keep them there, Ella knew the sales would come.

Leo had sat scratching his beard while she pitched her ideas, nodding thoughtfully. His eyes drifted to Roald at the front desk. Roald was leaning back on a stool, phone inches from his face, scrolling endlessly. He looked like a zombie.

He looked back at Ella. She nodded.

"He doesn't even like to read," Leo had said. "He told me that in his interview. He said he couldn't remember the last time he'd read a book. And he's always on that stupid phone machine..." He sighed. "He's not helping the situation, is he."

Ella looked at him for a moment. "What if I worked here too? Helped him out a little?"

She loved to read. It was the one thing over all the years that she'd never stopped doing. Even when she'd been practically bedridden with grief, with sadness after Jack had left her, books had always been there for her. They were like a friend who always knew the right thing to say. Ella would be able to help the customers with recommendations, to personalize their experience, something that Roald was unable to do.

Leo had hemmed and hawed when she refused payment. The last thing Ella wanted was to add to his financial burden. And besides, working here would give her something to do. The Seaside House was still in its early restoration stage, more foundational work. There wasn't a lot Ella was able to do at the moment. She could help revitalize the bookstore, and work alongside Roald to develop relationships with their local customers. Excitement stole through her as they planned. She ignored the little voice that told her she was using it as a distraction from her own flailing personal life. She was trying to help a friend, that was all. And the bookstore was also one of her last ties to Jack.

So in exchange for her help, since Ella wouldn't

budge on payment, Leo suggested that she could take out any books she wanted from the store for as long as she wanted. Ella loved the idea. When she had reached out a hand to Leo and shook his firmly, a smile rose to his face that didn't quite reach his eyes. He was...afraid. Ella could see it.

She didn't blame him. Change was hard. Brutal sometimes.

Ella chipped away at the lavender paint until it was completely dark outside. The rain wasn't letting up. She stretched and arched her back, wincing, and grabbed the broom to start sweeping everything up. She had to start somewhere.

"Oh no! No, no, no!" a voice called from behind her. Ella jumped and yelped, holding the broom in front of her like a weapon. She lowered it as she saw Leo standing there, drenched in rain, his eyes wide.

She laughed. "Leo! I didn't even hear you come in!"

"Ella, what are you doing?" he asked, rushing over to the wall, running his hands over it.

Ella's heart was still pumping hard. "What do you mean?"

He looked up at her, expression wild. Tears pooled in his eyes. "The paint! The paint! What did you do to the wall?"

"Leo..." she started, her face twisted in confusion. "We talked about this? The paint...it was old, moldy...it was peeling everywhere." She frowned, shaking her head. "We talked about repainting..."

Leo lowered himself to the hardwood floor, his hands pressed against the wall. "I didn't..." he started, his voice hoarse. His other hand twirled his wedding ring around on his third finger.

Ella sighed and sat down on the ground next to him, putting a hand on his shoulder. "I know it's hard, Leo. I know this is hard for you. I'm really sorry."

He closed his eyes, and two small trails of tears ran down his weathered face. "I was with Martha when she picked out this paint. I don't even know how many years ago it was." His voice wavered. "It's...just a shock, that's all." He looked up at her and wiped his eyes with his sleeve. "I'm sorry, Ella. I know it has to happen. It's what she would've wanted, I think. I know I have to let go."

Ella nodded and rubbed his back. "We can do this at whatever pace you want. This place hasn't changed in a long time. I promise we'll honor her with whatever we do change. We're just going to update things, clean it up. That will help keep her memory alive...making it so you won't have to sell the place."

He nodded, not removing his hand from the wall. Ella's chest tightened as she saw the pain etched across Leo's face. He had truly loved Martha.

Ella sat with him for a while before clearing her throat. "What do you miss the most about her?" she asked. Ella had always been afraid to ask about Martha, afraid that it would upset Leo or send him into a tailspin. But maybe if he could talk about it a little, with someone he trusted, it would make things a little bit easier.

Leo released his hand from the wall and sat back, blowing out a long breath. To Ella's relief, he smiled. "The sound of her voice. It was like...music. It was the sort of voice that made you feel all warm inside." He laughed as fresh tears rose to his eyes. "I'm sorry for getting all weepy, Ella. I know it's been a long time since she's been gone. But I really do miss her. I miss her more than I can say. It's like someone ripped a huge hole inside me."

Ella blinked back tears and smiled as she thought of Martha. How she'd always had a good story, how she was always singing, humming, floating around like she walked on air. Ella sometimes still couldn't believe she was gone.

"I miss her too," Ella said softly. She rested her head on Leo's shoulder and let the tears fall. The rain pattered softly against the front windowpanes, and a soft beam of moonlight illuminated the hardwood floor around them.

After a while, Leo cleared his throat. "What about you and Jack? What do you miss the most?"

A confusing ache stole through her. Ella couldn't quite place the feeling. It was like...anger and grief were intertwining, twin serpents coiling around her heart. She straightened her back and squeezed her eyes shut.

Leo looked at her, his eyebrows drawn. "Oh, Ella, I'm sorry—"

"No, it's okay," she said, letting out a shaky laugh. "I miss the way he used to hold me. His arms would wrap around me and I just felt...safe. He held me like he never wanted to let me go."

She wiped her eyes with the back of her hand. "It's so hard, isn't it? Remembering. I mean, I haven't seen Jack in twenty-eight years. But finding out what really happened, why he left us...finding out that he died...it was like..." She met Leo's kind eyes, and swallowed hard. Something loosened in her chest. "It was like losing him all over again. I'm angry with him for leaving, and my heart is broken for what he went through, all at once. If I'm being completely honest with myself…I think I've never really let him go."

Ella thought again of the last letter he'd left her, one of the letters Jack had given Fiona that he'd written for each family member. Each person he'd left behind. Her mouth was suddenly dry as she thought of that yellowed envelope, languishing in the top drawer of the old dresser in the bedroom.

She'd opened the envelope countless times, her eyes darting over his distinctive scrawl. Starting the first sentence over and over, the deafening pounding of her heart in her ears drowning out everything else around her. *Dear Ella,* it read. *There's so much I want to tell you, so much I've wanted to tell you, I'm not quite sure how to begin.*

And that was all she'd seen. She couldn't get past the first sentence. Her heart would lodge in her throat, the room would start spinning, and she'd shove the letter back into the envelope, back where she didn't have to face it anymore.

Leo's hand on her shoulder snapped her from her thoughts. She let out the breath she'd been holding, and their eyes met for a long moment. A surge of heat rushed to Ella's face.

After a while, Leo nodded once, and looked up at

the wall. He cleared his throat and gave her a small smile. "Well. Onward and upward, I suppose." He rose to his feet and held out a hand to help Ella up. "Why don't you head home for the night. I'll take it from here."

Ella nodded and stretched her arms over her head. "I'll see you tomorrow, Leo." She gave his shoulder a squeeze before turning to leave.

"And thanks, Ella," Leo said softly. "Thanks for everything."

"You're quite welcome," she said, returning his smile. Her heart fluttered strangely in her chest as she headed through the stacks toward the entrance.

Before she opened the front door, she turned back one last time. Leo was hunched over, scraping the wall with both hands, pushing with a force that seemed to take all his effort. Ella's heart broke as she watched him stripping away each layer, each movement like he was losing something, some essential part of himself. Leo was such a good man, such a positive force in her life...seeing him suffer made her stomach twist in pain.

She exhaled a shaky breath and pushed out into the rain, out where she wouldn't have to think about the parts of her life she was still clinging to, unwilling to start chipping away at them.

14

"And then you take the brush like this, really gently, like you're holding a feather, and then..." Ramona dragged the brush tipped in yellow softly across the pool of deep blue on the canvas. "Voilà. That's a gradient. This lighter shade blended with the darker blue makes a midtone, this really beautiful turquoise gradient. But it still needs to be wet, so you have to work fast."

"That's really cool," said Lily, her eyes fixed on the canvas. "That looks just like the color of the water by the north shore." She looked up at Ramona. "Is it okay if I try it now?"

"Of course!" said Ramona, a smile spreading on her face. The girl was just so sweet. "And don't be afraid to experiment! That's the real secret artists will never tell you." She leaned toward Lily in a conspiratorial whisper. "Most art is just a bunch of mistakes that happened to look really cool."

Lily grinned and took the brush from Ramona, dipping it in yellow and lightly dragging it across the pool of blue, biting her lip with her front teeth in concentration. Ramona leaned back on the picnic bench and listened to the wind rustling through the branches of the large oak tree poised over them in the expansive backyard of Danny's house.

The smell of burning charcoal wafted over from the grill, intermixing with the earthy aroma of the freshly cut grass that filled her with memories of backyard barbecues from her childhood. Watermelon, hot dogs, roasted marshmallows and sparklers, fireflies and bonfires and playing capture the flag in the dark. It was the stuff of summer dreams. Danny was in the house getting everything prepped for the barbecue, leaving Ramona some quality time with the girl she'd really come to love. There were times Lily felt like her daughter.

It was dangerous thinking, she knew. Lily wasn't her daughter, and she was treading carefully as she and Danny navigated their complicated new relationship. Her own losses in the past put her in a vulnerable spot, given how much she'd always wanted children.

But Ramona couldn't help herself. She saw so much of herself in Lily. She badly wanted to be a strong female presence in her life, someone Lily could count on. Lily deserved it. She certainly wasn't getting that from Caitlyn.

A prickling sensation danced across her skin. Caitlyn. She was going to be here in less than four hours to pick Lily up for a weekend in Providence, where she lived. It was the only downside to the perfect day they'd been having. Ramona planned to make herself scarce before Caitlyn arrived so she didn't have to talk to her.

The back door of the house pushed open. "Hey, Ramona, can you give me a quick hand in here?" asked Danny. He was wearing a white apron and holding a whisk, smiling at her in a way that made heat rush to her face.

"Back in a sec, Lily," she said. "You could try practicing more gradients with some of the other colors there. Maybe some of that red and light blue. See what happens."

Lily smiled and reached for the paint as Ramona followed Danny inside. The little girl had taken a real interest in painting after Ramona gave her the children's book she'd made. Lily had asked her a thousand questions about it, wanting to know every detail, the techniques she'd used, even how she'd come up with the story. Lily didn't know the painful history of the book, what it meant to Ramona.

It had been difficult to talk about at first, but there was just something about Lily that softened Ramona. She found herself telling Lily the truth behind it, or at least a version of the truth that was appropriate and would make sense to a nine-year-old.

When Ramona was finished explaining, her chest tight and her eyes wet, Lily had said nothing, but placed her tiny hand on Ramona's. It had been one of the most innocent and wonderful gestures Ramona had ever received in her life. Her heart had cracked in two, and her love for Lily grew stronger.

The screen door closed behind Ramona. "All right, what can I do for you—"

She was cut off by Danny reaching a hand to the small of her back and pulling her close to him. "Oh!" she gasped, grinning. "What's this?"

Their lips met in a strong, lingering kiss. Ramona ran her hands through Danny's thick hair and arched her back, pressing herself closer to him, fire rushing to her cheeks, her heart somersaulting.

He dropped the whisk on the ground as he wrapped his arms around her and kissed her neck. "Ramona," he whispered into her hair. Fireworks sparked across her skin, a sizzling heat.

After a few moments, Ramona reached behind him to the kitchen counter and lifted a bag of potato chips, tearing herself away. "Ah, so *this* is what you needed help with," she said, a playful smile on her lips. "Smart thinking. There's a hungry girl out there who needs snacks while her dad cooks us up a good meal."

Danny laughed as she sashayed out through the screen door. Ramona was grinning as she sat back down with Lily, opening the bag of chips and spreading them out on the red-and-white checkered cloth. "How's it going out here?" she asked, munching happily. "Oh, Lily," she said, stopping short as she saw what Lily had done.

In the space of just a few moments, Lily had filled a new sheet of canvas with a series of multicolored gradients, using swooping swirls of the brush to make frothy waves and a skittering sideswiping of highlights and shadows for the most beautiful painted skies Ramona had ever seen. "How..." Ramona started, leaning down toward the canvas.

It was brilliant. Lily had a natural talent, a talent

that certainly surpassed Ramona's. "This is really something, Lily. I..." Lily met her eyes. Ramona looked at her thoughtfully. It was something to explore with Lily. There was a lot she could do with talent like that.

"I'm not just telling you this to make you feel good, sweetheart. This is *really good*. I mean it...you should be very proud."

"Thank you," she said, blushing softly. "I just experimented, like you said. I get what you mean. Mistakes that look really cool. I started off trying to paint a mountain." She laughed, that beautiful tinkling laugh like music, and Ramona joined her, her heart nearly bursting at the seams.

Ramona watched Lily painting as Danny put hamburgers and chicken-and-vegetable skewers on the grill, the delicious aromas coursing through the backyard. Cicadas buzzed all around them, and the sun was just beginning to dip toward the horizon. Ramona breathed in deeply, and let the air out of her lungs in a slow exhale, closing her eyes.

But just as quickly as the warm sense of peace came, it was gone, poisonous ink spreading through clear water. Every time she let her guard down...it all came back. The reasons she wasn't allowed to relax.

So much had been happening all around her, a

storm of chaos, of grief and of fear. She was still reeling from learning what had really happened to her father, and was just beginning to walk down the winding path of grief over the long-ago losses of her pregnancies. The lawsuit from Fowler & Stoll was going to be hanging over her head for a long while. Just today, another bookkeeping client had sent her an email, letting her know they no longer needed her services.

The word about her lawsuit was getting out...and it was going to ruin her career if she didn't figure something out.

She'd wanted to reach out to her old bosses at Fowler & Stoll...to try to explain what had happened, what she'd been going through, maybe try to appeal to their sense of mercy. But the lawyer Charlotte had helped her find advised against it. Strongly. She'd decided to suppress her stubborn streak and listen to him. The worst part of it was mostly the fear of not knowing what would happen.

Samuel had still been calling her relentlessly. He'd even shown up once or twice at the Seaside House, but Ramona refused to listen to him. He'd been an integral part of the mess that her Uncle Patrick had gotten them all into. She wondered if Samuel really knew the extent of what his father had done. The fake charities, the embezzlement, the scams...Patrick had threatened to send Ramona invoices for all the restoration work he'd done before she kicked Samuel and his team out, work that he'd promised would be free. Ramona had no intention of paying them but knew that Patrick was a powerful man, a man with connections and a team of lawyers...and with a good percentage of their future earnings tied up in a written agreement, things weren't looking good for the Seaside House, whenever they managed to get it open.

If they managed to get it open. Christian was already working for free, and he was paying Keiran's meager wages out of his own pocket. Even with the discounts Danny was giving them from his supplies store, Ramona would be surprised if they ever got the inn open again.

"Mommy!" shrieked Lily from next to her, shooting up from the picnic bench and spilling paintbrushes and sheets of canvas everywhere. Ramona whipped her head around, her heart thumping hard against her ribs.

A slender woman with curly blonde hair and hoop earrings had opened the gate at the edge of the backyard, and was crouched down with her hands out. Lily jumped into her arms, and the woman pulled her up into a bear hug, smelling the little girl's hair. "Lily, baby, it's so good to see you," she said.

"Cait? What are you doing here?" asked Danny, heading toward her with a deep frown on his face. "You weren't supposed to be here yet—"

"I know, I'm sorry, Danny," she said, setting Lily down and pulling Danny into a hug that he didn't return. He looked over to Ramona, his frown deepening. "I got off work early, and thought I might stop over to catch up for a minute." She looked over at Ramona, her eyebrows rising. "I'm sorry. I didn't know you were having company."

"We're having dinner, Caitlyn," said Danny, forcing a patient voice. "I really wish you would've called first—"

But Caitlyn was already striding toward Ramona. Her stomach clenched. She'd successfully avoided all but the briefest encounters with the woman Danny married after Ramona had left him all those years ago, and had planned to keep it that way.

"Ramona, it's good to see you again," Caitlyn said as she approached, smiling. She wore a smart jean jacket over a tank top with a vintage patterned skirt and fashionable white sandals. The woman was gorgeous. A ridiculous flare of jealousy stole over

Ramona just as Caitlyn pulled her into a hug. She was chewing spearmint gum, and smelled like wildflowers and saltwater. "I'm really sorry to intrude," she said. "I should have called."

Ramona awkwardly patted her back and glanced at Danny, who was standing there with a confused expression. She had no idea what to say. She always assumed Caitlyn held animosity toward her, but this politeness, it seemed almost...genuine.

"It's all right," Ramona said, giving Caitlyn's back another pat before pulling away. "Ah, how have you been?"

"I'm doing great, better than ever," she said, sitting down on the picnic bench and pulling Lily onto her lap. "Oh! I almost forgot," she said, reaching into her purse and pulling out an orange teddy bear with a polka-dotted bow tie. "I thought this little guy was right up your alley, Lil."

Lily grinned and pulled the bear to her face, giving it a little smooch on the head. "Thanks, Mommy! I love him!"

"Caitlyn, can I talk to you for a minute in the kitchen?" asked Danny. Black smoke was pouring from the grill behind him in huge plumes. A sharp burning smell drifted over the light wind.

Caitlyn looked up at him innocently. "Sure thing,

Danny." She looked over the table. "Honey, did you paint these?"

Lily's eyes widened and she leaped up from the table, lifting one of the sheets to present to Caitlyn. "I have so much to show you! Miss Ramona has been teaching me how to paint! This is the ocean. Well, it was mountains, but I was *experimenting*. And this is a seahorse. And this is my friend Ashley."

Caitlyn wrapped her arms around her daughter, pulling her close. "Baby, you're so talented! These are really beautiful." She turned to Ramona. "Thank you for helping teach her, Ramona. I haven't got an artistic bone in my body...and neither does Danny." She laughed as she looked his way, beaming. He was watching her, his eyebrows twisted subtly. "I don't know where Lily gets her talent."

Danny cleared his throat. Caitlyn nodded. "Right. I'll be right back, sweetheart," she said to Lily, giving her a peck on the cheek. Lily's face broke into an enormous smile.

"Daddy, can Mommy stay for dinner?" she asked. Ramona's heart sank. She looked up at Danny. Lily came up to him, holding the orange teddy bear, her eyes like saucers. Danny looked at her with pain across his face.

"Oh, no, baby, I didn't mean to mess up your

barbecue or anything," said Caitlyn. "I've got a couple errands to run anyway, I'll be back a little later to pick you up. You guys have fun."

Lily's face fell. Ramona frowned and looked between Caitlyn and Danny.

Maybe she'd gotten Caitlyn all wrong. Looking at her now, you'd never know she had a long, checkered history, in and out of prison. She looked healthy, happy...her skin was practically freaking glowing. Caitlyn obviously meant the world to Lily, and who was Ramona to get in the middle of that?

"No, ah, you should stay," said Ramona. She glanced at Danny, whose frown was deepening. "You're already here, and we have plenty of food..." She regretted opening her mouth.

Caitlyn stood up and squeezed her shoulder. "Well, thank you, Ramona! That's very sweet." Ramona felt the corners of her mouth lifting upward of their own accord.

She was being so unexpectedly...*nice.* Caitlyn leaned in close, whispering in her ear, that smell of wildflowers blooming around her. "Listen, I think it's great, you and Danny. I always thought he'd never gotten over you." She glanced at him, winking, and lowered her voice further. "He's one of the good ones. I'm happy for you."

Ramona shook her head in surprise, and again found herself not knowing how to respond. Caitlyn patted her shoulder and began chatting with Lily. Ramona and Danny exchanged a glance. She shrugged, and he raised an eyebrow, as if to say, "If you say so."

And so they ate dinner together, laughing at the meat burned beyond all recognition, Caitlyn regaling them with stories from her job as a wedding coordinator in Providence, Lily happy as all can be. Once or twice, Ramona could swear she saw Caitlyn's eyes lingering on Danny for just a moment too long.

But she was probably imagining things. No matter how Ramona tried to fight it, flickers of jealousy licked at her. There was a complicated history there. At any rate, she knew Danny never wanted to get back together with her after she'd had that affair, the affair that led to Lily.

Caitlyn was nothing but polite, charming, lovely all night, before she took off with Lily. Caitlyn gave Ramona a big hug when she left, like they were old friends. And then they were gone, the night disappearing like a whirlwind.

Maybe she really had changed. People did change; Ramona knew that better than anyone.

There was no reason to be hostile to the woman. She may have been an inconsistent mother to Lily, but she was here now, and anything that made Lily happy was certainly good enough for Ramona.

It was possible, of course, that Caitlyn still had feelings for Danny. Ramona wasn't naive. Caitlyn had been married to him, after all...even if she did have that affair. If she did still love him, she'd been nothing but respectful the entire night, and there was no reason to worry about it.

But Ramona couldn't quite shake the feeling that there was something else she was missing...something she couldn't yet see. And that was a feeling she'd learned the hard way not to ignore.

15

"*Trevor! Where'd you go?*" Diane seethed in a whisper. She could barely see anything through the dense tangle of chaparral shrubbery. The coastal oaks and Monterey cypress trees overhead blocked the light of the moon that had been her guiding light.

"*Trevor!*" she repeated. She pushed forward, cursing under her breath as the sagebrush scraped against her arms. Her backpack pulled uncomfortably on her shoulders, and she was sweating through her gray T-shirt. She stopped short, whipping her head around. He was nowhere to be seen.

"Over here," said a casual voice from a few yards ahead. Diane shook her head and pushed through the sagebrush, ignoring the low sloshing of nausea rolling through her stomach.

She finally pushed through to a small clearing next to a stone wall that rose just above Trevor's head. He was standing there in his black tank top, the thick muscles of his arms glistening in the dim light. He brushed a lock of hair from his forehead and pointed to an oak tree next to him, wiggling his eyebrows.

"Oh no." Diane shook her head. "I can't climb trees."

"I'll give ya a boost. Trust me." He grinned at her, making her knees buckle slightly.

She sighed. It was hard to say no to Trevor. Not with that smile, that look in his eyes. She let him hoist her up, and she shimmied down a long branch, her breath catching in her throat, until she dropped lightly onto the perfectly manicured lawn on the other side of the stone wall.

A moment later, Trevor dropped down beside her, squeezing her shoulder. "See? I told you."

Trevor led her up the sloping backyard until the ground leveled off. In front of them was the most immense, sprawling mansion Diane had ever seen. To the far left was a tennis court next to a basketball court, and to the right was a huge, lush orchard filled with fruit trees and flowers of every color.

The back of the house was all expansive glass windows, all dark. A massive rectangular infinity pool glittered before her, dimly lit with ethereal dark blue and gold, making the water shimmer invitingly.

Diane turned to Trevor, who was admiring the house. He gave her a look, all danger and mischief and excitement. A thrill ran up her spine.

"How do you know they're out of town?" asked Diane.

He grinned. "I don't."

Diane never knew what was going to happen on any given day with Trevor. They'd head deep into the forest in the San Gabriel Mountains for a midnight hike, with nothing but the clothes on their backs and a wild sense of exploration. They'd sneak onto the roof of some apartment building near the shore and throw paper airplanes toward the sea, or dance under the stars to music only they could hear. He'd woken her up in the middle of the night once and driven her to Vegas, waltzing up to the Roulette table like he'd owned the joint and putting all the money they had between them down on black, just for the thrill of it. He'd won big that night, of course he had. They'd stayed at the top of the Bellagio, watching the city unfold beneath them, feeling young and free and utterly invincible.

It had all been a powerful, wonderful distraction from the car accident two years earlier. The accident where Diane had taken Trevor's sister away from him for good. The decision she'd made earlier that day, the mistake that had changed everything.

"How are you going to get in?" she whispered. It was hard to believe that an hour ago, she'd been sitting in the apartment they now shared in Santa Monica, quietly reading a book, when Trevor told her to pack an overnight bag. An hour later they turned right up a short road off the Pacific Coast Highway in Malibu, seemingly at random, Trevor arching his head left and right until he made some internal decision. He'd parked the car against the curb, took her hand, and pulled her into the thick chaparral, into the darkness.

Trevor walked up to the panoramic glass wall that looked to be part of the entrance. A thin line in the glass showed the edge of the sliding door. He stood there for a moment, thinking, then glanced back at her, winked, and lightly tugged on the handle.

The door quietly slid open. Unlocked, of course

it was. Diane laughed. Things just seemed to work out for Trevor. He was one of those guys.

He raised an eyebrow and disappeared inside. A minute later, bright white lights flooded the interior, spilling out across the infinity pool and over the long manicured grass lawn behind them. Trevor emerged a few moments later, a bottle of wine in each hand. He came up to her, uncorking one of the bottles, and passed it to her. "Bottoms up," he said with a grin, and they clinked the bottles together.

Diane drank deeply, trying to drown the steady drumming of her heart in her throat. The wide vista of the Pacific Ocean unfolded beneath her, sparkling and shining under the clear moonlight. The air was warm, and the beautifully clean and bright smell of saltwater carried over the light breeze.

This was a little crazy, even for Trevor.

But the risk of getting caught...it *did* something for her. All the things she did with Trevor distracted her from...well, from everything. From the accident. From losing her best friend. From the memory of the hollow look in Austin's eyes at Victoria's funeral.

And most importantly, it went a good, long way toward distracting her from the horror of her father abandoning the family that Christmas Eve. How long ago had that been now? Five years? Six? It was already getting hard to remember his face. She'd really buried herself in her work at the agency after that.

Her stomach somersaulted. Oh, no. Tomorrow was Monday, wasn't it? Work. She was going to have to take it easy tonight, which would be next to impossible with Trevor around.

But the feeling disappeared a split second later as she remembered, relief flooding her, that she'd left her job a while ago.

And Trevor had been right to talk her into quitting. He'd been pressing her on it for ages before she'd finally relented.

That place was eating up her life, anyway. What she wanted, more than anything, was more time with Trevor.

And he wanted Diane's time, too. He'd inherited a ton of money from his parents, and so Trevor hadn't worked for as long as Diane had known him. She'd moved into his fancy Santa Monica apartment near the coast, and it seemed every time he wanted to do something, she had to go to work. And all those late nights...well, it came down to a choice, how she was going to spend her time. And he was the love of her life. He'd been right to convince her to leave. You only had one life, right?

The very last thing she needed was for someone else she loved to leave her in the dust like her father had. She would do whatever it took to keep him around.

There was a tiny flash of something in the corner of her eye, up to the right. Her heart leaped as she scanned the houses far up on the hillside rising over the Pacific. She could just barely make out a small light that had flicked on in one of the windows.

"I think we should leave, Trevor..."

He set down his bottle of wine. "Nonsense. We're fine." He gave her a lascivious look and pulled his tank top over his head, exposing the deep grooves of his abs and the tight muscles of his chest. He looked down at her, beckoning, as he jogged over to the edge of the infinity pool and plunged in, hollering into the night air.

Diane laughed and pulled off her T-shirt and shorts, revealing a black one-piece bathing suit. He'd told her to wear something she could swim in. She'd known then the night was going to be a good one.

She sauntered over to the edge of the pool. He looked up at her, laughing.

"You look like an old hag in that bathing suit," he said, splashing water up at her.

Diane scowled. "Hey," she said. "Don't do that."

He shrugged. "What happened to that red string bikini I bought you? You looked hot in that." He narrowed his eyes. "You should take your hair out of that ponytail, too. It makes your face look...round. Heavy." He subtly flexed the smooth, hard muscles of his abdomen. "My fault for taking you out to dinner so much, I guess."

Diane pushed back the sour taste in her throat. She was afraid to start another argument...even when he was being insulting. She'd already been feeling him pulling away from her lately. The thought sent hot, short knives of terror into her stomach.

Without Trevor...well, she wouldn't have anyone left.

She stood there, debating, anger rising in her throat as she berated herself for letting him make her feel self-conscious. He leaned back and spread his arms, floating in the water, looking like a magazine model. Then he swam up to the edge, holding a hand up to her.

"I'm only kidding around, Di," he said with a smirk. "Don't take everything so personally. Come on in." He reached up and gripped her hand, pulling her toward the water. Diane felt something stir within her as she looked into those eyes pooling with something dark and dangerous, deliciously wrong but impossible to resist. She yanked her hand out of his grip, took three steps back, then jumped high into the water, splashing him as hard as she could.

He laughed and came up behind her, twisting her around to face him, and ran his hands through her dark, wet hair. Their lips met, pressed together hard, her body thrumming as she ran her hands over the taut muscles of his back and shoulders.

Diane pulled away for a moment. He looked momentarily irritated, then fixed a smile on his face. "What?" he asked.

"I totally forgot. I'm supposed to meet up with Bethany tomorrow morning. I'm helping her with her lines...her audition is tomorrow afternoon. We need to be back early. I need you to drop me off at her place."

Driving had become a real problem since the accident. Every time she'd gotten behind the wheel, her mouth dried up, her heart started jackhammering...she'd get that horrible feeling of vertigo, of the horizon tipping over, and her vision would start to gray at the edges. She'd pull over two or three times just to catch her breath, her hands trembling on the steering wheel.

Trevor pulled back from her. "Forget about Bethany. You're here with me." He gestured up at the house. "We could stay here for days if we wanted. Live it up. Have some fun."

She hesitated. "Maybe I could call her from a phone in the house tomorrow."

Trevor sighed and shook his head. She felt an uneasy stirring in her chest. "Look, Di, Bethany isn't your friend, all right? She's just using you."

"What?" Diane frowned.

He nodded solemnly. "I can see it. She just takes from you. Trust me on this. You don't need Bethany."

"She's been my friend for years, Trevor," she said, bristling. Had she been wrong about her somehow? Bethany had been another creative director at the agency. Diane had risen through the ranks quickly, and Bethany had been a mentor of sorts. She'd quit when she got a small role on a crime series, believing her acting dreams were coming true, but they'd remained friends.

"She doesn't like you," he said. "I can't believe you don't see it. I mean, look at what you just told me. You're going to leave tomorrow to run lines with her? When you have all this going on?" He shook his head. "What has she ever done for you?"

Before she could answer, he swam right up to

her, his gaze fixed on hers. Those beautiful X-ray eyes, dark, cryptic reservoirs. She felt naked when he looked at her like that. "Be with me tonight. Forget all the rest. All we have is right now." And he touched his lips to hers, running his fingers along the nape of her neck. "I love you."

He pressed his lips hard into hers, and she forgot about everything else, relishing in the surge of fire in her chest, the pinpricks of heat dancing all across her skin.

Then a blinding flash of light smacked her square in the face.

"*Freeze! Don't move!*" shouted a growling voice behind them. Trevor whipped his head around. Just beyond a glaring halo of white light piercing the darkness, coming from the far side of the house near the driveway, Diane could make out the rhythmic flashing of red and blue lights.

"*Go!*" Trevor yelled, grabbing her by the arm and yanking her toward the edge of the pool. He hoisted himself out in a single graceful motion and began bounding down the lawn toward the back wall by the time Diane had found purchase and flopped out onto the pool's edge.

"I said *freeze!*" the police officer yelled at her, his keys jangling as he ran toward them.

Diane's pulse pounded in her throat as she ran down the hill as fast as she could. Trevor was already climbing the tree at the bottom of the hill. Her bare feet slipped on the smooth grass, sending her tumbling forward, hitting the cool ground hard with her shoulder. She yelped and scrambled to her feet, whipping her head around. The police officer was less than fifteen feet away. Terror seized her as she pumped her arms. Trevor would hoist her up the tree and they would be fine.

But when she got to the tree, Trevor was gone.

"Trevor!" she screamed. She leaped up to grab the low branch hanging over the wall and missed. Her stomach twisted like a wet dishrag as she heard the thumping of Trevor's footsteps becoming fainter.

Diane jumped up again, but her wet hands couldn't grip the bark of the branch, sending her falling onto the ground on her back, knocking the wind from her completely. The officer stood over her, doubled over and panting.

"You're under arrest, miss," he said, scanning around for Trevor. He shook his head softly, then helped her to her feet and placed a cold pair of handcuffs on her wrists.

"HELLO?" a hoarse voice answered through a yawn.

Diane closed her eyes, crushing back the tears threatening to form. "Austin? It's Diane."

She heard the shuffling of blankets. "Diane? What's wrong?"

She squeezed the bridge of her nose with her fingers, dropping her voice so no one else in the holding cell could hear her. "Austin, I got arrested."

A hulking woman on a long bench next to her exploded in wet, hacking coughs. Harsh fluorescent lights drilled into her eyes, sending a dull throbbing ache through her skull.

It was her third phone call. The first two had been to the landline in Trevor's apartment. Their apartment, rather.

No one had answered.

Diane thought about calling Bethany, but she was frightened, and embarrassed. And Trevor's words about her were ringing in her ears...she didn't know what to think anymore. Her family was three thousand miles away, and she barely spoke to them anymore, at any rate.

She hadn't seen much of Austin after the accident, but Diane knew he would know what to do. He would help her, no matter what.

"Austin, I'm so sorry to call you this late, I didn't

know what else to do." She closed her eyes and tears fell down her cheeks. She shouldn't have called him. Not after she'd taken away the love of his life. What had she been thinking?

"No, it's okay, Diane." His voice was alert now. "Tell me what happened."

A FEW HOURS LATER, after Diane had been processed, Austin pulled up in front of the police station in his old yellow Chevy pickup. Diane was sitting on the sidewalk, shivering. Her bathing suit underneath her clothes was still damp. Every part of her was sore. Shards of the day's first light cut through the low-hanging clouds in the overcast sky, searing into her eyes. There was a low rumbling in the distance, and small droplets of rain began to fall.

"Hey," he said, helping her to her feet. "You okay?"

Diane's mouth wobbled as he helped her into the passenger seat. She shook her head.

Austin closed the door and slid into the driver's seat. He reached into the backseat and handed her a clean, folded T-shirt. For a horrible moment she thought it might be Victoria's, but as she unfolded it, she saw it was one of his. He looked away as she pulled off her damp shirt and pulled his on, already feeling a little better. When she was done, he handed her a hot cup of coffee from the cupholder, along with a small paper bag.

She took a long sip of the coffee, the hot steam glorious against her frigid, clammy skin. Inside the bag was an enormous lemon blueberry muffin from Penelope's Bakery. Her absolute favorite. Her eyebrows rose, and a smile of delight spread across her face.

"Austin...thank you," she said softly.

They drove in silence back up through the city to Trevor's apartment. Thoughts were coming slowly, all out of order.

It had been a wretched night. A long drive to the station, handcuffs digging into the smooth skin of her wrists, fingerprints, her first and hopefully only mugshot. Her muscles cramping terribly after hours sitting in that holding cell, doing her best to remain invisible to the other detainees. An interview hours later with an officer in a tiny, frigid room, her teeth chattering as she recounted what they were doing. She refused to give them Trevor's name.

The officer interviewing her sat down across from her, studying her shrewdly. After a long moment, he sighed. "Why do you think he left you there?"

Diane looked back at him, opened her mouth to speak, but couldn't think of a good response. He kept his gaze on her, his eyebrows softening. He shook his head softly.

"Look, kid, I'm gonna let you off with a citation for breaking and entering. You'll have some community service, an informal probation. We didn't find any evidence of anything missing in the house...I don't think you two were trying to steal anything. There was no property damage. I have more important things to do than chase after kids playing grown-ups in someone else's house, though."

He leaned forward, looking briefly at his hands spread on the table before meeting Diane's eyes. "Piece of advice from a father, though, take it or leave it. You might want to ask yourself if this sort of thing...is what you really want." He rose from the table and turned out of the room, leaving Diane in her swirling tornado of thoughts.

Austin's pickup rolled to a stop in front of Trevor's house, the wheels squeaking. He kept his hands on the wheel and glanced over at her.

"So, you and Trevor are still together, huh."

Diane frowned, instinctively defensive. "Yeah. Why?"

Austin's eyes went back and forth over hers. He let out a slow breath. "I don't know. Sometimes..." He looked out the front windshield, fingertips drumming on the weathered steering wheel. Rain pattered lightly against the truck. "I just don't know about him sometimes. That's all. As long as you're happy..." The sentence lingered in the air, unfinished.

Diane badly wanted to talk to Austin like she used to. To open up to him. They'd always been close...and when Victoria died, she'd lost Austin, too. Diane had kept a wide berth, feeling like her guilt would eat her alive.

She looked across Austin's face, across the days of growth on his cheeks, the dark, deep grooves under his eyes, his unruly hair. There was something missing in his eyes, a sort of hollow void that made Diane's heart fold in two. He would never get over Victoria. She didn't deserve his kindness.

A little smile formed on his lips. "Well. At any rate, I'm glad you're all right, Diane. And listen," he said, his eyes boring into hers. "If you ever want to talk...you know where to find me. I'm here for you, if you want."

She nodded as a tear fell down her cheek, words escaping her as he helped her out of the truck and drove away, leaving her in front of the high tower that housed Trevor's penthouse apartment.

Diane squared her shoulders. It was time to have a talk with Trevor.

THE ELEVATOR SLID open and she stepped forward to the front door of the apartment, pounding hard with her fists.

A moment later, Trevor opened the door. "Diane, thank God!" he said, wrapping her up in his arms. "I've been calling police stations for hours. No one will tell me anything."

Diane shook her head and pulled out of his grip. She pushed past him, throwing her damp shirt on the brown leather couch. "You weren't calling for hours. I called here, twice. No one answered."

His eyes lit with danger. "I pulled the phone off the hook for a couple hours to get a little sleep. So shoot me. I was exhausted." He scowled, and plopped down on the couch. "You were fine. What, a little stint in the drunk tank? You're a big girl. I couldn't very well turn up at the police station, now could I? That dumb cop saw my face."

"I was alone *all night*, Trevor," she seethed. She yanked a glass from the cupboard, poured some water, and drank it all in one go. "I can't believe you left me there."

He shrugged. "I told you to run. You didn't listen."

"I *slipped*, Trevor!" she shouted at him, surprising herself. He glared at her. "I was right behind you, and you left me. You weren't there for me." She looked at him, and pulled herself to her full height. "I'm going to find somewhere else to stay. We're through."

He laughed, sending a chill across the nape of her neck. "And where are you gonna go?"

Diane swallowed hard against the lump in her throat. "I can go stay with my family."

"Your family." He snorted. "Diane, I've told you a thousand times. Your family hates you. You abandoned your sisters when your dad left. You think they're gonna take you back?" He shook his head, a pitying look in his eyes. "You're not going to leave me. You need me. You're just mad. I said I'm sorry."

"Actually, you didn't. And I mean it, Trevor. I've...

I've had enough." Trevor's eyes became narrow slits. She let out a slow breath. "This is over."

Trevor shot to his feet and was suddenly upon her, towering over her. His chest rose and fell hard. "You have got to be freaking kidding me. You're leaving me? *You're* leaving *me*? *After everything you did?*" He was screaming now, his face beet red.

Diane burst into tears. She felt small, weak. "Trevor, I—"

"Victoria is *gone* because of you! My *sister!*" he shouted, his voice breaking. The cords of his neck were standing out. Diane couldn't breathe. "You don't listen, Diane! If you had listened to me, *Victoria would still be alive*! It's your fault she's gone! And now you have the audacity to *leave me* on top of that?" Tears glistened in his bloodshot eyes.

A sickening lurch tore through Diane. He'd really loved Victoria. She hadn't really thought this through. Trevor had been there for her when no one else had, after all.

Was she really throwing it all away over this?

She didn't want to be alone. Couldn't be. She thought of her father, the last time she saw him. The way he used to pull her up into his arms, whisper into her long hair, *I love you, honeybear*. A sob built in her throat.

"I'm sorry," she whispered. Now Victoria's face swam in her mind, that wild burst of red hair, her eyes crinkling when she laughed. It sent a spike shooting into her throat.

He scoffed and shook his head. "I need to take a walk."

Diane froze, a huge wall of terror crashing over her. "Trevor, no, you can't leave—"

"You can't keep me here," he muttered. "I can do whatever I want. You're crazy."

"We agreed you wouldn't leave the house when we're fighting!" she shouted. An image of Trevor being hit by a passing car tore through her mind. If he left and something bad happened to him, after she'd just threatened to leave him, it would be her fault. Again.

She couldn't have anything else on her conscience. It would ruin her.

Trevor turned to her, his face expressionless. "So you don't want me to leave."

Diane squeezed her eyes shut and pushed back the thoughts screaming at her in her head, telling her to walk away. "No. Please. Something could happen to you."

His mouth was a thin line as he approached her. Her heart pounded as he stood over her.

And then his face softened. He reached up and touched her cheek with his hand. She felt like a deer in headlights.

"You know I love you, Diane. And if you really love me," he said, tilting her chin up so she met his eyes, "you'll promise never to threaten me with leaving again. I don't want to be alone. And I know you don't either."

Tears streamed down her cheeks. "Trevor, I am so, so sorry about Victoria—"

"Shhh. Let's not talk about her anymore." He wiped the tears from her face with the back of his hand. He pulled her close to him, and she buried her face in his chest.

She didn't want to be alone. And Trevor...well, he was still grief-stricken. The accident had changed his behavior, hadn't it? He would change...she just had to be patient. It was the least she could do, to be there for him after what she'd done.

He would change. And then they'd be happy.

And Diane thought then that things were settled. That they could drop back into their old routines. Fighting, making up, seeking out thrills, fighting some more, a wild rollercoaster as always.

But a month later, she came home after a few days' perfunctory visit to Marina Cove to see

Ramona and Ella, grabbed the mail from the mailbox, humming to herself as she approached the front door to his apartment. Their apartment. A sheet of lined white paper was pinned to the door.

She dropped the mail. Her stomach flipped over as she tore the note down and read it with trembling hands.

There was only a single line in Trevor's chicken scratch.

Moved out. Going to travel for a while. Have to figure some things out. Have a nice life.

Her ears rang as she frantically knocked on the door. No answer. Her hands shook violently as she pushed her key into the lock. It only went in halfway. The locks were already changed. She stepped back and for the first time saw several cardboard boxes lined up against the wall next to the door. Her belongings.

Trevor had left her. Just like her father had. She was alone now. All alone.

The hallway started to tilt to the right, and she splayed her hands against the wall to balance herself. She heard the horrible screeching of twisted metal. Saw Austin's hand gripping the back of the seat, heard Victoria's screams. The ground approaching fast. Diane sat down hard on the ground and choked out a single sob.

She closed her eyes against the images, reaching around to grasp solid ground. Her hand brushed against the mail on the ground in front of her, bound by a thick rubber band.

She needed something to stop the horrible memories, anything to bring her back on solid ground. She twisted off the rubber band, gasping for air as tears fell onto her lap, and slowly slipped it over her wrist. The world was still spinning around her.

Diane pulled back the rubber band as far as it would go, and with a trembling breath, she released it with a loud and painful *crack*.

"Uh, Diane?"

Diane looked up from her cards. "Huh?" she asked. Her mind had been...elsewhere.

Charlotte frowned, and glanced across the picnic table at Ramona, who had been watching Diane. For how long? "What's up?" she asked.

Ramona let out a breath and turned to face her. "Diane, is everything all right?"

Diane shrugged. "Yeah, everything's good, why?"

Ramona looked back at Charlotte, her expression unreadable. Diane sighed. After several hours sitting at the wooden picnic bench in the side yard of the Seaside House, trying hard to work on her pitch for Larson Brands, she'd finally snapped her laptop shut and given up. She just couldn't focus...her heart wasn't in it. Charlotte and Ramona had come out with a pitcher of homemade strawberry lemonade, Oreos, and a red deck of their father's old Bicycle playing cards. They'd been playing rummy in the beautiful sunshine for a while. It was peaceful, but her mind was racing.

I mean, how was she supposed to care about a company that made vegan bratwursts, anyway? And for that matter, how was she supposed to care about any of her agency clients? Was she really making the world a better place, helping these giant companies sell more *stuff* to people? Was that what life was about?

She no longer understood her agency work. Not after the way she'd been feeling since she'd been back. Since Trevor. That *thrill*...it was addictive. How on earth was she going to go back to sitting in traffic on the 405 freeway, sitting in all those endless meetings, listening to freaking *Parker* again? Ugh.

Right now, it seemed impossible. She was restless.

"Diane," Charlotte said, setting down her cards and leaning forward. "Listen, you know we're here for you if you want to talk, right?"

Diane nodded slowly. She scolded herself for

being annoyed at the question. "Yeah, I know. I'm fine, though, really. Why are you guys asking me if I'm all right?"

Charlotte's shoulders dropped a little, and her gaze wandered down to Diane's hands. Diane followed her eyeline, and watched herself release the thick rubber band against her bright red, splotchy wrist with a *crack* that sent bands of pain radiating up her arm. She hadn't been aware she'd been doing that again. Diane looked between Charlotte and Ramona, not knowing what to say.

"We love you, Diane," said Ramona, tucking her hair behind her ear. "I know it's been a while, but it just seems like something might be...I don't know. Wrong. Like, you aren't really sleeping. And, um, that rubber band..." She glanced up at Charlotte for a moment, looking a little helpless. "Is everything good at home? Grant, the kids?"

Diane straightened in her seat. "Yeah, everyone's good. It's just work, that's all. I've been under a lot of stress. Big pitch coming up." A pitch that would determine Diane's future with the agency. She swallowed against a lump in her throat. "Don't worry about me. I just need a break from thinking about everything, that's all."

Diane chugged the rest of her lemonade and

shuffled through her cards, hoping that would be that. She wasn't really ready for a heart-to-heart with the sisters. Sure, it would be great...but after all the long years, they were practically strangers. You didn't snap your fingers and suddenly have a lovey-dovey relationship, just like that...it wasn't realistic.

Diane loved them, but things were happening too fast all around her. Besides, she didn't need to start obsessing about anyone else's safety...about being at fault for something again. She had no way to keep track of her sisters, her mother. They could stay at arm's length, just for now. It was for the best.

A crackling roar split through the air like an ax, sending the cards in Diane's hand all over the table. They all whipped their head toward the source of the sound. Someone in a leather jacket was tearing down the little street toward the Seaside House on a giant motorcycle. A snapping, sparking pool of excitement rippled up through Diane's stomach into her chest.

The tires pealed as the motorcycle screeched to a halt. The man casually stepped off, his dirty-blonde hair whipping gracefully in the sea breeze. Rays of waning red and gold sunshine illuminated his face as he walked toward them. Diane shot up from her seat and went over to meet him.

Trevor didn't look at Charlotte or Ramona as they rose from the table. "Well, howdy, Di," he said. His eyes glittered dangerously in the light. "Fancy a ride?"

Ramona cleared her throat. "Ah, Diane? Who's this now?"

Diane turned to her. "This is Trevor. You met him ages ago, when I was in high school. He's an old friend." She gave Ramona and Charlotte a quick hug. "You don't mind, do you? I'll be back later." Without waiting for a response, she waved to her sisters, sat behind Trevor on the motorcycle, and held tightly onto his chest as they peeled away from the Seaside House.

STARS WERE GLIMMERING in the sky by the time they made it to the top of the huge cliffs carved into the eastern shoreline. A huge stretch of grass led out to a massive drop-off into the sea. Diane yipped gleefully as Trevor cranked the accelerator, headed right for the cliff, before swiping the motorcycle to the left and skidding to a heart-pounding halt right at the edge.

"That was *incredible*," Diane said breathlessly.

Her mouth was dry, her hair windswept after he'd raced them all around Marina Cove, blasting his accelerator as they tore across the Loop, hollering into the sky. She'd felt like a teenager.

Trevor smirked and headed toward the cliffs edge without her. Diane pushed down the irritation bristling at her and followed behind him. As she watched his back, a memory popped into her mind like a balloon bursting. The time he'd left her at that house they'd broken into. How many years ago had that been? Diane shook her head. More than twenty. So much had happened since then. She could barely remember it.

Being with Trevor...it had always been like having a bright spotlight shining on her, like she was the only person in the world. She'd forgotten how intoxicating it was. How all-consuming.

But when he stopped shining that spotlight...it was a cold place to be.

Another memory tried to surface, the day he'd left her, but something huge blocked it, swallowed it whole. An overwhelming sense of guilt stole through her, her breath catching in her throat. It had been her fault, hadn't it? Trevor had finally given her what she deserved for taking his sister from him. She hadn't deserved him in the first place.

"Ow!" she cried suddenly. Without thinking, she'd already cracked the rubber band around her wrist, and winced at the pain.

Diane shook her head, rubbing her raw wrist. No sense in rehashing the past. She was here now, and she felt good. She needed to hang onto that. To something.

Otherwise...well. She had no desire to get lost again, lost in her own misery. No freaking way. She was done with all that.

"Hurry up," Trevor called gruffly over his shoulder. Diane frowned and picked up her pace. That edge was coming back to him. She'd been so caught up in seeing him again, she'd forgotten all about that side of him. The distant echoes of night after night of long arguments bounced back and forth in her mind.

Something had been needling at her for a while now...she couldn't quite put a finger on it. The effect Trevor was having on her seemed more...brittle. Spread too thin, or something. She clenched her fists and willed herself to enjoy the brief respite from her own miserable thoughts.

As she caught up with him, Trevor was inching out over a long sheet of rock that jutted out from the jagged edge of the cliff, holding his hands out to balance himself. Diane reached out her hands and opened her mouth in a silent scream as he wobbled for a split second before he looked up at her, grinning. He plunked himself down on the edge, his feet hanging over the sheer drop of hundreds of feet to the jagged rocks and the dark, shimmering sea.

He pulled out a flask from the inside pocket of his leather jacket and dangled it toward her. "Come on. I don't bite. You gotta check out this view."

Diane walked up to the sheet of rock, hesitating. "That could fall at any second. I'm not coming out there."

He laughed. "Come on. Stop being such a little baby. You need to trust me."

She again pushed down the irritation. But what did it matter, really? She wasn't marrying the guy. She sighed and inched out over the sheet of rock, praying she didn't lose her grip on the slippery surface. As she settled down next to him, she looked out over the water and brought a hand to her mouth.

"Oh, geez," she managed lamely. The moonlight cut a long silver path leading from the horizon all the way to the shoreline beneath them. A fine mist of saltwater brushed against her skin. She yipped as a colossal wave rose precariously and smashed against the rocks at the base of the cliffside, sending an explosive spray into the air.

This was why she was here. The rest didn't matter. It just didn't matter anymore. Trevor's shoulder brushed against hers and her heart skipped a beat. *This* was what it was all about. A break in the suffering. A beautiful, glorious pause.

Diane looked up to see Trevor watching her, those X-ray eyes boring into hers, darting back and forth over her. She could almost *feel* him reading her mind. His mouth tugged up into a smile as he returned his gaze to the water.

"You should move here." He took a drink from the flask and passed it to her.

Diane laughed. "I just might."

"I'll give you a job," he said, leaning back on his arms. "I don't really need to be in Chicago much, anyway. I like it a lot more here in Marina Cove. Especially since you've been back."

Diane's heart pounded in her ears. "Trevor...I—"

"Come work for me," he interjected, turning to face her. "I mean, do you really like it out there in LA anymore? All that smog, the traffic? Are you happy with that ad agency stuff?" He snorted. "My company could use a creative like you. You can bring Grant," he added, a smirk crossing his face.

Heat rose to her face. She opened her mouth to speak, but found she couldn't. She pulled a long drink, wincing at the burn.

Trevor laughed. "Well, it's your life, Di. You need to loosen up, though. Live a little, and stop being such a goody two shoes. I mean, you're out there all cooped up in your office, sitting in twelve lanes of traffic on the 405 all day, using that writing talent of yours to sell diapers and detergent and pizza rolls, when you could have so much more. Be so much more. You've always held yourself back from what you could really become." He shook his head and tossed a pebble over the edge of the cliff. "I know you're not happy. And that's a shame."

Tears rose to Diane's eyes. It was too close to home, too close to the truth. She reached her hand into her pocket and ran her fingers over the folded sheet of pink paper, squeezing back a sob. She looked up at Trevor, their eyes meeting. Fire rushed across her skin.

At that moment, her phone buzzed in her back pocket. Without breaking her gaze, she pulled it out and jammed the power button down as hard as she could.

17

"I missed you last night," Charlotte said, intertwining her fingers into Christian's. "So how has Old Man Keamy been, anyway?"

Christian laughed. "I think you can just call him John now. You guys are like old friends."

"Everyone always called him that growing up. They all thought he was a crazy recluse. It's going to be hard to undo that." She smiled.

After John Keamy had told them how her father had been the one who'd hit him with his car all those years ago, Charlotte had been terrified to join Christian for one of his visits up to Keamy's isolated cabin, visits he'd been making for years. Now that Christian was getting treatment for PTSD, he was trying to pass along some of what he was learning to Keamy, who was also a veteran.

But for some reason, Keamy seemed to adore Charlotte, and had even tried his hand at baking her chocolate chip cookies the last time they'd visited. Underneath his brash, grumpy exterior, he was a terribly sweet man.

"He's doing okay, I think," said Christian, frowning. "I wish I could get him out of his cabin once in a while. I think he needs...I don't know. Friends. Social interaction. Maybe a good woman. You know anyone?"

Charlotte laughed and shook her head. Her mother had given up on dating for the time being. Or at least that's what she'd said. Charlotte thought she'd sensed something between Ella and Leo, just once or twice...and who knew? She didn't want to interfere, just in case.

"You're one to talk." She raised an eyebrow at Christian. "You still live in that tiny little box you call a cabin all by yourself. You *just now* got a cell phone. You're a recluse, too."

Charlotte and Christian were walking just ahead of Mariah, Sylvie, and Nick. Charlotte had just finished up work for the day, and Christian had surprised her as they'd closed up the restaurant to walk home with her. Nick was telling some story in that booming voice of his, gesturing animatedly, and Sylvie and Mariah were laughing hysterically. The sun was just beginning to set over the water, the sky a stunning violet and gold.

He scoffed playfully. "Hey. It's not a tiny box. I built that cabin. I think it has tons of space. Luxurious, I'd say."

Charlotte rolled her eyes. "You have to climb over your bed to get to your table. Your *one* table, with the *one* chair. Your cabin, good sir, is a tiny box. And on that huge, beautiful lot you talked Keamy into selling to you." She moved closer to him. "We always used to talk about building a house on that lot someday."

He looked down at her. "I know." He moved his mouth to say something but closed it, shaking his head. His cheeks reddened.

Charlotte's heart fluttered. He'd never said it, but since she'd come back and discovered he'd bought the gorgeous plot of land that sat right on the shore and built his tiny cabin in the far corner, she'd wondered if he'd bought it hoping she would come back to Marina Cove one day. Warmth radiated through her as she squeezed his hand.

They got to the corner of Shoreline Drive and

Driftwood Lane. "Well, this is our stop," said Sylvie, taking Charlotte's arm and peeling her off Christian with a wink.

"So how are things going?" Sylvie asked, pulling her aside and lowering her voice. "I mean...you know. With everything going on."

Charlotte's stomach twisted. She was asking about Jack. She let out a breath and closed her eyes for a moment. Nick was asking Christian something about a plumbing issue they'd been having at the restaurant while Mariah snapped a few photographs of the shore.

"It's hard to explain," she said finally. "On the one hand, I feel like I lost my father...like, really lost him. When we didn't know what happened to him, I think some part of me always pictured him somewhere else, alive and, I don't know...happy." Tears pricked the corners of her eyes. "But now that I know what really happened, it's just a lot to process still. It's going to take time." Sylvie nodded and rubbed her shoulder comfortingly.

"On the other hand," said Charlotte, wiping her eyes with the back of her hand, "I can say honestly that I've never been happier. I don't want to jinx anything, but Sylvie...I'm *happy*. Things are going well with Christian, slow but well. And I adore my work at the restaurant. I look forward to going there every day...it's a dream job, and I still can't believe I get to do it." She pulled Sylvie in for a hug. "That's thanks to you, girl. I really can't tell you what that means to me. To have something of my own, something I can work toward, really dive into. For the first time I can ever remember, everything is just clicking together, you know what I mean?" She let out a laugh. "I'm having the time of my life, Sylvie."

Sylvie grinned and nodded, her eyes bright. "That makes me so happy, Charlotte, you have no idea. And listen, you're giving our restaurant a huge boost with your pastry magic. Business has been up every week since you've started. You're doing *me* the favor, and don't think I don't know that."

Charlotte returned her grin, then leaned forward and dropped her voice further. "So it seems like things with Nick are going a little better, huh?"

Sylvie glanced behind Charlotte at her husband, a glint in her eyes. Then her face turned serious. "We're working on it. There've been a lot of, ah, *talks* lately." She snorted a little laugh and looked back up at Nick. Charlotte's throat constricted as she saw the affection in her eyes. "He's one stubborn man, but he's also...principled. I've made it clear what I expect, and so has he, so we're working to meet in the middle. It isn't perfect...but, you know, I really do love him." She smiled and looked at Charlotte. "We'll get there, I think."

They all hugged and said their goodbyes. Nick wrapped his arm around Sylvie's waist as they walked down Driftwood Lane toward their house. Charlotte sighed happily as she took Christian's arm again, following Mariah as she led them toward the Seaside House, snapping photos as she went.

As the sun dipped toward the horizon and the beautiful fragrance of wildflowers followed them down the shoreline, Charlotte felt like her chest was bursting with a spooling bright light. It was a fleeting feeling that went as fast as it came, but it was something she'd never really experienced before. Something like excitement. Hope. She'd learned to stop trying to hang onto it, to stretch it and hold it tight, and just let it come as it did and enjoy it while it was there. She squeezed Christian's arm a little tighter, and grinned.

"Oh, my God." Mariah stopped short in front of them. The Seaside House was just up ahead. Ollie was bounding through the sand, his ears flapping gloriously, and stopped next to her, panting happily. Charlotte lifted a hand over her brow, squinting in the fading sunlight, her heart pounding.

Diane was standing on the front porch, both hands on the wooden railing, biting her lip. The front door pushed open, and Ramona stepped out, holding a pitcher of water and a glass.

And sitting on the front steps leading out onto the sand, dressed in an immaculately tailored dress shirt and black slacks, hair slicked back and a tentative smile on his face, was Sebastian.

"No. Absolutely not," said Mariah through gritted teeth. "I'll see you guys later." She turned in the other direction and began walking away.

"Mariah, wait," said Christian, but Charlotte placed a hand on his arm to stop him, not taking her eyes off Sebastian. Fire rose in her throat. She continued toward the house as he took the glass of water from Ramona, drank half of it, and returned it to her without looking up. He sat up and met them in the sand, his hands raised in supplication.

He looked...well, good. Tanned, healthy, vibrant. His outfit alone was probably worth weeks of her pastry chef wages. Charlotte's fists clenched at her sides.

"Sebastian, what are you doing here—"

"I know, I know, I'm sorry," he interjected. Ramona was looking at him from the porch with a grim intensity. A flood of warmth hit Charlotte at seeing her sister's protectiveness. "I should have called, but I knew you would just say no. Listen," he said, stepping closer. "I felt terrible about our last call, Charlotte. I just want to talk...and I didn't want you to have to come all the way out to Manhattan."

"Sebastian, I—"

"You must be Christian," interrupted Sebastian, reaching out a hand. Christian gave it a firm shake. "Good to finally meet you." He looked him directly in the eye. "I hear you and Mariah are making up for lost time."

Christian released his hand from Sebastian's, glancing at Charlotte. He raised an eyebrow. "You and Charlotte raised a wonderful girl," he said after a moment.

Sebastian nodded. Diane took Ramona by the arm and led them down the porch. "We're going to go grab a bite to eat," said Diane. "Ah. We'll see you later." Ramona gave Charlotte a single nod, a nod in solidarity. Charlotte nodded back. They were beginning to develop their own silent language, a language Ramona had with their mother for many years and Charlotte had always envied. Ramona glared at Sebastian as she passed him and headed down the sand with Diane.

"I should go too," said Christian. "Nice to meet you, Sebastian."

"No." Charlotte's voice was hard. "Christian, please stay. I'm not cutting my night short because of this." She turned to look up at Sebastian. "What do you want, Sebastian? Why are you here? You can't just turn up unannounced like this."

Sebastian ran a hand through his perfect salt-and-pepper hair. Ollie sat next to Charlotte like a guard, giving Sebastian the stink-eye. He reached out to pet Ollie but was met with a deep growling bark.

"Look," he said, his eyes darting to Christian and then back to Charlotte. "I've had some time to think. And, ah, I know that you don't want to get back together with me." His shoulders dropped almost imperceptibly. "I realize that I'm just going to have to accept that. It isn't what I want...but I want you to be happy."

Charlotte gritted her teeth. If he wanted her to be happy, he wouldn't have started a dalliance with one of his work subordinates. He *certainly* wouldn't have carried on a six-year relationship with her best friend.

Sebastian was smooth with words...but his actions told a different story.

He looked her in the eyes. "I don't want a complicated divorce, Charlotte," he said. "And, ah, I see that you're still in need of...ah, of money." He glanced up at the Seaside House, an eyebrow raised. Charlotte followed his gaze. Dark scorch marks still scored the side of the house from the fire. Her mind flashed to the one-star review Felix Caldwell, the ridiculous but well-respected critic, had left for them during his ill-fated stay. It seemed like a thousand years ago.

He stepped closer to her. Charlotte felt Christian tense up next to her. "I know we had that prenup," he said, not taking his eyes off her. "And I don't want you to come out of this empty-handed. Not after everything you did to support me over the years." He unbuttoned his sleeves and rolled them up. "I'm *barely* in the black, especially after we lost the deal with Ramona for this land, for the Seaside House..."

Charlotte's nostrils flared. "Sebastian, you—"

He raised his hands. "Please. Just listen. I told you then that I didn't know Alastair was planning on tearing the house down. I really was trying to help you. It didn't work out. I've moved past it." Sebastian sighed, a faraway look in his eyes. He shook his head and looked back at Charlotte. "Anyway, I have a proposition for you. Please, let's sit for a minute." He turned and walked up to the porch, sitting down in one of the wicker chairs.

Charlotte looked up at Christian. "I'm sorry," she whispered. "You don't have to stick around for whatever this is. Can I call you as soon as he leaves?"

"No, Christian, you should stay," said Sebastian from the porch. Charlotte turned to glare at him. "You may as well hear it from the horse's mouth."

Charlotte and Christian sat down on the wooden swing across from Sebastian. He topped off his glass of water and sat back, taking a long drink. Charlotte shifted uncomfortably in her seat.

"Like I said, I want to help you, Charlotte." He looked at her for a moment. A horrible image of him in Brielle's arms tore through her. She didn't think she'd ever get over that. "In order for me to help you, for you to get something in the divorce, I have to get a few things off the ground. I have a meeting in a few days with an investor. He owns a bunch of little pharmaceutical companies. He calls himself 'Tex'...three guesses where he's from." Sebastian laughed to himself. "Cowboy hat, spurs on his boots, the whole package. Been married for, like, fifty years or something. Anyway."

He leaned forward in his seat, his hands meeting at the fingertips. "He apparently only does business with people who have the same, ah, values as he does. Family values."

Charlotte felt Christian stiffen next to her. She furrowed her eyebrows. "Where are you going with this, Sebastian?"

His eyes bored into Charlotte's. Not long ago, that look would have made her melt inside. Now, it sent spikes of anger into her throat. "What I'm asking you is this...and I know what it sounds like, but please just bear with me. I'm asking you to come to the meeting with me, and just for this meeting, I want it to appear that we're still together. And not, uh, getting a divorce." His finger idly ran over the ring on his finger, the ring Charlotte hadn't noticed until just now that he was still wearing.

Charlotte was speechless for a moment. "That's ridiculous," she said finally. "No. Absolutely not. Why on earth would you think—"

"I know it sounds a little crazy, I know that," he said, cutting her off. "But Charlotte, this benefits both of us. If we can get Tex on board, then Carter Enterprises will get a nice influx of cash. We're back in pharmaceuticals, biotech, patents...our wheelhouse. I'll be able to take care of you. We can make this divorce quick and clean."

Charlotte stared at him. He unbuttoned the top

button of his dress shirt and wiped the sweat forming at his brow. "You don't have to answer now," he said softly. "Talk it over with Mariah. With Allie and Liam. With Christian. Whomever you need to. And if you don't feel comfortable with this, that's okay too, I understand completely." He rose to his feet and set the glass of water on the table. "I really do want to help, Charlotte. I know you don't believe me, but I want you to be happy, after everything I've done to you. I want to make things right...as well as I can, at least." He sighed, looked between them, and turned to leave. He looked like he'd aged ten years since he'd been sitting with them.

"And if Tex doesn't invest?" Christian asked, his voice tight. "What will you do then?"

Sebastian stopped short. After a moment, he turned back to face them. "Look. I know you're probably not my biggest fan, Christian. I'm not stupid. But despite everything I've done, I never stopped loving Charlotte. Or the kids. I've basically ruined my own life here. Mariah won't even talk to me anymore," he said, his voice cracking slightly. Charlotte's chest tightened.

Sebastian shook his head and cleared his throat, looking up at Charlotte. His eyes were heavy. "I have no intentions of holding things up anymore. I admire you for moving on, Charlotte. I wish...I wish I was having an easier time. But that's on me. You've been nothing but wonderful." He turned to Christian. "You're a lucky man. I wish you two all the best. Let me know what you decide. Whatever you think." A long breath rushed out of him like he'd been holding it, and he turned and walked away through the sand.

A long, uncomfortable silence passed. Charlotte finally cleared her throat.

"I'm not going to do it," she said softly. "I don't trust him. I'm not going to pretend we're still together just so we can get some money. I have my job at The Windmill now. I can get by without him..." She looked up at Christian and rested her hand on his arm. "I know that's the long way, Christian. That it means the Seaside House restoration will take a lot longer. I want to say it again, I don't expect you to keep working on it for free."

He shook his head. "You know I'm not doing it for the money. I never was. You see what my life's like...it's barebones. I have almost no living expenses, no possessions to maintain. I have my tiny box, as you call it. I haven't really needed money for a long time. I do it because I love the work...and because I love you, Charlotte."

Tears unexpectedly sprang to her eyes. "So you don't think I'm stupid for not agreeing to this?"

He looked at her evenly. "This isn't a decision I should be weighing in on at all, I think. I trust you completely. I want you to do what you think is right, and what will make you happy." He tucked an errant strand of her long hair behind her ear. "If you decide to go through with it, I fully support you, if that's something you're worried about. And if you don't, I fully support that too. Just listen to what your gut tells you, Charlotte. It won't steer you wrong."

She wiped the tears from her cheeks. "I love you too, Christian." She rested her head on his shoulder. "Despite what he says, I'm worried that if I say no, he's going to drag this divorce out forever. He could do it, too. He's already made it so difficult...I just want to move on." She sniffled. "I hate this."

He wrapped his arm around her shoulder and kissed the top of her head. "We'll figure it out together. I'm here for you, you know that. We'll get through this."

They sat there for a long time, Charlotte's mind spinning. It seemed like a small thing, just a meeting with an investor, hold his hand and laugh a little, and then she'd finally have some money. Money she deserved for supporting him for the entirety of her marriage, raising their family and keeping the household. Money she'd have if he hadn't slowly bankrupted Carter Enterprises.

But there was no trust there anymore. Charlotte felt in her gut that it wouldn't be so simple, no matter what he told her. She didn't want to go through with it.

A sensation of walls closing in on her brought that old feeling of panic, the pins and needles, the dizziness. Fear snaked and coiled through her body as the overwhelming feeling that she would never get out of this marriage consumed her.

uzz buzz. Buzz buzz.

Diane's heart was racing a mile a minute as she pulled her phone from her back pocket and swiped up to see who'd texted her.

Parker.

Her breath caught in her throat as she opened the text. It was three emojis in a row, little bombs exploding. Then, eloquent as always, *Lol.*

Well, that about summed it up.

Diane's hands were trembling slightly as she kneaded the dough on the kitchen counter. She closed her eyes and tried to listen to the sound of the waves lapping at the shore outside, to Frankie Valli on the old record player Charlotte had put on in the dining room.

Two hours earlier, she'd signed on to the video conference for her pitch to the Larson Brands executives. After spending all that time unable to focus on her pitch and going out with Trevor, she'd been... well, underprepared would be a kind way of putting it. Never in her life had she felt so put on the spot. She'd stammered through a series of ideas and thoughts that now, in retrospect, were ludicrous. It had been consummately unprofessional...and she'd known it the entire time.

Larson Brands had not been happy. Geoff and Lisa were both on the video call as well, their faces tight and grim. Parker had been grinning like a fool the entire time.

There was no one to blame but herself. Things weren't looking good.

"Okay, I think the dough's ready." Charlotte appeared at her shoulder, and Diane tensed up. "Should we start assembling?"

Ramona and Mariah began plating pepperoni, sliced green peppers, sausage, mushrooms, and olives on the counter around Diane. The oven behind her sent waves of heat that brought beads of sweat to her brow. Right now, it was like a prison in here.

They'd talked her into making homemade pizza and watching bad rom-coms tonight. She'd relented, but Ramona had taken her aside. "I think it might be good for you," she'd said. "Take your mind off things. It'll be fun, I promise."

Diane had bristled. Ramona had no idea what she was dealing with. But her stomach was rumbling after not eating all day before the pitch, and she figured it would help distract her from what she'd done. And what she worried it would mean.

"Mmmmm," said Mariah as she dumped spoon after heaping spoon of pizza sauce over her dough. She looked up at Charlotte, who had her eyebrows raised. "What? The sauce is the best part," she said with a giggle.

Buzz buzz. Buzz buzz.

Diane ran a hand through her sweaty hair and looked at the cracked screen of her phone. Her hands were shaking now. She gripped the phone harder so no one else would notice.

A call from Geoff. Oh, no.

Her finger hovered over the answer button, but she couldn't make it press down on his name. Geoff called again. Two more times. Diane's heart thundered in her ears.

What had she done? What was she doing?

A little red dot appeared over her email icon. Thorns of pain skewered into her wrist before she realized she'd yanked back the rubber band. "I need to look at this, back in a sec," she breathed to the others before going out onto the porch and opening the email.

Diane,

Tony from Larson called me after your pitch and let us know they were dropping us as a prospective client. I don't have to tell you what that means for the future of our agency. We're scrambling over here.

Since you're clearly no longer interested in your work, and with your continued refusal to answer our calls or attend our meetings, your time with Nicholls+Kline has come to an end.

This is terribly unfortunate. I wish I understood what's happened to you, Diane. You've put us in a real bind. Again. And after everything we did for you and Grant.

I expect your personal possessions to be removed from our office by the end of the week.

Geoff Lindsay

Diane felt all the air go out of her lungs. She'd been fired. She had no way of making money anymore, the sole breadwinner. She was on her own. Her fingers instinctively went to dial Grant's number before she sat down hard on the porch and tried to catch her breath.

Her skin was cold. She cracked the rubber band.

There was no way she was going to get through a night with the girls. She was the odd one out, and they all knew it, no matter how much they'd been trying to involve her. And Diane had no intention of spending the rest of her night thinking about how she'd systematically ruined everything good in her life.

She closed the voicemail and stared at her screen. Through the splintered glass, an old picture of Kayla and Jamie stared back at her, her phone background. Kayla was just a little girl, maybe five years old, and was mid-flight in an old blue plastic swing that Grant had hung from the large maple tree in their front yard. Jamie stood in front of the swing, his arms out, giving Kayla a push, laughter in his eyes.

Diane's chest tightened as she looked closer at Kayla. Her baby girl. She looked so happy. Her hair flew wildly behind her in the wind, her mouth wide open, her eyes sparkling with absolute glee.

Diane remembered so clearly the day she'd taken the picture. She remembered thinking, *I'm not ready for them to get older. Please, let things slow down, just a little. I'm not ready for this to end.*

Tears welled in her eyes as her fingers moved automatically to check the GPS tracking app, as they so often did almost unconsciously. The practiced swipe showed Kayla's car, driving near her school.

Diane wondered what she was up to. Who she was with. Was she having fun?

Was she happy?

Diane's fingers hovered over Kayla's number. She squeezed her eyes shut and shook her head. She couldn't. She couldn't affect things. What if she wanted to come visit again? It would change Kayla's plans, because she would feel guilty. And if something happened...well. Diane couldn't be responsible for that.

Her heart splintered as she swiped Kayla's number away. Hopefully she'd just see Kayla back in LA as she'd originally planned...she didn't know what else to do. She knew she was ruining her relationship with her daughter, as she'd already done with Jamie.

But at least she wouldn't have any more guilt on her shoulders.

A text appeared on her screen. Trevor. A warm prickling sensation ran across her chest.

Where are you? Want to hang out?

After a moment, she squared her shoulders and replied. *I'm at the Seaside House.*

A few minutes later, he responded. *Cool. See ya in a few.*

Ten minutes later, his motorcycle roared down the street and skidded to a stop. He wore a tight black T-shirt that clung to his muscles. "Hey, kid," he said, grinning at her.

Ramona pushed open the front door. "Hey, Di, the pizza's almost ready—oh." She stopped short at the sight of Trevor. "Hi, Trevor."

He kept his eyes on Diane. "You ready to go?"

Diane looked back at Ramona. A line appeared between her sister's eyebrows. "You're leaving, Diane?"

Diane opened her mouth to speak, but Trevor interjected. "I'll bring her back in one piece, don't you worry."

Ramona stepped toward him. "I have a better idea. Why don't you stay for dinner? Diane was helping us make homemade pizza."

Trevor snorted. "Sounds like a real party." He

looked down at Diane and offered her his hand. "Come on. Let's go."

Diane stood up and faced Ramona. She knew she was being rude, terrible, really, by leaving them when they were trying so hard...but she just couldn't think anymore. She was done *thinking* all the time. Suffering all the time.

But there was something in Ramona's expression that gave her pause. She was really trying. She let out a breath, and turned back to Trevor.

"Maybe we could stay for a little...you can meet my family. Then, after dinner..."

His mouth formed a thin line. He approached Diane, and leaned in to whisper into her ear. His breath on her neck rose goosebumps on her arms.

"I know you don't want to be here," he said, glancing up at Ramona. "I have something fun planned for us."

"Maybe just for a few," she whispered back.

He looked down at her. "They'll be fine without you. It's my last night in Marina Cove for a week. I've got business back home in Chicago." He leaned in closer. Butterflies fluttered in her stomach. "I promise you'll have more fun with me."

Diane glanced back at Ramona, whose eyebrows were furrowed, and shook her head, pushing back the burning behind her eyes. Ramona looked at her for a long moment before nodding and turning back into the Seaside House.

Diane closed her eyes and let the air out of her lungs in a huge *whoosh*. Trevor grinned and hopped on his motorcycle.

And before Diane followed him, she pulled her wedding ring from her third finger and set it gently on the wooden railing of the front porch, ignoring the bile rising in her throat.

"*Wooooo-hooooooo!*" Trevor yelled into the night air as he ripped off his shirt and dove headfirst into the black waves.

Diane laughed and pulled the bottle of wine to her mouth, taking a long drink. *This* was how to spend a night. Especially after everything that had happened today.

Guns N' Roses blared from the speakers of the speedboat and carried out into the endless dark water. A gleaming band of white moonlight cut across the waves and shimmered around them. Diane hadn't believed him when he said people left their keys in their boats all the time, but of course, he'd been right. She had yipped in delight as the engine roared to life and he took her out into the open sea, the wind billowing through her dark hair, carrying away all her worries and problems along with it.

"Come on in!" he shouted from the water, sending a splash her way. Diane shrieked as the cold water struck her skin. She took another long drink, looking down at her long navy maxi dress, and shrugged. She pulled off her jeans under the dress, and stepped carefully toward the back end of the boat. Plugging her nose with one hand, Diane leaped into the dark sea.

Her whole body seized up as the frigid water pierced her, sending tremors rippling into her arms and legs. Her lungs were on fire. Kicking as hard as she could, she finally broke the surface, and hollered into the night.

They swam and splashed around the boat, jumping again and again into the water. Diane felt alive, young, like she had all those years ago, before all her problems began. Her mind was a pleasant blank void. It was absolutely glorious.

Her phone buzzed from the white cushioned seating along the side of the boat. Diane pulled herself from the water, her dress clinging tightly to her skin, and lifted her phone to shut it off. Just before she hit the power button, she saw Ramona had sent her a text.

I'm worried about you. Maybe we can talk about it sometime?

Diane frowned. She glanced up at Trevor, who was watching her. "Who's that?" he asked, his voice tight.

She hesitated. "It's Ramona. My sister. I think they're upset that I left."

He scowled. "Why are you thinking about that right now, when you're here with me?" He swam toward the boat and lifted himself up, his powerful arms gleaming in the moonlight. "You've got to stop worrying so much, Diane. It makes you look weak. If your family cared about you, they would've done more to be there for you when you were in LA all those years."

Before Diane could register what he'd said, he slipped an arm around her waist. "They don't care about you like I do. Forget them. Have some fun instead. That's what you really want."

Grinning, he took her hand and guided her to the edge of the boat. Then he faced her and lifted her up, carrying her as though she were as light as a feather, and with a whoop, jumped straight into the water with her.

Diane screamed with laughter as they broke the surface, her arms around his neck. His heat radiated through the thin fabric of the dress plastered to her skin.

She looked up at him, his eyes blazing into hers. Her pulse pounded in her throat, her skin electrified. Grant's face emerged in her mind's eye, and she shoved it away with all her might. She was done thinking about all that now. Done. The world was beginning to slip and slide around her, tilting to the side, threatening to cast her off into the abyss.

And then everything around her disappeared as she closed her eyes and pressed her mouth against Trevor's in a kiss.

"WHAT DID YOU DO, DIANE?"

Diane stopped in her tracks on the porch landing of the Seaside House. Droplets of cold saltwater fell from her hair and dress, dappling the wood of the porch. She whipped her head around to the source of the voice.

Ramona was sitting in one of the wicker chairs,

in the dark, watching her. Diane's heart leaped into her throat. She just barely made out Charlotte sitting next to her.

"What do you mean?" she asked, a little too quickly.

Ramona stood up and held something out. A tiny glimmer in the soft moonlight.

Her wedding ring.

Diane gritted her teeth and bounded toward Ramona, yanking the ring from her hand. "It's none of your business." She turned and pushed on the front door. It wouldn't yield. She pushed her whole body against it until it finally squealed open.

"What's up with that guy, Diane?" Ramona asked, her voice softened.

Diane whipped around. "Nothing. He's just a friend, all right? I don't get why I'm being interrogated here. I'm sorry, but you guys have no idea what you're talking about." She wiped her mouth, her heart thudding against her chest.

Charlotte sat up and approached Diane slowly. "You kissed him."

The world seemed to tilt sideways for a brief, terrifying moment. She snapped the rubber band against the wet skin of her wrist and swallowed hard against something blocking her throat.

"Yes. I kissed him. Who cares? I'm a big girl. I don't need you two monitoring my every move."

"What about Grant?" Ramona asked. "What about your kids? Is this really what you want to be doing?"

Diane clenched her hands. "Don't you *dare* bring them up, you two have *no idea*, you don't know anything about me—"

"Then talk to us, Diane!" cried Charlotte. She reached for Diane's shoulder.

Diane shoved Charlotte's hand away. "You want to know what *I've* been dealing with? Huh? *Do you have any idea what I've been through?*"

She was screaming now. She yanked the folded pink sheet of paper from her jeans pocket, now damp with the water soaking through her dress, and pushed it against Charlotte's chest.

Charlotte frowned and unfolded the paper, her eyes scanning the short handwritten message. Ramona moved next to her and looked over Charlotte's shoulder.

Charlotte looked up at Diane, her face twisted in confusion. "I don't understand."

Tears forced their way into Diane's eyes, spilling down her cheek. She brushed past Charlotte and sat down hard on the wooden rocker, her face in her hands. Her sisters sat across from her, not saying a word.

After a long moment, Diane raised her gaze to meet theirs. She let out a shaky breath.

"Look," she said, her voice warbling. "There's something I haven't told you yet."

19

THREE YEARS EARLIER

Diane yawned as she took a long drink of black coffee from her mug and tilted her laptop away from the sun's glare on her back porch, swiping through another page of transactions. It had been a few months since she'd gone through their retirement accounts, checking the returns on their investments. Her investments, really, since Grant had still been unable to find work anywhere in town after Geoff and Lisa had let him go.

She pushed back the fire in her throat as she thought of Parker. That snake had ruined Grant's career. Everything had fallen on Diane's shoulders. She hadn't thought it was possible to work any more hours than she had been, but there were always more. She barely slept five hours a night, often waking at her desk and quickly changing her clothes and splashing water over her face before her employees arrived in the morning.

Their kids had really taken the brunt of everything, though. Diane barely knew them anymore. What they were doing in school, who their friends were, what they wanted to do with their lives. If they were happy.

It broke her. Her children had been the most important part of her life...and she'd had to give that up so they could all get back on their feet. So that her children could live in a nice home, eat healthy food, have dance class and baseball and stage crew and an opportunity to go to college. Everything she did was aimed at protecting them from the problems they had resulting from Grant's past.

After Diane had finally paid off every lender, she'd realized that she and Grant were going to be in serious trouble come retirement. They were no longer in debt, but they had nothing to their names. So Diane had been working furiously at the agency to start contributing to their empty retirement accounts again. It was slow-going, but at this rate ... they should make it. Maybe.

Diane scrolled through page after page of transactions. She'd been letting it fall behind for the last few months, checking everything. And if she was being honest, monitoring. She'd never really regained her trust in Grant and had kept a close eye on their finances ever since.

She got to July's statements, and frowned. The balance was beginning to drop. A slow chill scuttled across the base of her spine. She leaned forward. As the pages went on, money was being withdrawn, first in small amounts, but the withdrawals kept growing. And growing. Until the balance had dropped to almost nothing. Icy sweat broke out on her brow.

There was an explanation. Grant had transferred some money. That was all.

Diane closed her laptop and tried to catch her breath. Grant was at the bank right now, trying to get a loan. He'd had an idea to start his own agency, from the ground up, since no one would hire him. It was an idea Diane supported wholeheartedly, since it seemed his luck in finding work wasn't changing. Eventually, if things worked out, Diane could quit Nicholls+Kline and they could both work for the new agency. Start over. Have something of their own.

There was some reason the money had been withdrawn. Maybe he'd had to show the bank liquid assets, or something. But it didn't feel right. Her gut told her something was wrong.

Diane tossed her laptop onto the patio couch and swept inside the house, bounding straight through the kitchen and down the stairs into the basement Grant had made into his office. She sat down hard at the desk that held his computer, turned it on, and waited. Guilt tore through her, but she ignored it. She knew it was wrong, breaching his privacy...but what else was she supposed to do, after all the lies he'd told her? He had an addiction, yes, and she had supported his recovery. But the trust she'd lost...that wasn't so easy to rebuild.

Diane had to know.

She frantically clicked through his documents. Opened his browser and shuttled through his history, scanning for anything related to gambling, her heart skittering wildly.

Nothing.

She sat back, relieved. At least there was nothing immediately obvious. She'd just ask him when he got home. She ran her hands through her hair, and laughed.

And then her eyes landed on a little folder on the desktop. A little folder with a tiny lock in the lower right corner.

Diane felt the color drain from her face as she double-clicked. A prompt appeared, asking for her password. Her arms and legs felt numb.

She closed her eyes and thought. She tried *password, 12345, poker*. She tried *diane*. Her kids' names. Nothing.

Diane felt that feeling, like the floor was tipping, and reached for her rubber band. Grant loved their children, but he'd always had a special relationship with Kayla. She was a daddy's girl, that was for sure. A memory ripped at her, Kayla bounding up the stairs and into his arms after a day at preschool, singing "I love my da-da, he is the bestest da-da in the town, and I love him" in her beautifully off-key little girl voice.

With trembling fingers, she punched in Kayla's birthday.

The folder opened.

THE SKY WAS BEGINNING to darken as Diane heard the telltale squeaking of the old brakes that meant Grant's car had pulled into the driveway. She sat at the kitchen table, her arms resting on her lap, her eyes on the front door. Waiting.

A few minutes passed before the door quietly opened. Grant shuffled in, set down his leather satchel, and looked up at Diane, his face lined and weary. His shoulders were slumped.

He hadn't gotten the loan. She wasn't surprised.

Grant's dress shoes clicked across the hardwood floor as he approached Diane and sat down across from her, running his hands over his face. She watched him, tears already welling in her eyes.

Despite everything, she loved him. It broke her heart to see him so disappointed. To see everything he'd been through. He was a good man with a serious problem.

But that didn't change what he had done.

Again.

Diane lifted the printed sheets of paper from the table in front of her and tossed them toward Grant. He furrowed his brow, and lifted the sheets up. A second later, he looked up at Diane.

"Diane, I can explain this."

Diane slammed her hands on the table, making Grant jump. "*NO!* No. You can't. You can't explain this. You lied to me. You're *gambling* again, Grant! I can't believe it. I can't believe you."

"I need you to listen to me—"

"I don't want to hear it—"

"Please, Diane!" he cried. His face was pale. "Listen. I know it looks bad. You know we're trying to get this loan from the bank. But we need a lot...and I knew we needed to show more assets, to make it more likely that we'll get a loan." He let out a hard breath and splayed his hands on the table. "I was trying to help us. I really was. It kills me, sweetheart, seeing what you've had to do, all the work...I thought...I don't know." He ran a hand through his hair. "I thought if I could get a couple of good wins in, just a few well-placed bets...I could take the work off your shoulders. I could help give you back the life you wanted. I just needed a couple of good wins—"

"That's how you lost everything, Grant!" she screamed. "You can't stop when you start! That was the whole point of all that therapy, all the help you got, all that work you did! You weren't supposed to gamble *ever again*, because of the slippery slope! I've spent years, *years* working, working, working, all because of the mess you got us in. I know you have a problem. I know that, Grant, but what am I supposed to do here? Do you have any idea how this affects me? It's *ruined my life, Grant!*" She choked out a sob.

Grant closed his eyes. "You're right. And I'm sorry—"

"You were sorry back then too! And look at my life now," she said, scoffing. "*I* paid the price for what you did. I never see my children. Jamie barely talks to us anymore! I feel like I barely know them because *I'm always working*. It's killing me, Grant...I gave up my family." Her chest heaved, and she gasped for air, swiping the tears from her cheeks. "I gave up my family because I love you and I supported you, but here you go again. You went behind my back and you lied to me again, Grant, you lied to me, you're gambling again and that money..."

She clenched her fists and squeezed her eyes shut. "Just tell me. Where's our retirement money. Tell me you still have it somewhere. Tell me it isn't gone. Please, please tell me it isn't gone."

Diane forced her eyes open and looked into the eyes of the man she loved. Grant looked back, the horrible silence stretching between them, engulfing them. He hung his head.

Diane opened her mouth wordlessly and stared at him. She thought of sitting in twelve lanes of traffic on the 405 every morning, the harsh sunlight slicing its way through the windows into her bleary eyes. Night after night of the lights flicking off one by one in the office as employees left, leaving only the single shaft of hot fluorescent light pooling over her desk. She thought of the look on Kayla's face, the slow nod of disappointment, every time Diane told her she wasn't able to make it to her play, her recital, her parent-teacher conference. That heartbreaking look, her daughter robbed of a mother who could be there for her in so many ways, who had so much to offer.

A black scream built in Diane's throat. She couldn't stop seeing that look. Everything around her was all coming crashing down again. Before she knew what she was saying, the words came tumbling out.

"I want a divorce."

Grant paled under the dim light of the kitchen. Somewhere outside a child screamed with laughter, followed by the patter of sneakers against the pavement. Diane's chest rose and fell hard.

"You don't mean that," he whispered. His eyes welled with tears.

Diane's thoughts skittered around in her mind. The kitchen seemed tiny now, the walls marching closer to her, boxing her in. Her blood was boiling.

She couldn't trust him anymore. How on earth was she supposed to come back from this? What was she going to do? She was going to be stuck working her life away until she died.

No way could that happen. She'd lost enough.

She kept her gaze on him, her eyes blurred with tears. Words were trapped in her throat.

A lone tear stole down Grant's cheek. He slowly rose from the table and turned toward the front door.

"Where are you going?" Diane asked. Her heart skipped a beat.

He stopped at the door, one hand on the knob. "I need to go. I need to think."

Diane bolted up from her chair, sending it skidding across the floor. "Don't you dare, Grant! Don't you dare leave this house during an argument!"

Her vision was starting to tunnel. If he left now and something happened...it would be her fault. She couldn't have it happen again. "We need to talk this through. Don't leave."

His shoulders slumped. "You can't force me to stay here, Diane. You just told me you want a divorce. I need...I need to think right now. I need to be on my own."

Diane stormed through the hallway and put her hand on the front door. "You promised me you wouldn't leave the house during an argument. You can't do this, Grant..." She was crying now. The room was beginning to tilt. For an instant she saw the look of horror on Victoria's face, Austin gripping the seat. The guardrail, the ground approaching beneath her. She thought of Trevor screaming at her over Victoria's death, blaming her for all those years. Leaving her behind because of what she'd done. She yanked the rubber band and cracked it against her wrist, making her wince. "You *promised me*. After everything I went through...you can't do this to me..."

He shook his head. "Diane, that whole system of yours...it doesn't make sense—"

"*Don't lecture me*, you have no freaking idea what it's like for me—"

"—I think you need to cool off. I don't blame you. But I have to think about what you said, I need to be alone for a little while—"

"*Please!* Grant, please, I don't want it to be like this, I can't have you leave, what if something happens—"

"Nothing is going to happen, Diane!" he yelled. "I'm going. I'm an adult. You can't stop me. I'm sorry, Diane. I'm sorry for everything I did. I understand if you want a divorce, I really do. I don't want one, but I'm positive I deserve it. We both need space to think right now, to calm down so we don't do anything rash, okay? I'm leaving."

He pulled open the front door. Diane let go of

her grip. "Fine! Then *go!* Get out! *Get out!*" She slammed the door behind her, shaking, then swept through the hallway and sat back down at the kitchen table, trying to catch her breath. The turn of his car engine cut through the quiet blanketing the house, followed by the gunning of his accelerator as he drove away from her, leaving her behind, alone.

Her throat seized up. She sat there for a long time, watching the sky darken, wringing her hands.

What had she done? He'd broken his promise to her, but she'd caused it. What did she expect? She'd threatened him with divorce. She was still in shock about what he'd done, but the exact situation she had successfully avoided all these years, the one she feared the most after the accident, had now come to pass.

If something happened to Grant now, it would be her fault. It was life-and-death.

She whipped out her phone and dialed Grant's number. Straight to voicemail. She dialed again, and again. Nothing.

Where would he go right now? Why did he shut his phone off? She stood and paced around the kitchen table, thick fear wrapping around her chest, tightening with each passing minute.

Diane raced out to the patio to get her laptop

and returned, setting it on the table, hands shaking wildly. She opened the tracking website, the one that pinged the GPS tracker she'd argued with Grant to have placed on his car long ago. Just in case. She'd never used it yet.

It showed him driving along the Pacific Coast Highway, traveling north. She breathed a sigh of relief. The little dot was still moving. He sometimes drove the stretch all the way up to Carpinteria, or sometimes even Santa Barbara, when he wanted to think. Which had always been fine, because Diane hadn't sent him to do it.

This time was different.

Diane opened up two more tabs. One for the weather, one for the California Highway Patrol accident reports. She groaned. It was supposed to rain, of course it was. She sat back, rolling through the tabs one by one, hitting refresh, scanning the CHP reports for a dark blue Ford Explorer. She dialed his phone every minute, on the minute.

She'd made a terrible mistake. What had she done? She didn't want a divorce. It had flown from her mouth before she'd realized what she was saying. She loved him. She would figure something out with him. He'd relapsed, that was all. He'd relapsed and what had she done? She told him she wanted a divorce.

An hour passed. Rain pattered outside intermittently at first, but was now falling hard. Her wrist was covered in angry red welts. Grant's car had continued past Carpinteria, but hadn't updated in ten minutes. She knew that could happen...the GPS wasn't perfect, was it? She dialed his phone again. He *knew* he was supposed to keep his phone on when he was gone; he knew that, didn't he?

After twenty minutes without the little icon pinging on the map, Diane began to sweat profusely.

There was no way her worst nightmare was coming true. The nightmare she'd been terrified would come true for so long. There was no way.

Raindrops pelted against the windowpanes of the kitchen and seemed to slice into her mind like tiny splinters. Nothing on the CHP reports. Nothing on the local news sites. Should she call the police? No, that was crazy. What would she even tell them? They'd laugh her right off the line. Maybe she should go out in her car, find him? Had she put gas in the car? She could be up there in an hour, less if she was speeding...

She couldn't breathe. The room was tilting around over and over. She spread her hands out over the kitchen table, moaning, tears falling from her eyes. Time passed by her without any meaning.

She would do anything to make this feeling stop. Anything. Anything. Anything.

A knock at the door shot her to her feet. She laughed with glee. He'd come home. Tears of relief poured from her eyes. "Grant! Oh, my God, Grant, thank God, thank God," she whimpered as she raced to the front door and pulled it open.

Grant stood there, a grim look on his face. The rain poured from the sky behind him.

Something was wrong, though. Everything was coming into Diane's field of vision slowly, one slice at a time. Time crawled to a stop.

She glanced behind him, toward something flickering in her periphery. Blue and red lights, flashing intermittently in the pouring rain. She squinted, her skin cold, her arms and legs numb, locked in place, cemented. A police cruiser was parked in her driveway.

Strange. What had happened, she wondered? Her eyes slid through molasses toward Grant.

But the man standing in front of her wasn't her husband. It was someone she didn't recognize.

A man in a police uniform.

No.

Diane shook her head to clear away the bad dream unfolding before her. Horribly, a giggle escaped from her throat. This wasn't happening. No. She was dreaming. That was all. She squeezed her eyes shut and forced her body to wake up.

When she popped them open, the man was still standing there. His mouth was moving, he was telling her something, but she only heard a hot buzzing sound. Darkness pooled at the edges of her vision.

Diane watched her hands softly close the front door on the man as he was still speaking. She watched herself press her back against the door, and watched herself slide to the ground. Hot tears streamed down her face as her mouth fell open in a silent wail.

"**O**h, Diane," whispered Charlotte from somewhere. Diane rubbed her eyes with the back of her hands. Tears fell from her eyes and dappled her dress. "Diane, I'm so sorry—"

"Don't," Diane said in a hoarse voice. "Please... don't." A hard sob choked out of her before she shook her head. "I don't want to think about it anymore. He's gone, and it was my fault, and that's all there is to say."

Ramona knelt down next to her. Diane bristled, but didn't move. She was too tired. "Diane, it's not your fault."

"Yes, it is," she said simply. "He wouldn't have driven away that day if it wasn't for me. My husband would still be alive if I hadn't told him I wanted a divorce. I'm responsible, and there's nothing more to be said. I knew something like this would happen again."

Ramona furrowed her eyebrows. "Again?"

Diane pressed her feet into the ground, willing the world to stop tilting. No way was she getting into *that*. "It doesn't matter. I just..." Fresh tears trickled from her eyes. "My life hasn't been going well, I can tell you that right now. I can't sleep. I don't taste my food. Ever since Grant's accident...I'm constantly checking where Kayla is, tracking her like a crazy person. I'm stuck. I can't bear the idea of causing something to happen to her too...so I never ask her to visit, I never influence her plans, I don't even call her in case something I do changes something and she gets hurt. Because it will be my fault again, and I can't handle it, I *can't do it* after Grant, after..."

Her face crumpled and her body shook with grief. "Jamie doesn't talk to me because I drove him crazy after Grant died, trying to track his every move. I wasn't there for him. I pushed him away and now he doesn't talk to me. Kayla is all I have left, and I've pushed her away too. She wanted to come visit me, you know. Out here. She was all ready to go, and I stopped her. And you want to know the worst part?" She looked between Ramona and Charlotte, her eyes wide. "I know what I'm doing is crazy. I know that's not how it works. The rational part of me *knows* that I'm still influencing them by trying to avoid influencing them. I tell Kayla not to come here, and maybe she gets in a car accident at school when she was supposed to be here instead. But here we are. I'm totally lost. This is my life now. I'm always going to be like this. And I'm tired. I'm so, so tired."

After the accident that had killed Victoria, Diane had spent so much time trying to prevent a situation where she'd be responsible for anything bad happening to someone else. Avoiding influencing situations, in her own twisted logic. But after Grant, everything had ratcheted up to a fever pitch. It was her worst nightmare made real.

That was when she'd started the obsessive checking, the obsessive mental looping. Everything had been in a downward spiral since then.

Diane let out a harsh breath and reached for the pink lined sheet of paper Charlotte had been holding. She slowly unfolded it. The ink had started to run, wet from her dress leaking through her jeans pocket. Her heart folded as her tear-streaked eyes ran over the few but precious words.

Hey sweetheart, went to the store, we needed milk. Back later.

I love you.

G

She stared at the note for a moment. "Grant pinned this to the fridge the day before he died. It's the last thing he ever wrote. It's the last time he told me he loved me." Tears fell from her cheeks as she gently folded it and carefully placed it back in her pocket.

Ramona wiped her eyes and leaned forward. "Diane, I don't know what to say. I can't even imagine...I'm so sorry. How can we help you?"

"You can't." Diane sat back, running her hands over her face. "Look. I only told you because I knew you weren't going to stop hounding me about Trevor. So you see? It's been three years. Three long years. Grant's gone. I'm allowed to see someone else. I'm tired of stopping myself from moving on, from worrying that I'm not supposed to move on. I didn't do anything wrong by kissing Trevor. I told him about Grant before we kissed, so he didn't do anything wrong either. So honestly, I don't want to hear anything else about it, because you know what? I'm *so sick and tired* of feeling guilty all the time, and I don't care anymore. I'm doing what *I* want for a change."

Charlotte moved her wicker chair closer and placed Diane's hands in hers. Diane tried to pull away, but Charlotte held on. A fresh sob built in Diane's throat.

"Diane, of course you're allowed to see someone. We had no idea that Grant...we didn't know what you were dealing with. We just..." She looked at Ramona, trailing off.

"Trevor just doesn't seem like a very good guy, that's all," said Ramona. "We're just looking out for you. He's rude. Really rude. He's ignored us both times you introduced us. He monopolizes your time. And I heard what he was whispering to you, Diane. When he took you away on his motorcycle. All that about how you didn't need us, how it was his last night and all. He's trying to isolate you. There's something...off about that guy. I just don't want you to get hurt."

Diane scoffed. "Blunt as always, Ramona. Look. You two really don't know what you're talking about. I think I know him a little bit better than you and your what, thirty seconds of knowing him?" She let go of Charlotte's hand. "All I know is that when I'm with

Trevor, I'm not suffering anymore. I don't think about work. I don't think about Grant. I don't think about having to track Kayla all the time. Or how Jamie doesn't talk to me anymore. I'm not cracking this *stupid rubber band* against my wrist all the time just so I can stay on solid ground. I'm not checking, and checking, and checking all the time, terrified of being responsible for someone's death again, needing to know where everyone is at all times. I've ruined my relationship with Jamie and I'm doing it with Kayla too."

Diane wiped the tears from her eyes and pulled her hair back behind her. "With Trevor, I feel *alive* again. I feel alive, and you know what? I don't care what that costs me. *I just don't*. When you two find yourselves responsible for someone's death, then you can talk to me. Until then, this is my life, and this is what I've decided."

Ramona and Charlotte glanced at each other before they both nodded slowly. "We're here for you, Diane," Ramona said in a quiet voice. "We love you."

Diane closed her eyes and nodded. She pushed back the voice in her head that screamed at her to listen to her sisters. The voice that reminded her the times Trevor had made her feel weak, small. How he had that side to him...the selfish side, the side that sometimes came out when Diane least expected it.

But Diane certainly wasn't perfect. When she thought about how she deserved to be treated better, she remembered how she'd taken away Trevor's sister. He'd loved her, really loved her. She could tolerate his issues, for now anyway. It was the least she could do to be there for him after what she'd done. She wasn't going to get all caught up thinking about the long term anymore. All that did was drive her mad.

He had a lot to offer, at any rate. He made her feel like the only woman in the world. She thought about his offer. To come work for him, to leave it all behind. He'd been joking...but what was stopping her now?

There was nothing back home for her anymore.

At any rate, Diane had made her bed and now she had to lie in it. She took back her wedding ring, the ring she'd been unable to bear taking off, even after all this time, and put it in her pocket next to Grant's note. She gave her sisters a hug goodnight, the scar on her arm throbbing horribly, and trudged up the stairs to the bedroom floor they all shared, impatient, waiting for the next time she could see Trevor again, for the next time her grief and fear and suffering would go away for a little while.

21

"Thanks again for the recommendations, Mrs. Keller," said the young woman as she handed Ella her credit card. "This will keep me busy for weeks."

"Oh, you can call me Ella, dear," Ella said with a smile. "And it was my pleasure, really. I love talking the Brontë sisters with someone else who loves them as much as I do. Next time you're in, we'll have to talk about Virginia Woolf."

The young woman laughed and lifted the giant stack of books into her canvas bag, heaving it over her shoulder and waving to Ella. Roald didn't stir next to her; he was swiping away on his phone again.

"Ah, Roald, maybe we shouldn't be doing that

when customers are at the register," she offered, fixing a smile on her face.

He glanced up at her and grunted before looking back down at his phone. Ella sighed and scanned the bookstore.

What a difference just a bit of time had made. It was unbelievable how much *clutter* had accumulated around the bookstore over the years. Each day, she scraped, cleaned, and painted, ignoring the stiffness of her muscles and creaking of her old joints, always waiting for the time when Leo would arrive after his shift on the ferry, eager for the company. They'd put on some music and work together, laughing and having great conversations. Ella had finally been loosening up after everything that had been going on. It was an incredible relief, a feeling of freedom.

Ella looked over by the fireplace. Charlotte and Christian were snuggled up on the old couch, laughing, flirting. Ella felt the corners of her mouth turn up. It was so good to see her daughter happy. Christian was a good man. He took care of her.

She watched them out of the corner of her eye, her heartbeat drumming, before averting her eyes. The hard sting of loneliness spiked into her throat. Charlotte looked up and waved to Ella, her eyes shining with happiness. Ella waved back, forcing a smile on her face, and willed back the tears pricking the corners of her eyes.

It had been their new relationship, after all these long years, that had first prompted Ella to want to find out what had really happened to her husband. She'd had no idea the rabbit hole that decision would take her down.

And now...well, she was happy for Charlotte, admired her courage to put herself out there again, especially after what that piece of work Sebastian had done to her. But Ella just wasn't ready to take that plunge. She needed to be able to trust a man again first...and that wasn't going to happen overnight.

The front door burst open, and Leo swept in like a hurricane, looking windswept as he always did in his captain's uniform. He cut quite the striking figure. Like...a Viking conqueror or something. A silent giggle spread within her, filling her with warmth.

"Ella!" he said, his deep, gruff voice sending a curious rush through her. "You're looking lovely this fine evening. Roald." He dropped his voice. "You're looking like you'd better *get off that telephone machine.*"

Roald dropped the phone and shoved it into his

pocket, muttering an apology. Leo shook his head. Charlotte and Christian were heading over, a small stack of books in Charlotte's arm.

"Mr. Sutherland! I mean, Leo," Charlotte said with a small laugh, giving him a hug. "How've you been?"

"Oh, you know." He grinned, his eyes sparkling as he shook Christian's hand firmly. "Gettin' older every day, but I've still got a skip in my step." He demonstrated by jumping up and clacking his heels together.

Charlotte laughed as she handed the books to Ella to ring them up. "This place is looking fantastic, guys," said Christian. "We'll be spending a lot more time here, that's for sure."

Leo was smiling at Ella. "It's all this one, she's one smart lady. I think we just might have a shot at keeping this place open." His gaze dropped on Ella. "Speaking of which, ah...I was thinking maybe I could, ah, take you out to dinner tonight. To thank you for all your hard work so far." He rubbed the back of his neck with his hand. "Doesn't have to be tonight, uh, or dinner, for that matter—"

"That would be lovely," Ella interjected. "Thank you, Leo." She suppressed a giggle as Charlotte winked at her, shaking her head and shooing her with her hand. There was no harm in dinner with a friend, was there?

Leo smiled, his cheeks a little pinker. He turned to Charlotte and Christian. "You're both welcome to join us, of course," he added. His cheeks were bright red now.

Christian looked at Charlotte, something passing between them. Charlotte frowned. "Actually, I have to get back to the Seaside House...Mariah's almost done with her shift at The Windmill and said she wanted to talk to us about something." Something flickered in her eyes. Worry? "Next time, though. Thank you, Leo. You two have fun," she said, taking her new books from Ella.

As Charlotte and Christian left the store, Leo shuffled on his feet. Ella cleared her throat. "So where would you like to go?"

The awkward expression melted from his face. "I know just the place."

AFTER A BEAUTIFUL STROLL together toward Marina Cove's northeast shore, the sunlight dancing through the trees and the warm breeze caressing her skin, Leo turned left on Elm Avenue, and Ella's stomach twisted. Oh, no. Directly ahead of them on the right was Fitzpatrick's Irish Pub.

Ella suddenly felt like she was walking through molasses. Jack had been here, his feet had walked the same sidewalk, he'd gone into that bar for years without Ella's knowledge. He'd quietly nursed his alcohol problem in that bar, suffering in silence for who knew how long. He'd left that bar one night and permanently disabled John Keamy.

And then he'd left them all forever.

"Are you all right?" Leo asked from somewhere very far away.

Ella couldn't speak. But then they passed Fitzpatrick's without stopping, and the cloudy haze that had filled her mind began to recede.

"Oh, yes, sorry," she said. Her voice sounded small, shaky. "I was just remembering something." She looked up at him. "So where are you taking me?" she asked, trying to inject a light tone into her voice.

A smile spread across his face. "I know this great place...it's up ahead here..." He looked around, looking momentarily lost. "Somewhere...anyway, the music is wonderful. And the food..." He rubbed his stomach. "Forget about it. You're gonna love it. It's called The Blue—"

"—Trombone," Ella said, laughing and shaking her head.

"Oh, you've been there before?"

"Yeah. It's where I had my nightmare date with Skip."

He turned to her, eyes wide. "Oh, no! I'm sorry, Ella! Listen, there are a dozen great places around here. Why don't we go somewhere else—"

"No, no, it's fine, Leo," she said, squeezing his hand. "It's a terrific place. I'd love to rehabilitate my memories of it."

He smiled and squeezed her hand in return. Then, straightening his posture, he swept his hair back and bent his arm at the elbow for her to take. "Well, might I have the honor then, ma'am?"

She giggled and took his arm. "Why, I'd be delighted, good sir." Ella felt warmth surge through her as they approached The Blue Trombone. He held the door open for her and the maître d' guided them to a small, circular table with a candle flickering in a small glass jar in the center.

The room was less crowded than when she'd been there with Skip. A few couples danced on the floor as the band played, the leader singing Sinatra, "Fly Me To The Moon." Leo pulled a chair out for Ella as she sat down. "And what would you two like to drink tonight?" asked a member of the waitstaff who'd appeared next to them. Leo looked up at Ella, a patient smile on his face, waiting for her to place her order. What a gentleman. She shook her head as she remembered Skip barking his drink order before Ella could even sit down.

They had a wonderful meal, a meal that Leo felt no need to provide a star rating for, a relief after her last experience. They fell into a spirited conversation about the future of the bookstore, some of the things Ella had planned.

"I just reached out to this local author, her name is Clare Torres," Ella said, taking another bite of chicken. "I've been reading her stuff for years, she's fantastic. She has a new book in her Mountain Ridge series coming out. Anyway, we talked, and she's up for a launch event at the bookstore! She'll be there to talk with readers, sign copies of their books, all that. I think it'll draw a lot of people; she's got a good following here on the island. Might even get some people from the mainland. If it goes well, this could be the start of us hosting more of these sorts of events."

Leo was listening to her as he finished eating, his eyes glimmering in the candlelight. "I really can't thank you enough, Ella. I mean it. I can already see a difference in our sales." He leaned forward and took her hands, sending a prickling sensation across her skin. "I don't know what to say. I can't tell you what this means to me."

Ella blushed and squeezed his hands. "It's my pleasure, Leo. I honestly love having something to work on. Something to..." She almost said *distract*, but shook her head. "Something to look forward to."

He nodded, opening his mouth to say something. The band dropped to a slower, gentler melody. The leader began to sing "Unforgettable" by Nat King Cole.

Ella shivered. It was one of her and Jack's favorite songs, one they'd danced to on countless occasions. She watched the couples dancing on the floor, her mind drifting to Jack.

A figure was standing next to her. She looked up to find Leo with his arm stretched out to her. "May I have this dance?" he asked her, a lovely smile on his face, his eyes crinkled.

"Yes," said Ella, before she knew what she was saying. Her heart was beating hard for some reason. Leo took her by the hand and led her out to the dance floor. Her mouth was dry as he placed a hand delicately on the small of her back, her fingers resting softly in the palm of his left hand. She lifted her other hand and placed it on his right shoulder. He kept a polite but friendly distance between them, guiding her in a graceful foxtrot.

Ella raised her eyebrows. "You can dance," she said.

He laughed, warm and deep. "You sound surprised."

He swept her across the dance floor, the music swelling around them. *Walk, walk, side, together. Walk, walk, side, together.* Her heart was fluttering. She could smell his aftershave, something coarse and earthy, like the air before a rainstorm. Ella looked up at Leo. He met her gaze. She'd never noticed how shockingly blue his eyes were. They shone like diamonds.

What was happening here? A thrill stole across her skin as they maintained eye contact, sweeping across the floor. *Walk, walk, side, together.* Leo was... well, he was a good man, she knew that, but he'd never gotten over Martha. Had something changed? A confusing twist of emotions swelled through her. She winced as she felt the smooth metal of his wedding ring on his third finger, the wedding ring he still wore. Against her will, Jack's face swam in her mind. What would he think of Ella right now, in the arms of another man?

The singer's voice threaded through the room all around them, the candlelight flickering and the music soaring. She moved closer to Leo, could feel the heat of his body, the slight intake of his breath. *Walk, walk, side, together.* The room was disappearing around her, the thoughts swirling around in her mind melting away.

There was just Leo, and the music. It was like they were dancing in a sea of starlight.

Ella looked back up into his face, and her heart caught in her throat. His eyes were blazing into hers, a wild intensity in them she'd never seen before, joy and grief and electricity. She felt like she couldn't catch her breath. "Leo..." she said. His eyes darted back and forth across hers as he pulled her closer to him. Her chest was heaving up and down.

Then the song suddenly ended, and people around them were clapping. Ella looked around to see what had happened only to find the other couples had cleared space for the two of them. The band had lowered their instruments and were clapping as well. Heat rushed to Ella's face. The clapping trailed off and the band began an up-tempo song that Ella couldn't quite place at the moment.

Leo cleared his throat as they weaved their way back to their little round table. Ella kept her eyes fixed on the floor. He pulled her chair out and sat down across from her, watching his hands carefully.

Something had shifted. She hadn't imagined it out there. They'd had a moment. But now...

"Leo?" she asked tentatively.

He stared at the tablecloth, his hands fidgeting with the edges. Then he slowly rose his eyes to meet hers, and Ella's throat constricted. He had a hollow expression, like...he'd been emptied out. Like he was defeated. Or afraid.

Ella reached out and took his hands. "Leo," she said, her voice firm now. "I want you to talk to me. Is it Martha?"

He shook his head, not breaking eye contact. "What is it, then?"

Leo exhaled slowly and shook his head again, returning his gaze to his hands. "Ella..." His voice was soft, tired. Weary. "Ella, you're a wonderful woman..."

"But?"

His shoulders dropped, and his mouth moved, searching for the words. Ella was again struck with the feeling that there was something else going on with Leo, something he was hiding.

Maybe it was Martha, maybe he felt guilty...but

Ella had known Leo a long time. Something else was holding him back.

Her chest tightened as she reached out a hand and placed it over Leo's, patting it softly.

"It's all right, Leo," she said softly. "It's all right."

Their eyes met. Something indelible was scratched across his expression. Whatever it was, she couldn't look at it anymore. It was like staring into the sun. It hurt to see him going through this...whatever it was.

She looked at their hands for a long moment, ignoring the thrumming in her chest, the queasy feeling she had as she thought of Jack. The fear that Leo was leaving her in the dark about something, just like Jack had. And then she slowly released them, placing her hands in her lap.

Horribly, she felt something like relief. As she'd felt herself step tentatively out on a ledge, felt her defenses falling as she danced in Leo's arms, a distant part of her mind had been screaming at her to stop, to go back to safety, where she didn't have to feel so vulnerable, so exposed.

But now that the moment they'd shared was gone, all Ella could feel was heartbroken.

22

D iane turned onto Mariner's Way, huffing and puffing, her cotton shorts rubbing uncomfortably between her thighs. She couldn't remember the last time she'd gone on a run. Grant had still been alive.

She ignored the blisters forming on her heels and pumped her arms in front of her, pushing herself faster. The cool morning breeze sweeping over her skin was incredible, cleansing. An older woman riding a bicycle smiled and waved to her as she passed. People were so friendly here.

Diane passed a bakery, the delicious aromas of baked bread and pastries spilling out onto the street, beckoning her. She narrowed her eyes and sped past it. No more lemon blueberry muffins for this lady, no sir. If she was going to be seeing Trevor again, she'd need to be in tip-top shape, just to keep up with his adventure-seeking.

It didn't help that he'd always had the appearance of being carved out of solid rock by a master sculptor, and that he'd only aged like a fine wine since she'd last seen him all those years ago. He was a beautiful man, and he knew it too. Diane had always felt unattractive around him, like people wondered what they were doing together. Did wonders for the ol' self-esteem.

Diane slowed to a jog and turned onto Beachcomber Avenue. Out in the distance, a deep rumble of thunder rolled through the sky. She'd ended up somewhere on the eastern part of Marina Cove. Somewhere around here was Austin's restaurant.

She wondered what he'd been up to. Maybe she could drop in on him sometime to say hello. Trevor wouldn't be back in town for another week, so she had a lot of time to kill. The thought sent a shudder down her spine. What was she supposed to do for a week?

The hair on her neck suddenly rose. That horrible feeling of being watched stole over her. She stopped, heaving to catch her breath, and whipped her head around.

There. It was him. The man who'd been following her, wearing the same red baseball cap and vintage sunglasses.

No way was this a coincidence. She wasn't anywhere near the Seaside House. He was definitely following her.

She pulled out her phone, trying to look nonchalant, but her mind was racing. Suddenly she turned and began walking in the opposite direction.

Why was he following her? Did Grant still owe someone money? She was positive they'd paid everyone off. And if this man wanted money, why hadn't he confronted her yet?

It was like he was...keeping tabs on her.

Her fingers went to call Grant instinctively, as they so often did, before she froze, her throat constricting.

Oh. Right.

She crossed the street, turning right at the next intersection. As she reached the end of the street, she cautioned a quick glance behind her.

He turned onto the street directly behind her and raised a newspaper in front of him. Pretending to read.

Should she call the police? Maybe she could call Trevor. She lifted her phone and scrolled through her contacts, her finger hovering over his name.

No. Trevor would just think she was crazy. What would she even tell him?

She turned left at the next street, and then right, running now. Her footsteps echoed across the narrow cobblestone street, people glancing up as she passed them. Tears pricked the corners of her eyes. This was the last thing she needed right now.

Diane ducked into a little antique shop. Her breath was coming in short gasps. She needed help.

She lifted her phone and called Austin. He would know what to do.

"HERE. DRINK THIS."

Diane took the steaming mug from Austin, shivering despite the warmth. She brought it to her lips, and let the warmth course down her throat.

"Ooh. What is this?" she asked, leaning back on his couch, letting the steam wash over her face. Her heart was still hammering.

"It's just lemon tea with honey." Austin smiled and sat down at the other end of the couch. "When I was little, and I was upset about something...my mom, well, she never really knew how to talk about things, but she'd always give us something hot to drink, me or my brothers. Or my dad, when he was still alive." He leaned back and stared at the ceiling. "Told us it would help us calm down. It was her fix for everything. That, and brownies." A little smile curved his lips. "To this day, it's what I think of first when someone's upset."

Diane turned to face him. "Oh, so you've got brownies, too?" she asked, wiggling her eyebrows.

He laughed, a deep, warm laugh that felt like a blanket around Diane. "Fresh out, sorry. If you ever stop in at my restaurant, though, I'll be sure to hook you up."

Diane laughed and pulled her legs beneath her, sipping the hot tea and feeling better with each passing minute. Austin had answered on the first ring, and had immediately left work to meet her at the antique shop where she was hiding from whoever was following her. He'd been there in under five minutes, but by the time he found her hiding in the back by the old furniture, she was trembling like a leaf. He'd taken her back to his house to calm down, just a few blocks away.

"Are you sure you don't want me to call the police?" Austin asked, furrowing his brows. "I'm worried, Diane. I mean, if someone's been following you..."

Diane shook her head. "No. Thank you, though. I'm sure." She closed her eyes and swallowed against the lump blocking her throat. "I'm honestly probably just imagining it. My husband..." She closed her eyes. "He had some gambling troubles in the past. He'd been borrowing money from some unsavory people, I was never really part of that. I thought maybe it was someone who wanted money...but we paid everyone back. I really think I'm just paranoid. I've been so out of it, ever since..."

Diane looked up at Austin, tears welling in her eyes against her will. He got up and sat next to her, resting a hand on her forearm, and said nothing. He simply sat with her.

It was such a simple thing. She'd felt so alone lately. She thought of how close she and Austin had been, before the accident. How he was always such a good listener. Victoria had been very lucky to have someone like him.

Something in Diane broke. A tiny moan escaped her lips, and before she knew what she was doing, she buried her face in Austin's shoulder and shuddered, tears pouring from her eyes. She couldn't get words through the pinhole her throat had constricted to. He put an arm around her and held her, letting her cry.

Diane cried for losing Grant, for losing her job, for ruining her relationship with her children. For Victoria, and for taking her from Austin, from Trevor. For the loss of the wonderful friendship she'd had with Austin.

She cried for being adrift for the last three years, unable to properly grieve, unable to let go. She cried for the long, long nights without sleep, for the loss of the taste of food. For being so utterly, utterly alone, floundering, stuck in a cycle of obsessive thoughts aimed at trying to control everything and everyone to keep her life from running straight off the rails.

After her crying died down, she pulled away from Austin. "I'm so sorry, Austin," she stammered. He reached over to the end table and pulled out a tissue, handing it to her. "I don't know what came over me."

He nodded. "Well, listen. I'm here if you want to talk about it."

She looked at him, really looked at him. There had always been something in Austin's eyes that made her feel safe, let her know she could trust him.

Diane blew out a long breath, and then she told him about Grant.

THE SUN HAD DROPPED below the horizon by the time they'd finished talking, disappearing behind a thick gray cover of clouds. Rain pattered against the large window behind them, and thunder lightly rattled the windows. Silence stretched between them, each lost in their own private thoughts.

Austin had apparently been wondering if something had happened to her husband, given the way Diane had been acting since she'd been back, but he thought maybe they'd separated, or got divorced. He'd held her as she cried some more, and listened as she told him about Kayla and Jamie, about losing her job. With each passing moment, she felt lighter and lighter, unaware of just how heavy the burden had been. Diane really hadn't wanted to talk about Grant ever since he died, but it felt wonderful to open up her heart about everything she'd gone through.

Now in the wake of it, however, she felt the sting of regret pinching in her stomach. She hadn't thought of it as they'd been talking, but talking about Grant's car accident had undoubtedly made him think of Victoria. Diane had been so consumed by finally feeling safe enough to talk to someone about how she was feeling that she hadn't stopped to consider how it might affect him. How she'd taken away the most important part of his life. Diane wondered if he thought about that night as often as she did.

Austin cleared his throat, breaking the silence and the flood of guilt beginning to pool within her. "Well, I know words don't mean much, but again, I'm really sorry you had to go through that," he said softly. "I appreciate you talking to me about it, Diane."

She turned to face him, her fingers idly picking at the loose threads of his couch. "No, it means a lot, Austin," she said. "Thank you. Just for listening. I haven't..." Her voice warbled. She took a breath to steady herself. "I haven't really had anyone to talk to. I miss this. I've missed you."

The corners of his mouth turned up in a smile. "I've missed you too."

Diane held his gaze for a moment before blowing out a long breath and pulling her hair back in a ponytail. She looked around his living room, really seeing it for the first time. The room was clean, sparse. Several acoustic guitars lined the far wall, and a couple of electric guitars were propped up next to two large amplifiers. A drum set filled the far corner.

Her eyes wandered to the dining room. A few posters of bands Diane didn't recognize hung on the wall, and a large vintage record player sat next to a huge old wooden table in the center of the room.

Diane laughed. "I'm surprised Kate let you decorate the place like this. I like it. Very bachelor-pad." She turned to him. "When do I get to meet her?"

His eyes slowly met Diane's, and she knew instinctively. Something hollow in that gaze.

He nodded, briefly closing his eyes. "When Trevor asked about her, I didn't feel like updating him. He and I don't really talk these days." He ran a hand through his hair. "It's been a few years since we divorced."

Diane shook her head. "I'm sorry. I had no idea. You were talking about her at the restaurant..."

He leaned back against the couch. "Yeah. Not a great situation. But we'd always wanted to open a restaurant together. We wanted something more stable." He laughed mirthlessly. "We had no idea how brutal the restaurant industry is. How hard it is to open a successful restaurant, let alone run it."

Diane nodded. "I can't imagine how hard it would be to have to work with your ex all the time."

He smiled and shook his head slowly. "It's less than ideal, that's for sure."

Diane watched him for a moment. "You said you wanted something more stable? What did you do before the restaurant?"

He glanced at her sideways before an unreadable expression crossed his face. A moment passed before he looked up at the ceiling. "Kate and I were in a band together."

Diane raised an eyebrow. "Really? Anything I might have heard of?"

He shook his head. "Probably not. We had a moment in the indie scene...never made it huge, though, obviously." A blush rose to his cheeks. "Silver Hollows?"

Diane gawked at him before laughing. "Good one. I used to hear them on the radio all the time."

"No, really." He looked at her evenly before rising to his feet and disappearing into the hallway. Emerging with a CD, he slid it into the stereo system next to the television.

A moment later, an acoustic guitar plinked out a melody that Diane already knew by heart. After the first four bars, a swell of electric guitars and cellos joined, with crashing drums and a playful bass line. A beautiful, coarse voice filled the room.

"I can't believe it!" Diane yipped over the music. "I've heard this song a thousand times, I can't believe I never recognized your voice!" Her feet tapped to the rhythm, and a grin spread across her face. "Oh, man. We used one of your songs for a commercial I wrote the ad copy for! Oodly Noodly!"

He winced and laughed. "Yeah, that was a big mistake in hindsight. Flavored macaroni and cheese wasn't really our vibe. Tanked our street cred a little, selling out like that." He shuddered. "To be fair, we were told it would only air in Japan. We didn't know it would go viral."

Diane giggled. "I can't believe it. I'm in the presence of indie rock royalty here." She grinned and grabbed Austin's wrist as he tried to get up to turn the music off.

"I only wanted to show you I wasn't lying."

"Well, I stand corrected." She was silent for a few moments, listening as the final chorus kicked in, Austin's voice plaintively swelling against the violins and electric guitars spiraling into a huge finish. As the song rang out, Diane looked over to him.

"Not to be fawning, but your voice is..." She searched for the right word. "Emotional. Like...I believe you're actually feeling what you're singing about. Authentic. You got really good."

The next track came up, and Austin told her stories of his time on the road. First playing in little bars here and there, but eventually selling out larger venues, then finally getting a contract with a respected independent label. Diane listened intently, enjoying the time spent with him, feeling the distance of all the long years between them closing a little. They eventually turned to the old times, back in LA, after they'd all graduated and moved out, bright-eyed and trying to conquer the world. Diane was surprised at the ease with which he spoke of Victoria. Like she was still around, alive and well somewhere, an old friend.

"Remember that camping trip up in Big Sur that last summer?" Austin asked.

Diane cackled and raised her hands to her mouth, nodding furiously. "I *totally forgot* about that! We had nothing, like, I don't think we brought food, we didn't have tents—"

"We literally just pulled over on the road trip, no hotels in sight—"

"I think you pointed up the hill and said, 'How about up there?'" Diane said in a playful mocking imitation.

"Remember the wolf howls?"

A burst of laughter escaped her. "That was your

idea. You and I kept taking turns sneaking away from the fire and howling—"

"How did they not put it together?" Austin was laughing hard, his face red. "Trevor and Victoria were totally spooked. I mean, we'd kept coming back all, 'Did you hear that?'"

Diane wiped a tear from her eye. "Victoria figured it out. Trevor, though..."

Austin shook his head. "He didn't find it very funny. I think he got up and left, didn't he?"

Diane nodded. "I think he didn't like not being the one coming up with the ideas for once." Another song cued up, this one a simple acoustic melody underneath Austin's coarse, wavering voice. It sent a chill up Diane's spine.

"So what happened?" Diane asked, sitting with her legs beneath her and facing Austin. "To the band?"

He shrugged. "It just sort of...fell apart." After a moment, he sighed. "It was fun while it lasted."

Diane pulled out her phone. "I want to see you perform."

He reached out to take her phone. "No, that's really not necessary—"

She laughed and turned, pulling up a search and

clicking the first video. "I still can't believe that's you—"

He groaned and sat back on the couch as the video started. A spotlight came on in the darkness of the stage, and sure enough, there was Austin, looking a little younger and a little less world-weary, tentatively walking up to the microphone as the audience clapped and cheered. The camera pulled back as more colored spotlights illuminated the other band members. As a woman pulled a bass guitar over her head and began to play, Diane's heart stopped beating. She felt all the color drain from her face.

The long red hair, the slender frame, the dream-like way of moving. Dark eyes that held both playful-ness and mystery.

She was a dead ringer for Victoria.

Diane clasped her hand to her mouth as she looked up at Austin. She recalled when he turned up at the Seaside House to bring her shoes back and saying he had to get back to the restaurant, calling his ex-wife Victoria instead of Kate.

A knowing look crossed Austin's face. He nodded once. "Yeah." He averted his eyes to the floor.

Diane set the phone down. Austin's plaintive

voice spilled quietly from the stereo. Her stomach was twisted like a wet dishrag.

He hadn't gotten over Victoria. The love of his life. The one Diane had taken away when she'd made that terrible mistake while driving that night.

A terrible silence pooled between them before they both looked up at the same time. Diane willed her voice to remain steady. "Did you..."

Austin shook his head. "I didn't realize it, no. Not for far too long. And once I did..." He lifted a shoulder. "Things weren't the same. We drifted apart. We were never right for each other, anyway."

The sound of the rain falling against the window filled the silence as the song ended and another began, this one a simple cello and piano. Austin had his head turned toward the window, watching the rain.

"Before all that, we'd had an idea to open a restaurant, something that we thought would be more stable if the music ever dried up...and dry up, it did. Things got strained between us, and she left the band. I wrote the music, and she wrote the lyrics. As things fell apart between us, she couldn't write anymore. But we still had the restaurant. So now... we work together. And there you have it."

An electric shot of guilt pulsated from her

stomach into her chest over and over. Her hands shot out against the couch as the room began to tilt to one side, her heart jackhammering wildly as she recalled the accident. The blinding headlights of the truck on the wrong side of the road. The car spinning out of control, flipping over the guardrail...

"Diane?"

Austin was seated next to her and had her hands clasped in his. She shook her head, trying to steady her breath.

As she stared into his eyes, the room steadied itself. She felt his hands against hers, the callouses of his fingers, the heat of his body, that sense of solid ground, of safety. Her breathing stabilized as his eyes wandered back and forth over hers.

Tears rose to her eyes as everything they'd lost stretched between them, all the years of grief and loss and growing up and getting older and trying, desperately trying to move on, to find some happiness or peace in this life. A lightness descended upon her, a curious warmth.

She squeezed his hands as she disappeared into those eyes, Austin but not Austin. Her stomach fluttered as she found herself unable to tear her eyes away from him.

Austin broke the gaze, clearing his throat and

running a hand through his hair, his chest rising and falling hard. The final song ended, and Austin quietly walked to the stereo and ejected the CD. A heavy silence blanketed the room, punctuated only by the gentle pattering of rainfall outside.

He sat back down on the couch, his hands fidgeting in his lap. "So," he said, not quite meeting her eyes, "how long are you here in Marina Cove?"

Diane let out a breath. Her heart was still thumping hard. "Actually, I'm not sure," she said. She reached for her tea, now cold, and took a long drink. "I, ah, I've been hanging out with Trevor quite a bit, actually." That thrill of excitement, of danger danced across her skin, dulled now for some reason but still there.

His eyebrows rose. "Really? More adventures since we broke into the pier, huh?"

Diane nodded. "I think...we're sort of, uh, seeing each other again."

She furrowed her eyebrows as Austin's mouth opened, his face paling. "What?"

She tilted her head. "Is that bad? I mean, I'm not married anymore, it's been three years. I know he's a little rough around the edges—"

Austin stood up suddenly and ran his hands over his face as he disappeared into the kitchen for a moment. Heat rose in Diane's throat. What did he care if she started seeing Trevor? It really wasn't his place to judge.

He returned, pacing the room for a moment, drinking from a glass of water. Something ran across the back of Diane's neck, a prickling sensation. "Austin? What is it? You're scaring me."

He set his water down hard on the coffee table and sat down, looking up at her. "Diane," he said softly. Her heart leaped into her throat. She shook her head slowly as his eyes softened.

"I don't want to see you hurt, so I need to tell you something he obviously hasn't been honest with you about." Sorrow glimmered in his eyes. Diane couldn't breathe.

"Diane," he said, his voice tight, "Trevor is married."

Time slowed to a stop. Every moment she'd spent with him since she'd been back on the island flashed through her mind, a twisted cascade of images that drilled into her skull and reverberated like a gong. Nausea sloshed through her. He'd told her he never married. She'd asked him on the Ferris wheel.

All those things he'd said to her, all the attention he'd been showering on her...the lingering gazes, the fingertips brushing against her skin, the flirtatious quips. Inviting her to come work for him, to stay with him. The long, passionate kiss they'd shared.

It all meant nothing to him.

Diane was nothing but another thrill.

A memory surfaced, one she'd shuttered away long ago in the rarely frequented passages of her mind. The night he'd left her for good, the callous note he'd pinned to the door.

Have to figure some things out. Have a nice life.

He'd tossed her aside then when he was done with her. And sooner or later, when she stopped being thrilling enough for him, he'd do it again. Only this time, he was already married to someone else. Some other poor soul out there who had no idea how Trevor had been spending his nights lately.

Short knives of heat rose into her chest and face. All this time...she should have seen it. Why had she let herself fall prey to him once again? Why had she refused to remember what he'd done all those years ago?

She sat back hard against the couch as she replayed everything from the last weeks again, only this time seeing it with fresh eyes. She'd been so intent on *forgetting*, on distracting herself, on blinding herself from her grief over Grant, her career falling apart, the constant checking on Kayla, everything, all of it, that she hadn't seen what was right under her nose.

The last words he'd said to her before he dropped her off at the Seaside House, after they kissed, rang in her mind. *I can't wait to see you again, Di. To see what happens next.*

Trevor wasn't at all the person she'd thought he was. He never had been. He was selfish, arrogant. A liar. He'd used Diane, used her for his own cheap thrills. She meant nothing to him. Probably never had, even all those years ago.

Well, there was no way she was going to stand for that. An idea formed in her mind.

Trevor might have pulled a fast one on her...but maybe she could stop someone else from suffering the same inevitable fate that she had.

Diane sat upright in her chair, her mind now strangely calm, a placid, steady void. She knew what she needed to do.

"Austin," she said, "I'm going to go to his house in Chicago. He's there the rest of the week. I'm going there, and I'm going to find him. I'm going to give him a chance to tell his wife about everything that's happened between us. And if he refuses...well, let's just hope it doesn't come to that." Her fists clenched at her sides. "She can make up her own mind what to do about it, but at least she'll know. He had no intention of stopping things after we kissed. I'd want to know if it were me, that's for sure. She deserves to know what kind of man he is."

Austin watched her for a long moment before he nodded firmly, his expression grim. "That's something I can get behind," he said. "The guy's gotten away with too much for too long. I'm so sorry, Diane. I really am."

Diane shook her head. "Not me. Things would have fallen apart eventually. Better now than later. I was just too blind to see things how they really were."

She debated for a moment before taking his hand, resolved. "Will you come with me, Austin? I know it's a huge favor to ask, but I'm sick and tired of trying to do everything myself all the time. I could use some support. I don't want to do it alone."

One corner of Austin's mouth turned up in a slow smile. "I'd love to."

23

R amona took a long, slow breath and focused on the sound of her shoes against the sidewalk. *Step. Step. Step. Step.* Her face was hot, her skin clammy. A light rain fell from the sky dark with clouds, dappling her shirt and making her shiver. She opened her umbrella and turned onto Sandpiper Street in the direction of the Seaside House, the session she'd just attended with her counselor ringing in her ears.

They'd spent the first part of the session recounting some of the struggles Ramona had been having in the last week. They talked about Danny, Caitlyn. Lily, sweet Lily. What was great about Pauline was that they didn't actually spend much time talking about Ramona's sobriety, at least not directly. They spent most of their time exploring what had led to the behavior in the first place, and what Ramona could do about it. She was still getting used to the idea of seeing a counselor at all; it went against her nature of refusing to ask anyone for help, but everything was changing. The proof was in the pudding. Ramona had been feeling better since she'd gotten help.

After they talked about Ramona's fears over her bookkeeping clients slowly dropping like flies, as word was undoubtedly spreading through the grapevine about the lawsuit against her, Pauline asked Ramona if she was ready to talk about her father. It hit her like a slap in the face. She'd opened her mouth to answer, but a cold spike had shoved its way into her throat. She looked helplessly at Pauline, her limbs paralyzed.

There was so much going on in Ramona's life that she really hadn't been able to process everything she'd learned about her father. What it meant. It was a matter of reconfiguring an entire adult life's worth of understanding...no simple task.

After a long moment, Pauline nodded softly and told Ramona that they would take things slow, that they'd go at her pace. She reminded her again, as she often did, that a house was built one brick at a time.

Ramona closed her eyes and let the muscles of her stomach unclench slowly, unballed the fists she hadn't realized she'd been making. She looked up from her feet and took another long, slow breath. Things were going to take time, but she didn't want to spend the rest of her life miserable, wondering what would've happened if she'd only tried to sort through her issues.

Her phone buzzing in her pocket tore her from her thoughts. She pulled it out and glanced at the screen.

Samuel, again. When was he going to get the freaking message? They didn't want to hear whatever he had to say. He and Patrick had really screwed them over badly. Was he just trying to bilk them for more, somehow?

Joke was on him. They had nothing left to give.

As she pressed the end call button and looked up, she stopped in her tracks. Down at the end of the block was Caitlyn.

She was crossing the street under a bright orange umbrella, wearing a gorgeous leather jacket over a trendy vintage dress, her blonde curls bouncing in the light wind. Despite how unexpectedly polite and sweet Caitlyn had been when she'd turned up at the barbecue, Ramona still hadn't been able to shake the feeling that there was something else going on, a reason behind her change in behavior. She wanted to give Caitlyn the benefit of the doubt; Ramona was changing for the better, and there was no reason to think that Caitlyn wasn't going through positive changes of her own.

But still. Ramona couldn't help but feel fiercely protective of Lily. The girl was just...precious. She was the most wonderful little girl, and Ramona had come to feel that she would go to great lengths to protect her.

Ramona frowned as she stepped behind a large foldout sign on the sidewalk outside the restaurant next to her, just out of Caitlyn's view, and peeked around it. Caitlyn was hunched over slightly as she crossed the street, and was looking back and forth, her eyes scanning all around her. She glanced back in Ramona's direction, and Ramona slipped back behind the foldout sign.

Something flitted across the back of Ramona's mind. There was something in Caitlyn's expression.

Ramona's heart began beating harder as she

thought of Caitlyn's checkered past. All that time she'd been in and out of Lily's life, sometimes gone for months at a time, sometimes ending up in jail, sometimes no one knowing where she'd been. All the missed birthdays, the missed holidays, Lily disappointed over and over again with a mother who was unable to be there for her like she deserved. All the while creating a terrible situation where Lily only pined after her more, desperate for the love and affection from a mother who hadn't ever seemed all that interested in providing it.

Before she knew what she was doing, her feet had taken her in Caitlyn's direction, careful to stick close to the shops and restaurants next to her should Caitlyn hazard a backward glance. Caitlyn turned left at the next intersection, her body language that of someone hiding something, going someplace where they didn't want to be seen or heard. Ramona's chest tightened as she turned to follow her, ignoring the doubt pooling in her stomach.

She shouldn't be following Caitlyn...she knew that. But right now, she didn't care. Caitlyn's demeanor was suspicious, and Ramona was consumed with a need to know if she was somehow falling back into her old ways. Lily's beautiful, shining face kept appearing in her mind.

Caitlyn wrapped her leather jacket around herself and turned right onto a narrow, darkened street. Ramona paused at the intersection, holding her breath and slowly inching her head past the old brick wall of the building next to her.

A man was leaning casually against the side of the building, smoking a cigarette, flicking ashes to the cobblestone street. A mess of dark hair fell over his eyes. A smile broke across his face as Caitlyn approached him, her arms spread out to greet him. He pulled her in tightly, and he glanced up over Caitlyn's shoulder, right in Ramona's direction. Ramona gasped involuntarily and pressed her back against the brick, out of sight.

What was Caitlyn doing? Who was this guy?

She looked around to make sure no one was watching her before she slowly cautioned another glance around the corner. Ramona couldn't hear what they were talking about, but she saw him reach down into a green leather satchel and pull out a small bundle wrapped in dark cloth. Caitlyn slipped it into the inside of her leather jacket, reached into her pocket, and handed him a small white envelope. Dread pooled deep in Ramona's stomach.

Caitlyn reached up and hugged the man again, kissing him on the cheek, before waving to him and turning back in Ramona's direction. Ramona whipped her head back around the corner and bolted back in the direction she'd come, sprinting halfway down the block before dipping into a little café, her heart pounding.

Something was going on. And it wasn't good.

Her mind raced as she considered what to do. But before she could do anything, Caitlyn passed across the sidewalk in front of the café, that suspicious look still etched on her face.

Ramona gave it a few moments before she got up. She pushed down the voice screaming at her to stop now, that it was none of her business, that there was probably some explanation.

All she could think of was Lily.

Ramona needed to know what was going on. She kept a careful distance, and continued to follow Caitlyn.

THE RAIN HAD DISSIPATED as Diane and Austin turned onto Seaside Avenue, the first glimmers of starlight shimmering in the dark sky. A quick stop at the Seaside House to grab a few things, then off to the ferry. There were no flights to Chicago for days, and Diane didn't know exactly how long Trevor would be home. She didn't want him to weasel his way out once he came back. It would be too easy for him to lie to her and say he'd told his wife. Diane needed to know herself.

Austin didn't own a car or have a valid driver's license anymore, since he lived full-time on Marina Cove, and Diane no longer drove at all, so they'd have to take a rideshare all the way to Chicago. It would be pricey, but Diane was determined.

She could've asked her sisters for help...but she was too embarrassed by what she'd learned about Trevor, after she'd defended herself so fiercely to them. Besides, neither of them owned a car. What were they going to do? She might be able to get away with never telling them about this new development at all. No sense in feeling any worse than she already did.

She pushed down the words ringing in her ears. *We're here for you, Diane,* Ramona had said after she'd told them about Grant. *We love you.*

Diane just wasn't ready to go there with her sisters. To get so personal...she was too ashamed. They'd tried to tell her that something was off about Trevor, and she'd ignored them.

Her skin tingled with a heady mixture of fear

and excitement. It felt good to stand up for herself. Her mind felt clearer than it had in a long time. The man who'd been following her, her lost job, Parker and his stupid sneer, it all seemed a million miles away. None of that mattered right now.

It was time to set things right. Trevor's wife didn't deserve what he'd been doing to her. She needed to know.

Diane looked over to Austin, who met her eyes and smiled reassuringly. Flickers of warmth stole through her. "Thank you again for helping me, Austin," she said quietly. "It was a huge thing to ask...I hope it doesn't cause too much trouble with the restaurant."

He laughed. "I haven't taken a day off in months. I think they'll manage. Besides..." he said, his voice dropping. "I think it's pretty awful, what he's done... the way he's always treated you and everyone else around him. I never wanted to say anything when we were younger, when you guys were dating...it wasn't my place. But the way he is...it's why I've kept my distance from him all these years." He put a hand on her shoulder and squeezed. "I'm proud of you."

Diane smiled, a blush rising to her cheeks. "Thank you."

They walked in comfortable silence for a few

minutes before Austin turned to her. "So, not to ask a dumb question, but how do we find Trevor's house?"

"Oh, I found it in like ten seconds," she said, shaking her head. "Blame the internet. Way too much information about people, just up for grabs. His home address was listed in real estate sales records a few years back that were publicly posted. So much for privacy anymore."

Austin laughed. "Well, that's unsettling."

"Oh, my God." Diane stopped in her tracks.

Austin stopped too. "What's wrong?"

Diane began running toward the Seaside House, her shoes smacking against the wet ground. She yanked her phone from her pocket. There was no way. She would've been alerted. She frantically tapped open the GPS app, and there it was. The little dot sitting right where it should be.

But here she was.

Moonlight pooled across the driveway, illuminating the silver Honda Civic in a hazy glow. Sitting cross-legged on the hood of the car next to a striped umbrella, raising her hands in supplication, was Kayla.

"*Kayla!*" Diane shrieked. "You aren't supposed to—"

"I know, Mom, I know," she said, sliding off the

hood of the car. Her long, wavy hair fluttered in the breeze. "I'm sorry, but I wanted to see you."

"How did you—"

"I just took off the tracker," she said, biting her lip. "To be honest...I've been taking it off regularly for a long time."

Diane pulled her daughter into a fierce hug. "I'm glad you made it okay."

Kayla buried her face in Diane's hair. "It was completely fine, Mom. I know how to drive. And I don't know how much it helps, but you didn't change my plans or influence me to come here. I'm here of my own volition, so if anything were to have happened, it wouldn't be your fault."

Diane pressed her eyes shut. Hearing it back, it sounded ludicrous. But nevertheless, here she was. It didn't matter how she got through the day, what she had to tell herself or what she needed to control. All that mattered was getting through it and trying to get to sleep at night.

That's all she could do.

Kayla gently pulled away. "I'm sorry to just turn up like this, but I have a short break and I, uh..." Her voice wavered.

"What is it, honey?"

Kayla looked at the ground, wiping her cheek. "I

just...I miss Dad. So much. And I'm gone at school and you're out here...and I'm just..." She exhaled a long breath, shaking her head. "I just hate what's happening. I feel like...like we have all this distance. I know Jamie doesn't call you anymore, he doesn't return my calls either." She looked up at her mother, her eyes glistening in the moonlight. "We're all we've got left now, you know? I felt horrible when I wanted to visit last week, and..."

Diane reached for her hands. "I'm so sorry, Kayla. I don't know what to say." She closed her eyes. "To be honest with you, sweetheart, I'm having a very hard time myself. I know I've only made things worse since your father, since he..." Diane arched her back slightly, wincing. "I've been spiraling off the freaking planet, Kayla, is what I'm doing. I don't know what I'm doing anymore. I'm sorry I haven't been there for you. It's...hard to explain."

Diane had been far too ashamed and terrified to tell Kayla exactly why Grant had left in the first place, how Diane had driven him away, how it was her fault. What if Kayla never spoke to her again? She couldn't do it. And her kids certainly didn't know about the accident she'd caused that had killed Victoria. How would she ever explain how the fear of being responsible again, of having to hold that guilt and look at herself in the mirror in disgust, had changed her, shaped her?

Kayla let go of Diane's hands and glanced over her shoulder. "Who's your cute friend?" she asked under her breath.

"Oh!" Diane exclaimed, whipping around. Seeing Kayla had driven everything else from her mind. Austin was standing back politely, shifting from one foot to another, like he was wondering if he should leave. "Sorry, Austin! This is my daughter, Kayla. Kayla, this is Austin. He's..." She looked up at him, into his eyes. He smiled at her. Her heart beat a little harder. "He's an old friend of mine, a very good friend from way back when. Back when I was just a kid."

Austin approached her and offered his hand. Kayla grinned at him. "Very nice to meet you." Her gaze quickly flashed over Austin before she looked at Diane and subtly wiggled her eyebrows. Diane barked a laugh and shook her head. "How long have you been sitting here?"

Kayla laughed. "Most of the day. No one answered the door. I figured someone would turn up eventually."

Diane ran a hand through her hair. "I'm sorry,

honey. I'm so glad you're here now, but..." She looked back at Austin.

"I'm dealing with a little, uh, personal problem... Austin and I were actually just leaving for Chicago. We were planning to get a rideshare on the mainland..." Diane's stomach twisted. "We were going to leave tonight..." What was she supposed to do now?

Kayla stepped closer to Diane. The smell of her coconut shampoo drifted over the breeze, sending a painful stab of affection through her chest. "Well... maybe I could tag along. We could..." Her cheeks reddened slightly. "We could spend a little time together, I don't know. You don't have to tell me what's going on, obviously. And this is my idea, so you don't need to feel responsible if something happens."

Diane's throat constricted. "Yeah...but...you wouldn't be coming with us in the first place if I didn't...if I..." she stammered. She suppressed the urge to reach down and crack the rubber band on her wrist and instead turned to Austin. He stepped closer and gave her a warm, reassuring look. The tightness in her chest loosened a little.

There was something about having him here... she no longer felt like she was going to slip off the world.

Diane looked back into her daughter's eyes, her heart folding as she took in her earnest expression. Kayla had always tried so hard to get closer to Diane, to stay close, no matter what Diane had been going through. There was still hope for them.

The girl had lost her father...and she hadn't deserved to lose her mother, too.

Diane put her hands on Kayla's shoulders and looked her directly in the eyes. "I'm a little messed up right now, Kayla," she whispered, willing back her tears. "I think...that I'm going to have to work on that. Right now it seems insurmountable. But if you're sure you want to come, then I would love to have you with me."

A grin spread across her face as she hugged Diane. "I love you, Mom."

"I love you too, baby," Diane whispered into her hair.

Kayla pulled back and looked over at Austin. "When's the last ferry out of here?"

Austin glanced at his watch. "We've got twenty minutes, give or take."

Kayla nodded and blew out a breath. "We can take my car. So. Who's ready for a road trip?"

AFTER THEY DROVE AWAY from Hyannis Port, Kayla pulled over to get gas. Diane and Austin went into the convenience shop attached to the gas station. After filling three large cups with burnt coffee, she found Austin with a huge armful of chips, soda, candy, and beef jerky. "What?" he said. "Road trip food. It's the best part."

Diane laughed. This reminded her of the road trips they all used to take back in LA all those years ago. Singing along to music blaring from the radio, windows down, that feeling of invincibility they'd thought would last forever.

Comfortable quiet filled the car as they pulled back onto the highway. Kayla had the radio on low, tapping her fingers on the steering wheel to Billy Joel. She glanced up in the rearview mirror. Austin, happily munching on potato chips, gave her a thumbs up.

Diane wrung her hands in her lap. She wanted to talk to her daughter, tell her what had been happening...about Grant, about her job, all of it. But something huge was blocking her throat.

Kayla wanted to get closer to her. And she'd been the only one really taking steps so far.

Maybe Diane could take a small step. She could at least tell her the purpose of their trip. About everything between her and Trevor since she'd been back. She didn't have to go into detail...or go into their long past. Just about the relationship he'd started with her, their kiss, all while his wife waited for him back home, unaware.

"Kayla," Diane said, her voice husky.

Kayla looked over at her, her brows furrowed. "What's wrong?"

Diane took a deep breath and let it out. "I want to tell you about why we're going to Chicago. I want to tell you about a man named Trevor."

RAMONA'S SHOES were soggy as she strode through the wet grass, trailing behind Caitlyn as she turned into Sunflower Run Park, the sound of the creek floating over the evening breeze. The creek she'd just been splashing in with Danny and Lily what seemed like only yesterday. Caitlyn was going somewhere with a purpose.

Ramona's heart hammered as she followed behind, hoping against hope that Caitlyn wouldn't turn around. There were no buildings to duck behind or stores to turn into out here in the expanse of the beautiful park. A few people strolled around casually, mothers with their children, couples holding hands. Part of Ramona was thrilled, and didn't really care if she was caught. She would confront Caitlyn if need be, find out what was going on here.

Caitlyn was approaching the huge, intricately carved fountain of aged stone that stood in the center of the park. The old wishing well encircled the fountain, where generations of people flicked pennies and quarters to make a wish. Beams of light pointed at the fountain, a fine mist floating into the sky and sparkling like starlight.

Ramona picked up her pace, having no clear idea what she'd say to Caitlyn if she turned around. Caitlyn circled the fountain once before looking to her left, her face lighting up.

Ramona froze in her tracks as she saw who was approaching Caitlyn, her mouth suddenly dry.

It was Danny, holding Lily's hand.

Ramona couldn't move as Lily ran up to Caitlyn, her hair flying behind her. Caitlyn lifted her off the ground and twirled her around, kissing the top of her head. She gave Danny a small wave and smiled, and he nodded to her.

They hadn't noticed her standing there, just far enough away that she hadn't been spotted yet, but if they looked in her direction, there was nowhere to hide. If she started running, they'd see her for sure. Her feet remained planted on the ground, her thoughts tumbling through her mind.

Danny hadn't said anything to her about meeting Caitlyn. Those flickers of jealousy licked at her again. She shook her head. Danny didn't owe her an explanation...he hadn't done anything wrong. Caitlyn had probably just turned up out of the blue like she always did and wanted to meet them for a walk in the park. She was Lily's mother, after all. She had every right to see her.

Still, it didn't explain her suspicious behavior. What was in the bundle? Who was the man she'd hugged? Was it money in the envelope she'd handed him?

Caitlyn squatted down to Lily's level and said something that made her little cheeks crinkle in a grin.

And then she reached into her leather jacket and handed Lily the bundle wrapped in dark cloth.

Ramona wanted to leave. Obviously she'd been wrong. But she couldn't move. The way Lily's eyes widened, the way she looked at her mother... Ramona couldn't help but yearn for that look herself. She watched, transfixed, as Lily opened the bundle to reveal a beautiful set of wooden paint-brushes.

Ramona's breath caught as she took in the polished glimmer of the wood, the bristles flowing into the perfect taper, the gleaming brass ferrules. Even from a distance, Ramona could see they were extremely high-quality brushes, handcrafted impeccably.

Ramona had been wrong, dead wrong. Another wave of jealousy sloshed through her. Painting was the way Ramona had been bonding with Lily, spending all that time teaching her, painting with her, getting to know her...it had been their thing. And Caitlyn was swooping in and taking Ramona's place.

She shook her head and scolded herself. She had no right to be upset with Caitlyn over trying to support her daughter. It wasn't a competition, anyway. If Caitlyn was supporting Lily now, if she was trying to be a better mother, Ramona had no intentions of getting in the way of that, no matter how uncomfortable it was having her back in Danny's life like this. She only wanted what was best for Lily.

Lily's eyes were like saucers as she ran her hands over the brushes and reached her arms around her mother, pulling her close. Caitlyn held her tight and breathed in her hair. She stood up and, before Danny could react, pulled him into a hug too. He didn't return it.

Just as Ramona began backing away, desperate to leave without being noticed, Caitlyn's eyes landed directly on her. Ramona took in a sharp lungful of air. Her eyes locked on Ramona's, and didn't let go.

And after what seemed like an eternity, her eyes narrowed and her face pulled into a knowing smirk. She pulled Danny more tightly against her body, the dangerous smile widening.

Ramona was unable to tear her eyes away from Caitlyn's as Danny pulled away from her, and the three of them turned to the fountain. Danny handed Lily a coin, and she closed her eyes before tossing it into the wishing well. Ramona turned around and ran, blood pounding in her ears, ice running down her spine as she fought to stop that knowing smirk tearing at her mind as it all became clear.

Caitlyn hadn't changed. She was staking out her territory, and Ramona was the competition. She was going to squeeze Ramona out of Lily's life, and Ramona knew in her bones that she was going to try to squeeze her out of Danny's life, too.

Again, Ramona found the ground beneath her

pulled away, again found herself with no idea what she was supposed to do.

A THICK, heavy silence blanketed the car as Diane finished telling Kayla about Trevor. Kayla kept her eyes locked on the road, not saying anything for a long time.

Diane glanced up in the mirror at Austin. He returned her gaze and mouthed, *It's okay.*

Diane nodded, desperately wishing the horrible tightness in her throat would loosen. Hopefully Kayla could forgive her for even being interested in another man after her father.

Kayla pressed the knob to turn off the radio, and to Diane's surprise, reached out and grabbed her hand, giving it a squeeze. "Mom, that sucks," she said. "I'm so sorry he led you on like that. He sounds like a really terrible guy."

Diane's eyebrows rose. "So you're not mad that I was..."

Kayla looked at her, confused. "What? Of course not." She shook her head. "I want you to find someone, Mom. It's been three years, right? You loved Dad, but there's nothing wrong with trying to move on, is there? You deserve some happiness. I'm just sorry this guy ruined the first time you put yourself out there." A smile rose to her lips. "I'm proud of you for sticking up for yourself like this."

Diane let out a huge breath she hadn't realized she'd been holding. A small laugh escaped her throat. "Oh, Kayla," she said softly. "I can't tell you how relieved I am to hear that."

Kayla smiled and returned her eyes to the road, opening her mouth to speak but then closing it. Her eyebrows furrowed.

"Kayla? What is it?" Diane asked.

Kayla didn't answer, but after a moment she exited the highway. She turned onto a long, deserted street that bordered a neighborhood blanketed in darkness, and pulled over against the sidewalk.

"Everything all right?" asked Austin.

Kayla kept her hands on the wheel, chewing her bottom lip. Diane was struck by an image of Kayla as a little girl, getting ready for her very first dance class, so beautiful in her tiny blue dress, chewing her bottom lip nervously. *It'll be all right*, Diane had whispered to her, pulling her close. *I'll be there for you the whole time.*

Kayla nodded to herself, then looked at Diane. "I think you should drive."

A horrible shudder crawled across her spine. "What?"

Kayla unbuckled her seatbelt and turned in her seat to face her mother. "You don't have to, of course. I don't know when you stopped driving, or why, but I imagine it has something to do with the reason you were always fretting whenever Dad drove, and how much worse things got with your, uh, checking on me, after he died." Her eyebrows drew up in concern. "You said yourself that you were going to have to work on things...I just think that you're already going to confront this guy, stand up for yourself...I think it's the perfect chance to face this. To see that it's okay."

The horizon behind Kayla began slipping to the side, and Diane's breath caught in her throat. Her pulse thundered in her ears. "You don't understand, Kayla," she choked out in a distant voice.

Kayla shook her head. "I know I don't. You can say no. I'll keep driving. But I know you don't want to live like this, Mom. It wasn't your fault that Dad died."

The words pierced the air and drilled into Diane's heart. "What do you mean?"

Tears shimmered in her eyes. "I think that maybe you're blaming yourself for what happened to Dad.

You told us you had an argument and he left. I've heard you two arguing before...I know you made him promise never to leave during an argument. So I think it must've been a bad one. And Mom," she said, her voice thick, "no matter what happened, *it wasn't your fault.*"

Diane burst into tears. "It was, Kayla, it was—"

Kayla shook her head furiously. "*No*, Mom. It wasn't. Bad things just happen sometimes. You can't control it. You can't control everything. I don't care if you pushed him into the car, turned the ignition, and forced him to drive away. What happened was not your fault. No one could have ever predicted that would happen."

Diane could barely hear Kayla over the buzzing in her ears. The image of the ground rushing up toward her filled her mind. She couldn't catch her breath.

She reached down to yank back the rubber band, needing to anchor herself to something, before a hand reached out and stopped her. Diane looked up in surprise to find Austin holding her arm, firm but gentle. His eyes bored into hers. "It's okay, Diane. We're here, right now, in this car. You're not in the car accident. You're here, with Kayla. With me."

Tears spilled from her wide eyes, her chest rising

in hard bursts as she tried to catch her breath. She felt Kayla's hand on her other arm.

"Kayla," she heard herself say from a million miles away. "I was in a car accident a long time ago. I think...I think it really messed me up." Breath whistled out of her throat as beads of sweat fell into her eyes and burned like fire.

She saw Kayla nod slowly through the dark blanket that had formed around her vision. Austin moved his hand to her shoulder. "Diane, the same thing used to happen to me, all the time. I had to learn what to do. You aren't in any danger right now, okay? You're here. You're having a flashback." The words rang through the air as he let out a breath. "Try to focus on what's happening around you right now, instead of fighting the feeling."

Diane watched herself clamp her eyes shut. Instead of fighting back the need to yank back the rubber band, she gritted her teeth and tried to just watch it for a moment. Her stomach lurched as she focused on the way her hand felt encased in Kayla's tender grasp. She focused on the sound of the radio, the breeze carrying in through the open windows, how it gently brushed against her skin. The way Austin's firm hand on her shoulder sent a swell of warmth through her, like it was pushing away the darkness that had pooled inside her. She opened her eyes and locked them on her daughter's.

The final darkness in her vision receded. The jackhammering of her heart began to slow. She pressed her feet into the ground and exhaled all the air that had been trapped in her lungs.

She'd spent so long fighting the sensations when they'd come up, a terrible tug-of-war when the horizon would start to tilt and she would see the ground rushing up, smacking that stupid rubber band like it was a magical talisman, something that would pull her back into reality.

But when the feelings went away, they were always lurking, always waiting for her guard to drop. It hadn't ever occurred to her that she could just drop the battle altogether. Stop fighting it, and redirect her focus on what was happening around her. To ask for help when she needed it. She really wasn't alone, was she? Grant was gone, but she had Kayla. Austin. Her eyes burned as she thought of her mother, her sisters. Hadn't they kept trying all this time to help her? To be there for her?

It was time to change. She didn't have to do everything on her own. She'd spent so long trying to suppress her guilt over Victoria, to get her family out of the spiral Grant had gotten them into that she'd become someone who just barreled forward, head down into the wind, getting through the days at any cost, learning that she couldn't rely on anyone else. Only it wasn't really true. Grant, despite his problems, had always been there for her. He'd been a wonderful husband.

Diane felt alone because she'd unwittingly pushed everyone else away.

She took a long, slow breath, and before she could change her mind, unbuckled herself and walked around to the driver's side. A grin spread across Kayla's face as she got out and handed Diane the keys. As she sat down in the driver's seat for the first time in many years, her pulse pounded hard in her ears, her hands trembled. Kayla sat down in the passenger seat and placed a hand on her back. Austin reached out and held his hand against her upper arm and squeezed.

"I'm so afraid," Diane whispered.

Kayla squeezed her hand. "It's okay, Mom. I'm here for you right now." She looked over at Austin. "We're here for you."

Tears sprang to Diane's eyes as she turned the key in the ignition. The road stretched out in front of her into infinite darkness. The ground began to tilt, but she took a breath and focused on Kayla, on

Austin. On the way her hand released the parking brake. How her foot pressed gently against the gas pedal. Her hands turning the wheel ever so slightly, taking them away from the curb.

Her heart was a jackrabbit as she pulled onto the street, felt the wind on her cheeks. Tears fell onto her lap. Kayla yipped next to her. "You're doing it! Mom, you're doing it!" She glanced up into the mirror to see Austin grinning.

"*Wooooooohooooooooo!*" he yelled out the window into the open sky.

Diane held her foot down against the gas pedal, laughing. It was like she was flying.

I'm not alone.

The dial on the speedometer passed twenty, thirty, forty, and they were approaching the onramp to the highway. Diane gripped the steering wheel and leaned forward, her teeth clenched, her stomach twisting, pins and needles popping and cracking all over her body. She focused on the feel of Kayla's hand on her back, on the warmth of Austin's hand gripping her shoulder. A slow groan built in her throat that rose to a yell.

And then they were suddenly free, untethered and floating on the beautiful, infinite stretch of highway, the stars glittering like diamonds in the sky and the wind billowing against her skin through the open windows. Diane's body shook with laughter and gleeful tears as they drove out into the great wide open, into possibility, into redemption.

She'd done it. She was finally free.

24

A dull ache throbbed in Diane's lower back as she turned onto the quiet suburban street in Clarendon Hills, where Trevor lived with his wife. Her eyes seemed to squeak as she opened and shut them. They'd driven all night and all day, hitting heavy traffic on their way into Chicago. Weak fading daylight shone through heavy cloud cover, and a cool wind whipped through the windows.

Diane slowed the car as she peered around for his house. Kayla's gentle snores drifted through the car interior. Diane caught Austin's eyes in the rearview mirror. She'd never really noticed how the light caught little threads of gold stitched throughout his hazel irises. Her stomach fluttered.

And there it was, up ahead on the right. She double-checked the address on her GPS and pulled the car against the tree-lined sidewalk. A little girl in pigtails riding a pink bicycle went past them, followed by a boy trying to catch her. "We're here," she whispered, gently touching Kayla's arm. Deep sleep lined her face as she yawned and stretched.

"You drove all the way here," she said, rubbing her eyes. "I'm so proud of you, Mom."

Diane grinned. "Thanks, honey. Listen, you don't have to come with me if you don't want. I don't really know what my plan is..."

Kayla shook her head. "If you're okay with it, I'll be there."

Austin leaned forward from the backseat and rubbed Diane's shoulder. "Are you ready?"

Diane took a deep breath and nodded. She squeezed Kayla's hand, and got out of the car, then the three of them crossed the large slate-brick circular driveway that led to the mansion in front of them. The meticulously kept lawn was bordered by a rose garden and carefully landscaped bushes. The house loomed above them, stone facade with huge windows and a large circular turret. She glanced back at Kayla and Austin before raising her hand to the dark wooden front door and rapping her knuckles against it.

Thoughts tore through Diane's mind. What was she going to say? What if Trevor didn't answer, but his wife? She leaned over to peer into the front window. Lights were on somewhere further back in the house.

This had been a bad idea. A poorly planned bad idea. What was she hoping to accomplish? Was it even right, forcing Trevor to confront what he'd done? She'd been rash about things. Hurt. Maybe she should let it go completely...just tell him whatever he was hoping would happen between them was over. Maybe his wife didn't need to know? She felt like a crazy person, driving all night to turn up at his doorstep.

Diane turned on her heel. "Guys, this was a huge mistake, let's get out of here before they see us—"

The front door squealed open. Diane closed her eyes, and then slowly turned around, wincing.

Standing at the door was a young, beautiful woman with dark, wavy hair. Her low-cut dress hung perfectly across her slender frame. Her eyes wandered across Diane's body, making her feel like she was being examined, before they fell over Austin and Kayla. "Can I help you?" she asked, narrowing her eyes.

The words were lodged in Diane's throat. She looked back at Kayla and Austin, her eyes wide. A thought split through her mind, just turning and bolting in the opposite direction. They both stepped closer to her. Kayla gave her a wink.

Diane sighed and pulled back her shoulders. No. His wife deserved to know, didn't she? Why should this poor woman spend any more time with a man who was planning on starting a relationship with someone else? Who had already kissed her? If Diane were in her shoes, she certainly would want to know about that.

But she would talk to Trevor first and give him the chance to do it.

Diane turned back to the woman. "Can I please speak with Trevor?"

She crossed her arms in front of her, the line between her brows deepening. "Who's asking?"

Diane met her gaze, unflinching. "I'm Diane."

The woman's arms dropped limply to her sides as her face crumpled. The hair rose on the back of Diane's neck. Tears clouded the woman's eyes, and she frantically wiped them away with the back of her hand.

"So you're the one, then," she said, her voice small and wavering.

A thousand thoughts drilled into Diane's mind. She shook her head in confusion as invisible bands cinched around her chest. "What?" she finally choked out.

The woman eyed her up and down again. She turned into the foyer out of sight, and emerged a moment later with her purse, keys clenched in her hand, then pushed past Diane. "I hope you'll be enough for him," she muttered. "I never was." She opened the door to the SUV in the driveway, turned the ignition, and peeled away.

Diane shook her head. What was happening? She slowly turned back to the front door, stunned.

Standing there, one eyebrow raised and that winning smile on his face, was Trevor.

"Diane? What are you doing here?" he asked, stepping down to meet her. He pulled her into a hug. "I'm glad you're here, though." He looked past Diane. "Austin, my man, what's the good word?" he asked casually. He said nothing to Kayla.

Diane was speechless as Trevor stood back, running a hand over the perfect stubble on his face.

"What's going on, Trevor?" Austin asked, his voice tight.

Trevor's grin widened. "Come in. See for yourself." And then he turned and went inside.

Feeling like she was trapped in a dream, Diane followed him into the house. To the right was a large room with white carpeting, filled with designer furniture and an enormous black grand piano. A dining room with an expansive wooden table that looked to seat fifty people stretched to the far wall, and glittering chandeliers dappled the room with warm light. Directly ahead, a giant marble staircase rose imperiously to the second floor, spiraling out in both directions.

At first, Diane couldn't pinpoint what was off; her thoughts moved through mud. She shook her head, and then placed it.

The house was littered with brown cardboard moving boxes.

Diane crouched near one of the boxes at the base of the stairs. Scrawled across it in red marker was *Sienna clothes, formal.*

Diane felt rather than heard Austin and Kayla come up behind her. A hot ringing sound filled her ears. She turned to Trevor.

"What is this?" she asked quietly.

Trevor came up to her. She could feel the heat of

his body. Her skin tingled as she smelled his aftershave.

"Diane, I have a lot to tell you," he said, standing over her, his X-ray eyes scanning hers. She felt naked. His mouth turned down into a slight frown. "I haven't been totally honest with you, but that ends now. I was going to tell you once I got back to Marina Cove...but this is even better. I'm so glad to see you."

He placed both hands on her shoulders, sending a hot thrill over her skin. "Diane," he said, "as you can see, I haven't told you yet that I'm married. And I'm sorry about that, I'll explain." His eyes lingered on hers. "That was Sienna. She's moving out."

Diane shook her head. "Trevor, what—"

"Diane," he interrupted. "I'm getting a divorce. And it's because of you." His lips curved into a smile. "I love you."

He blew out a breath. "Whew! Can't believe it's all happening. Look, Diane," he said, taking her hands in his. Blood pounded in her ears. "When we ran into each other after all these years...I felt something. Something powerful. And as we started to spend time together, I couldn't help it, but..." He looked at her almost bashfully. "I was falling in love with you all over again. I really couldn't help it. I was so, so stupid to leave you all those years ago. I was just a kid, you know? I didn't know what I wanted, I just..."

He ran his hands through his hair. Diane felt lightheaded. "I just don't know what I was thinking," he continued. "But I love you. I think I never stopped loving you. And I know that you love me, too. I know you're ready to move on from Grant. I want to be with you. So I told you I had a work trip, but I was really coming here. To end my marriage with Sienna. We were never right for each other. She was on her way out anyway. And now we can be together. Just you and me. Like it used to be. Like it's supposed to be."

Austin cleared his throat behind her, like he was trying to get her attention, but he sounded faraway, like he was on the other end of a long tunnel. Diane fought to make the muscles of her mouth move. The faded scar on her arm burned like wildfire. "Trevor, I don't, I don't know what to say—"

Her stomach somersaulted as he stepped closer. "Say that you'll be with me. I'm selling this house, Di...I'm moving to Marina Cove permanently. I want you to come work with me at my company. I was serious when I asked you the first time. And if you don't want to live in Marina Cove, if you want to move back to LA, or move to Tokyo, or France or Brazil, I don't care. That doesn't matter to me, I can do my work from anywhere. I'll give you everything. I have more money than I know what to do with, you don't even need to work anymore, if you don't want to." His eyes were deep, dark hollows, endless pools of electric intoxication. Diane couldn't look away.

"I'll follow you anywhere, Diane, to keep you with me."

Diane's mind spun frantically. Thoughts collided like bumper cars. She was stunned; she'd never seen this coming. He was ending his marriage...for her? Everything he'd done since she'd been back, all the talk and the flirting and the kiss...it hadn't been at her expense. It had been real. He wasn't using her for just another cheap thrill, after all.

Her brows drew together as she fought to put her thoughts in order, but she couldn't make sense of anything. Maybe she'd gotten him wrong all this time? It wouldn't be a great start, him being married and all, but he said Sienna was already on her way out. So what was the harm there?

If she went with him...well, it solved everything. It wouldn't matter that she lost her job, wouldn't matter that she couldn't stand another moment in her LA home, the memories pushing against her, closing in, suffocating her. She wouldn't have to think about Grant at all, or worry about checking on Kayla or suffering her guilt over Victoria or anything at all, because when she was with Trevor, everything else melted away. When he took her with him, out on whatever adventure he planned, her problems disappeared.

For better or worse, when she was with Trevor, she was distracted. He was the perfect drug to take away her pain, if only for a little while.

Diane startled as Austin appeared next to her, tearing her from her thoughts. He looked at Diane hesitantly as she turned to him.

"Diane," he said in a low voice. "All I want is for you to be happy. And if this is what you want, then you should be with him. But I think you should think about this before you...decide anything. Before you do anything you might regret later."

She could feel the hair on her arms standing on end. The walls seemed to march in on her, the moving boxes closing in and suffocating her on the landing.

Diane looked up at Trevor. His eyes were narrowed to slits as he dropped her hands. He stepped toward Austin, their faces mere inches apart. When he spoke, his voice had dropped into that deep, almost growling baritone that sent memories hurtling into Diane's mind, memories long forgotten. Trevor used the same voice when he got so angry that he reminded Diane how she'd taken Victoria away from him. She barely registered the words as they left his mouth, her head spinning at the guilt punching through her stomach.

"You don't get to weigh in on my life," he seethed to Austin. "Not after what you took away from me."

The words sliced viciously into the air, heavy and dangerous and volatile. Diane's brow furrowed as she looked to Austin. His eyes had widened slightly. Diane could feel the rage pouring off Trevor in hot waves.

After a long moment, Austin's breath hitched and he stepped back, hanging his head and closing his eyes. Ice water plunged into Diane's stomach as she watched two tears trickle slowly down his cheeks.

The words echoed in Diane's mind, reverberating from her past and into the present. She'd heard those words before. Diane froze, her breath caught in her throat.

"What is he talking about, Austin," she said in a low, carefully controlled voice.

Austin watched the floor and shook his head. Trevor was still standing before him, his chest heaving, hostility slashed across his expression. Diane stood between them, pulled Austin's hand into hers, and used the other to tilt his face up.

"Austin, talk to me," she said softly.

Austin slowly met her gaze, his eyes bloodshot, weary. He'd aged ten years in a moment. Lines she hadn't seen before etched their way into his face.

"He's talking about Victoria," he said, his voice just above a whisper. He squeezed his eyes shut and shook his head. "How I'm responsible for her death."

Diane couldn't breathe. She dropped his hand and stepped back like she'd been smacked. Kayla reached out and grabbed her forearm, her eyes imploring.

All at once, for the first time since the accident, Diane's mind replayed what had happened, how they'd gotten there.

Jumping into the Pacific. Sitting around the campfire, Austin strumming his guitar. Victoria's lithe silhouette dancing against the dimming sky.

Trevor beckoning her. *Come on, it's time.*

Diane shaking her head. *No. I don't want to do that.*

Trevor pressing, more insistent. *Don't be a little baby. We won't have to work for years. You can quit that stupid job of yours and spend all your time with me.*

Diane whispering back as Austin watched them, narrowing his eyes suspiciously. *No. We'll get caught. No, Trevor.*

Trevor sulking. Austin asking Diane what was wrong, Diane shaking her head. Trevor would give her the silent treatment for days, now that she'd said no to him and his latest idea. She'd always been game, loving the thrill. Only this time, the plan had escalated too far.

A wealthy friend of his father's lived up in Ventura, up above the water in a mansion, and apparently owned dozens of valuable paintings. Trevor had concocted a plan to break in and steal one. *He'll never even notice, he's so rich and stupid*, he'd kept telling her.

Their escapades hadn't ever harmed anyone. So far, at least. Diane had no intention of relenting. They'd gotten in that old Plymouth Duster, Trevor sulking, his fists clenched at his sides. Diane's heart pounding. He wasn't used to not getting his way.

As they drove north, Trevor was seething in the

passenger seat. Austin and Victoria sat in the back, pretending not to notice. Trevor insulting her under his breath, making her feel small. They turned onto Mulholland Drive toward the San Fernando Valley, the city far below them, winding along the serpentine road, lights twinkling like fireflies in the darkness.

Diane had enough. She turned to him, her hands steady on the wheel. Words came tumbling out of her mouth before she could stop them. How he was pathetic, how he couldn't push her around. How she was sick of the way he treated her. Trevor breathed harder and harder.

And then he grabbed her arm and squeezed.

Hard.

Don't you dare speak to me that way, he growled.

The next moments happened slowly, pieces filtering in one at a time. Diane's eyes wide, the sting of pain drilling from his fingertips into her soft skin. Looking up at Trevor in shock. Austin leaning forward and tearing Trevor's arm away from Diane's, growling into his face to let go. Diane glancing back to see the fury in Austin's eyes, the protectiveness.

To see Victoria's face twisted in horror.

What? Diane asked, or tried to. Nothing came

out. Trevor's hand now on her shoulder. Austin gripping the seatback. Diane whipped her head around.

Two bright headlights. A beat-up red and silver pickup truck, on their side of the road. Swerving erratically. Diane looked into the driver's face. Slow terror inched up her spine as she saw his closed eyes.

Diane's hands moved across the wheel of their own accord, cutting left as hard as she could. The tires screeched on the pavement as the red pickup slipped past them in a buzzing drone. And then the horizon began to tilt, sending Diane over the edge of the world as the car rolled over the guardrail and into the ravine below.

And then darkness.

Diane stared at Austin, her entire body thrumming, before turning back to face Trevor. Fury split across his face, his cheeks bright red as he glared at Austin.

It all clicked into place.

"You blamed me for Victoria," Diane said to him. Her voice was tight. "You blamed me for changing our plans that night, because I didn't want to break into that house, I didn't want to steal anything. You told me Victoria would still be alive if I had only listened to you. You blamed me for taking my eyes off the road. For not seeing the truck." She watched Trevor as his eyes slowly widened. "You blamed me *for years!*" she shrieked.

Trevor stepped backward, nearly tripping over the stairs behind him. "And after all this," she said, gritting her teeth, "after I've *tortured* myself about it for almost twenty-five years, after I've been so terrified of changing anyone's plans, of being responsible for causing something else bad to happen, I find out that *you blamed Austin?*"

She was shaking as she stepped toward Trevor. "You put the blame on us separately, without us knowing you'd blamed the other. You manipulated us."

Trevor's face had slackened, his hands raised. "Diane, I—"

"*Don't!*" she screamed. "Stop talking. You listen to me. You blamed *me* for her death. I didn't want to go break into that house, I said I didn't want to go, and you wouldn't listen. You never took no for an answer, you just had to get your way. And when I stuck up for myself, you grabbed my arm. You never should have laid a hand on me. And Austin," she scoffed, her voice hitched up an octave, "all Austin did was try to help me. He didn't do anything wrong. And I changed our plans, yeah. I took my eyes off the road.

After *you* crossed the line, and made Austin intervene."

Diane's body was clenched tight as she took another step toward Trevor. He looked like an animal backed into a corner. Everything was tumbling through her mind, a lifetime of guilt and shame and self-hatred reconfiguring into a new pattern.

She thought of the shock she'd been in after the accident. How Trevor had placed the blame on her. How the memory of that night had become fuzzy in her mind, her own way of protecting herself against the trauma of what she'd gone through. How she'd spent all those years suppressing the memory, cracking that godforsaken rubber band to snap her back into reality, back to where the memories couldn't hurt her.

She thought of how every time she'd pulled away from him, he'd sensed it, and held Victoria's death over her, made her feel small, weak. How the guilt had caused her to write off his manipulation. His possessiveness. He'd talked her into quitting her job, ending her relationships with her friends. All Diane's time had become about Trevor. He wanted to own her.

He'd made Diane feel guilty to keep her bound

to him. And Diane's grief had been too strong to fight it.

And he did it so that he wouldn't have to be alone. She thought of how Austin had disappeared from their lives after the accident, and realized that Trevor had pushed him away, blamed him for Victoria to keep Diane close, to isolate her further.

He'd taken away one of her best friends without her realizing it.

Diane looked into his eyes, those shrewd, knowing eyes of his, and for the very first time, she saw cracks in the facade. Trevor wasn't the confident, self-assured man he presented. Behind that mask was a boy who was afraid, a boy who felt guilty for what had happened to his sister. He'd been blaming himself.

Diane moved closer to Trevor, and he sat down hard on the wooden stairs. She looked down at him, her breath squeezing against her lungs.

"Austin wasn't responsible for Victoria's death, Trevor. And neither was I."

Trevor's eyes brimmed with tears. "Diane, I'm sorry. I'm really sorry. Austin, you too, I don't know why I did it, I had to blame *someone*, she just couldn't be gone, she *couldn't*..." A strangled sob escaped his throat. Something wild took over in his eyes, and he shook his head fiercely. "You don't know what it's like, okay, you don't understand—"

"Trevor, shut it," Diane said through gritted teeth. "There's nothing you can say right now."

Trevor wasn't to blame for Victoria's death either, not really. He shouldn't have grabbed her arm, shouldn't have been pressuring Diane for so long, but he hadn't done it not caring if they got into an accident. He'd loved Victoria. It had devastated him beyond understanding. But he handled his own guilt by placing the blame on others. By manipulating people into staying close to him, terrified of being alone.

Diane thought of Grant, and a frigid chill ran through her bones. She thought of the three years she'd spent blaming herself for what happened to him. How it had cemented the behavior that had been building for her entire adult life. The behavior designed to control her fear of being responsible for another death. The constant checking, the fear of influencing people, the terror she had over Grant leaving during an argument, the accident reports and GPS apps and weather tracking and everything else, how she'd driven Jamie away with her obsessiveness. Kayla's words rang through her ears.

Bad things just happen sometimes. You can't control it. You can't control everything.

She wasn't responsible for what happened to Grant. Or, she was as responsible as anyone else could be, including Grant himself. She may have said something she didn't mean, but she didn't make him walk out that door. She'd asked him to stay. He'd made his own decision. And that didn't make him responsible, either. He hadn't known getting into that car would end everything.

To try to place blame...it was folly. It was meaningless. Life just didn't work that way. To think those things could be controlled was a delusion. An understandable delusion that covered the deeper knowledge that so much of life happens for reasons unknown.

She looked deep into Trevor's eyes, through the facade, and saw herself reflected back in them. Since she'd been back, she'd unwittingly been allowing Trevor to manipulate her like he had all those years ago. He'd been possessive of her time, isolated her. He'd thrilled her, offered to whisk her away and solve all her problems, only under the condition that she would be his.

He wanted to own her, so that he would never have to be alone.

Trevor was a drug, a powerful one. When she was with him, her problems seemed to disappear. But they never really had, had they? They were just...delayed. And like a drug, Trevor took a little more of her each time they were together.

Diane turned to Kayla and Austin. Kayla had tears in her eyes. Austin was as pale as a sheet.

"Austin," Diane whispered. Their eyes met. She put her arms on his shoulders. "Austin, what happened was not your fault." His face was tight. She shook him. "Listen to me. It wasn't your fault. You were only trying to help me." He looked at her, weary and grief-stricken, like Diane was a life preserver. He said nothing.

As she looked at Austin, something shifted within her. Something significant. She suddenly saw him in a new light.

All this time, he'd done so much for her. He'd been the one who'd answered the phone when she was in jail after Trevor bailed on her, bringing her favorite lemon blueberry muffins. He'd pulled Trevor's hand off her in the car. He'd saved her from choking at Trevor's party. He'd held her on the couch while she poured her heart out about Grant, about her life falling apart.

And when she was running from whoever had

been following her, she hadn't gone to Trevor. She'd called *him*.

Because deep down, she'd known that it wasn't Trevor she could trust. It wasn't Trevor who would be there for her.

It was Austin.

She thought about what Austin said just moments ago, before he told her to consider her next move with Trevor.

All I want is for you to be happy.

Not once in all the time she'd known Trevor had he asked Diane what she wanted. What would make her happy.

Her heart fluttered as her eyes wandered over Austin's. This was a real man. Someone reliable, caring, trustworthy. All this time, right in front of her, he'd been there for her in so many ways. This wonderful, selfless man. She pulled him against her in a tight embrace, running her hand through the back of his hair. Tears spilled from her eyes, and she felt his body shudder against hers. She held him and cried for all they had lost together.

After some time, she gently pulled back from Austin, gave Kayla a reassuring look, and turned to face Trevor. He was sitting on the stairs with his head in his hands, rubbing his eyes with his palms.

"Trevor," said Diane. He slowly looked up at her, his eyes bloodshot. "I'm sorry about Victoria. It wasn't my fault, and it wasn't Austin's fault. And it wasn't your fault either. I've spent my whole life blaming myself for what happened because of you, and obviously so has Austin. I'm going to have to figure some things out...and I suggest you do the same."

Anger and then grief flashed over his expression before his face fell. He looked exhausted. He opened his mouth to speak, but then closed it.

She stared at him for a moment, recalling the last line of the short note pinned to the apartment door, the note he'd left her weeks after she'd threatened to leave him. *Have a nice life.* He'd sensed that she had one foot out the door, and had decided to act before she was able to. Just like he had with his wife now. Diane had been a perfect opportunity to make sure he wouldn't be alone.

She felt sorry for him.

"Goodbye, Trevor," said Diane. She took one last look at him, turned on her heel, and nodded to Austin and Kayla, heading out through the front door with them. With each step, she felt a little bit lighter, the long and terrible burden finally beginning to lift.

Diane opened the driver's seat door to Kayla's car, and gently removed the rubber band from her wrist. She held it in her fingers for a moment, then tossed it into a cupholder in the center console. She didn't need it anymore.

Then she looked up and her eyes met Austin's, and they both smiled.

25

Charlotte's hips swayed as she set the sliced apples on the stainless steel pastry table and reached for her copper saucepan, singing along loudly to "Stand By Me" playing on the radio. She was the only one in the back of The Windmill; everyone else had gone home. After stopping home to walk Ollie and catch up with Allie and Liam over the phone, she'd come back to prep a few things for the next day, including taking another stab at making tarte Tatin. The first couple of tries hadn't been quite right.

Not that Charlotte was complaining. Sampling each concoction was her favorite part of the job. She grinned as she turned on the heat, added the water and sugar, and began stirring. People didn't realize how difficult it was to get caramel right. A little too long over the heat, just a matter of seconds, and you got a burned, sticky mess that was impossible to clean.

Charlotte still couldn't believe this was a job. A job that someone handed her real money for. It was truly a dream come true. Each day was different than the last, in the pursuit of exploring new recipes, mastering old ones.

It was just...right. It was a feeling she'd never known was possible. A feeling that grew each day she got to come in and explore her creativity. And it didn't hurt that the creativity yielded delicious treats.

The song ended, and "Unchained Melody" came up. Charlotte's heart immediately twisted at those first soulful notes. She and Sebastian had danced to this song at their wedding. A million years ago, it seemed. But also somehow like it had been only yesterday.

Charlotte's mind wandered as she used a pastry brush dipped in water to brush away the sugar crystals forming on the sides of the pan. Everything he'd said during his visit had been playing through her mind like a record endlessly looping.

She and Christian hadn't spoken much of it. Charlotte had told him that she wouldn't agree to pretend they were still together just so he could make his deal with that guy Tex. Charlotte didn't need his money. She had her job at The Windmill. She wasn't making much, but as business expanded, Sylvie had worked it out so she got a percentage. It was a pretty sweet deal, and would have to be enough.

That old feeling scraped at her insides, pooled within her, that feeling of doubt, of despair. She thought of how little progress had been made on the Seaside House, how much it was going to take to get things going again. Christian couldn't work on it alone forever, he'd never get done. She thought of Patrick's threats looming over them...not to mention Charlotte's promise to help Ramona and their mother with their seemingly endless pool of debt. It hadn't helped that Ramona's house was foreclosed on, and she was contending with a lawsuit against her.

Things were a mess. But there was light at the end of the tunnel.

Charlotte looked around. It didn't look like much back here, but she sensed something...big. Possibility. She knew that she could really make a go of things, could really bring The Windmill to a whole new level. She just needed time.

What bothered her most about Sebastian's offer was that she didn't trust him, not even remotely. She'd be a fool to think that his suggestion came without strings attached. It scared her that she didn't know what those were.

Despite what he'd said, he had more than enough power and influence to delay their divorce as long as he pleased.

If Charlotte refused, was that what he would do? He'd been doing everything he could to delay things already...this sudden change of heart made her uneasy.

And rightfully so. The man couldn't be trusted. He may have said he was ready to move on from Charlotte, and only wanted to help her...but that sinking pit of doubt still pooled within her.

It was a feeling of helplessness. A feeling that she'd been working so hard to overcome.

Mariah's face flashed in her mind. She'd asked to talk to Charlotte a couple of times, but then when Charlotte reminded her about it, Mariah kept brushing it off, saying it was nothing. She didn't want to push her daughter...but there was something going on. Was it something about Sebastian? Something else entirely?

The double doors leading to the kitchen burst

open, and Charlotte shrieked. She dropped the spoon she'd been stirring with. Smoke poured from the copper saucepan, the caramel long burned while she was lost in her thoughts.

"Charlotte," breathed Sylvie as she strode across the kitchen, her hair disheveled, mascara running down her cheeks. Charlotte pressed her hand to her heart, trying to stop it from pounding right out of her chest.

"Sylvie, what happened?" she asked. Sylvie came up next to her, breathing hard, and leaned forward against the pastry table, pressing her hands into the surface.

"It's Nick," she said, her voice faltering. Fresh tears pooled in her eyes as she squeezed them shut. "He's gone again."

Charlotte squeezed her shoulder. "Okay. Tell me what happened."

Sylvie gritted her teeth and slammed her fists against the table. "I can't believe he's doing this to me again." She turned to Charlotte, her expression shifting, her eyes wide. She was terrified. A chill ran down Charlotte's spine. "This time is different, though. I always know when he leaves, where he's heading. Always different suppliers, all over the place. So far, the problem has been he doesn't tell me when he stays longer, or changes his trip, or whatever, so I'm left here to worry what happened to him. And he's always like, 'Relax, babe,'" she said in her sarcastic imitation of Nick's deep voice. Charlotte drove her tongue into the roof of her mouth, trying desperately not to giggle at how spot-on it was.

"But this time, I turn over to kiss him in bed this morning, and I grab air," she said, her voice pitching up. "He isn't answering my calls. His calendar doesn't show any meetings with any suppliers. No emails this time. None of the staff knows where he went. Charlotte," she said, putting both arms on her shoulders, "what am I supposed to do here? Do I call the police? Do I wait?" Her eyes widened further. "I don't know what to do!"

Charlotte pulled Sylvie into her arms and smoothed her hair with her hands as she began sobbing. As her mind raced, trying to decide how to respond, Sylvie pulled away, frantically wiping the tears from her face and shaking her head. "I thought we were past this, you know?" she said. "We were doing so much better. We spent *so much time* talking about all this. I was crystal clear with what I expected, and he was changing, Charlotte, he was. The last day trip he took to Boston, he texted me every step of the way. I thought we were on the right track."

Sylvie touched her wedding ring with her thumb and let out a long, slow breath. Charlotte could feel her pulse throbbing in her temples. She pushed back the acid in her throat as she thought of Nick, how selfish he'd been. Her estimation of him was now at an all-time low. Sylvie deserved so much better than to be left like this, alone and terrified. "I'm so sorry, Sylvie. What can I do?"

Sylvie shook her head again. "I know he's just being selfish and probably forgot to tell me about a meeting with a supplier somewhere," she said, clenching her eyes shut and forcing steady breaths. "This is just...he's never done this. Never since I've known him. I'm not going to file a missing persons report when he's basically been keeping me out of the loop for years. I'm just really worried, and I...I feel so helpless. So *stupid*, for some reason. I didn't know who else to talk to."

Charlotte pulled her in again and held Sylvie close. "Well, I'm here. You know I'm always here," she said softly. She felt Sylvie nod against her chest and let out a hard breath.

"When he gets back home...there are going to be some changes. One way or another," she said, and then a bubble of laughter escaped her throat. She stood back against the pastry table and looked at Charlotte. "What a mess. At least I've got you."

Charlotte smiled. "I'm sure he's fine, honey. But I do hope you lay into him good for this one. He can't keep doing this to you."

Sylvie nodded, then turned her head toward the sound of knocking. She frowned, and they left through the kitchen to find the source.

Charlotte peered through the darkened restaurant. She could just barely make out a familiar figure knocking on the glass front door. She jogged past the booths and tables, her stomach tight. What now?

She unlocked the door and pulled it open. "Mom, what are you doing here? Did something happen?"

Ella waved her hand. "No, no, no, I'm sorry to turn up like this and scare you. Everything's fine, I promise." She looked past Charlotte's shoulder. "Hi, Sylvie, dear, how are you?"

Sylvie grinned and locked arms with Ella, guiding her toward the long bar counter, Charlotte in tow. "Oh, I've got a selfish beast of a man on my hands who thinks it's okay to skip town without telling his awesome wife where he's going, but other than that, I'm fine. More importantly, how are you, Mrs. Keller?"

"Oh, no, Nick's at it again?" Ella frowned sympathetically. She sat down on a barstool as Sylvie went to work pouring her a cup of coffee and placed a raspberry Danish on a small plate in front of her. "That's awful. I'm sure he's okay, dear...I'd hoped he was past this sort of thing." She looked at Sylvie evenly. "When he gets home, you tell him to come talk to me. I'll set him straight. He'll never see it coming."

Sylvie barked a loud laugh. "I'm absolutely going to take you up on that." Ella gave her a satisfied smile and took a large bite of the Danish.

"So, Mom, what brings you to The Windmill?" Charlotte asked.

Ella lifted the coffee cup to her lips and took a long, slow drink. "I just wanted to drop in and see you, is all. I have a lot on my mind...I suppose I didn't feel like being alone tonight."

The corners of Charlotte's mouth turned up. Her heart felt very full. "Well, I'm glad you came. I was trying to make a caramel apple tart, but I ruined the caramel on the first try. Maybe we can try again?"

Ella patted Charlotte's lap. "That sounds wonderful."

Sylvie lifted Ella's Danish and snuck a quick bite from the back end. "Do you guys mind if I stick around a while?"

Ella waved her hand in the air. "Oh, Sylvie, you don't need to ask that. The more, the merrier!" She looked around the kitchen. "You two have quite the operation going here. I'm so proud of you."

"Well, I owe you big time for giving birth to this girl over here." Sylvie squeezed Charlotte's shoulder. "Her pastries are gonna make us rich. And I guess she's a good friend too, or whatever," she said with a grin. Charlotte and Ella laughed. "So, should we do this?"

As they rounded up the ingredients and cranked up the music, Charlotte felt a sense of peace settle into her, like she'd slipped into a hot bath at the end of a long day. It was like being home. Every day she felt the space between her and her mother shrinking. In all the years she'd spent in Manhattan, she hadn't realized how much she yearned for this feeling. The feeling only family could provide.

But the peaceful feeling evaporated and quickly replaced with something else, something dark and knotted pooling deep in her stomach. Despite agreeing with Sylvie that Nick was probably just being careless again, she couldn't ignore that pit of doubt. It was a heavy feeling of foreboding, like the faint whispers of a looming thunderstorm on a sunny afternoon.

Hopefully she was wrong, but a voice inside her kept needling at her. Something felt different this time.

She had no choice now but to wait, and see.

26

Warm morning sunlight shone through the trees and dappled the sidewalk as Diane walked toward Heather's, her favorite café, dying for a cup of hot coffee. And maybe a lemon blueberry muffin. Her back ached from another long night on the hardwood floor of the Seaside House, still camping out with Charlotte and Mariah, Ramona and Ella in another room down the hall. Diane was going to get them some beds, or at least a couple of cots until they all figured things out. She winced as she stretched her arms over her head and yawned. This was getting ridiculous.

Kayla had only been able to stay another day before she had to get back to her classes. They'd spent the time catching up, walking along the beach. They talked about her school, the boys she was interested in, her life that Diane didn't know enough about. They remembered Grant together.

Diane was surprised at how easily conversation came, how well they were able to make up for lost time. It was a good start.

She thought of Charlotte. Of Ramona. How they'd all missed so much together, each caught in their own turmoil for all those years. How they were all here now, together. Right there, at the Seaside House. She thought of how she'd been keeping them at arm's length since she'd arrived.

She was done turning everything inward, forcing herself to do everything alone. It was time to change all that. They were here, now, ready to be there for her, ready to take the next steps. They'd opened the door for her. All she had to do was walk through it.

She stepped into Heather's, the delicious aroma of freshly ground coffee filling her with delight, and then stopped in her tracks. It felt like all the air had been siphoned from the room.

Sitting right there, a cup of coffee in hand and reading a newspaper, wearing his vintage sunglasses and that stupid red baseball cap, was the man who had been following her.

He looked up from the paper, and his mouth fell slightly open. His eyebrows rose. Diane met his eyes, not looking away. She squared her shoulders and stepped toward him, her legs encased in cement, heart thundering in her ears.

And then she sat down on the chair directly across from him.

His head darted back and forth, looking for an escape, before Diane snatched the newspaper from his hands and set it on the table.

"Hi, there," she said, looking at him evenly. "I'd like to know why you've been following me."

He opened his mouth to speak, but then shook his head and got up. Diane gripped his wrist.

"Please. I'm not going to call the cops. I just want to know what's going on. Does Grant still owe you money? Because I thought we paid everyone back. I can work something out. You don't need to do this."

He paused, looking at her through his dark sunglasses, and then sat back down. He ran his hands over his face and removed his baseball cap. Then, with a sigh, he removed his sunglasses.

Diane's breath hitched. His eyes. So similar, only with slightly fewer lines carved into his skin by age.

She would know those eyes anywhere. They were exactly like Grant's.

"Oh, my God," she whispered. "You're Grant's brother. You're Scott."

He nodded, his eyes clouding with tears. He cleared his throat, and when he spoke, it sent chills down Diane's spine. It sounded so much like him. It was like talking to his ghost.

"I'm really sorry, Diane," he said. His shoulders slumped. "I'm not very good at this. I never knew how to go about this."

Diane gripped the tabletop to steady herself. "What are you doing here? I thought...I didn't think you and Grant spoke anymore. Why on earth have you been following me?"

He let out a long, slow breath, and took a quick drink of coffee, wincing at the heat. He spread his hands out on the table, watching them. "It's sort of a long story. We hadn't spoken, not for years. The reason isn't important now. But he called me up out of the blue one night. Said he was in a terrible bind. It was his gambling troubles. He told me everything, about stealing all the money from the ad agency, how you two had worked for years to pay it all back. How much it was affecting you, how everything he'd done had really torn your family's life apart. He said he was desperate, that he needed to borrow some money."

Diane tried to take a breath, but her chest was bound up too tight. Scott closed his eyes and continued. "He said that he hadn't gambled in a long time, that he'd gotten help...but that he'd slipped. That he'd slowly cleaned out your retirement accounts to try to get enough capital to get a loan from the bank. I guess he'd wanted to start his own ad agency or something, because someone had apparently leaked what he'd done, and it stopped him from getting work anywhere. He'd been desperate to get you out of the situation he'd put you in, working all the time and missing everything." He sighed deeply. "He said he had no one else to turn to, that he'd turned to some, uh, less than savory lenders in the past, and while they were all paid back, he was always worried that it would somehow come back to bite him. He said he felt like he was always looking over his shoulder. He wouldn't go down that road again."

Diane nodded, remembering having the same fears. Grant hadn't really understood what he was getting into, but she knew they'd been in a desperate situation.

He clenched his fists as tears fell down his cheeks. "I told him no, Diane. I turned him away. I wasn't ready to talk to him...I didn't think I'd ever talk to him again. Grant and I..." He frowned and bit his bottom lip. "We have sort of a...bad history. Our family...there are a lot of, uh, problems there." He fiddled with his hands, his voice wavering. "A story for another time. It doesn't really matter. When Grant needed me most...I refused to be there for him."

Scott slowly raised his eyes to meet Diane's. "When he died..." His voice cracked. "I think I always thought I'd have more time. Time to make amends, to get to know him. I always thought..."

He paused for a few long moments, watching the people pass by through the café window. "I was worried about your family when he died. I wanted to make sure you were...I don't know. That you were all okay. That no one came around looking for money, or whatever. That things wouldn't just fall apart. I don't really know what I thought I could do, but I didn't know how else to make the guilt go away, after leaving him high and dry. So I thought I'd sort of keep an eye on you guys every now and then. From a distance. You know, just drive past and make sure everyone looked all right. That you guys were safe, and moving on and whatnot. I don't know." He shook his head. "It sounds creepy when I say it all out loud. But I just wanted to do something. The guilt was tearing me apart."

Diane exhaled all the air from her lungs. She hadn't expected any of this. "Why didn't you just...I don't know. Come up to me, and talk to me?"

He fiddled with his hands, wincing. "I...Grant and I, we didn't want anything to do with each other. It was all mostly my fault. Things were said, that old story. Your own family can hurt you more than anyone else, you know? I didn't want to go against his wishes. I tried...I tried to honor what he wanted." His eyes moved back and forth over Diane's. "Honestly, I haven't really known what my plan is here. Everything seemed fine, but then you up and disappeared one day. I got nervous. I eventually stopped by your office...I figured I'd just come out with it. I didn't know what happened...I guess I sort of panicked. Some kid named Parker heard me asking for you at the reception desk, and he sort of sauntered up and told me you'd 'scurried off to Marina Cove for a little vacation.'" He smiled humorlessly. "The guy seemed like sort of a rat."

Diane shook her head. Freaking Parker. A small spark of warmth lit inside her as she remembered that now she wouldn't ever have to see him again. Even if it took getting fired to make it happen, it was a fantastic consolation prize.

"So are you okay, Diane?" he asked, leaning

forward. "Your family? Are you guys going to be all right?"

Diane looked at him for a long moment, thinking. And then she nodded.

"We will be," she said, thinking of Kayla. Of Jamie. She would find a way to fix things with them. "Not yet, but I think we will be."

He let out a breath and nodded. Unspoken grief passed between them as Grant's face flickered in her mind. She thought of the last time she'd seen him, the pain in his eyes as he left their house for good. Her chest tightened.

"I just wish I got to know him," he said in a warbled voice. "He was right there, alive and well for all those years, and I don't know anything about him. What he was like, what he loved, what he hated. His dreams, his fears. Nothing. He was my big brother," he said, clenching his eyes shut as fresh tears formed. "He was always there for me when I was a little boy. And I wasn't there for him. And now I'm never going to see him again."

Diane watched him as her mind whirred. She thought of how she'd pushed down her grief every time she thought of Grant over the last three years. How it was easier to chastise herself, to blame herself for what happened to him rather than accept the fact that sometimes bad things just happened, and that he was gone. That there was nothing she could do to control it. She thought of how she'd yearned to talk to someone about him, but the guilt had driven her into silence, into turning into herself and leaning forward into the headwinds and barreling through each day like it was a battle to be won, something to get through. Something to survive.

Maybe she could start small. Maybe this was a chance to open up, to face her grief over her husband head-on. To deal with the problem rather than avoiding it, stuffing it down. To accept that he was gone, that she had loved him, that she could remember him and grieve and just be *sad*, that it was okay to be sad. It was her chance to see that maybe facing it wouldn't actually tear her down like she always feared it would.

Diane reached across the table and took both of Scott's hands into hers. A small line appeared between his eyebrows as he looked up at her, his eyes red and glistening.

"Scott," she said softly, allowing a tear to fall down her cheek. "Maybe we could talk about him. About Grant. I can tell you all about him. And maybe you can tell me all about what it was like growing up with him. Maybe you can talk to me about what happened between you two, what happened in your family." She leaned forward, letting the tears fall. "Maybe we can remember him. Together."

Scott pressed his eyes shut and clutched Diane's hands with trembling fingers. He nodded as tears streaked down his face. "I'd like that," he said, his voice barely above a whisper. "I'd like that very much."

Diane took a long, deep breath. And then she told him of the man she'd loved so much. And she was relieved to find that once she saw the shape of her grief, it wasn't quite so scary.

The unknown, that was the real terror.

She reached out and touched the grief, and saw that while her heart had been broken, it wouldn't last forever, now that she knew what she was working with. It wasn't insurmountable like she'd thought it would be. She would be okay, someday.

27

Charlotte raised a hand over her face to shield her eyes from the early morning sunlight streaking through the trees lining Main Street. She pulled her light blue T-shirt with the old-fashioned windmill printed on the front over the shirt she'd slept in and broke into a jog. Her phone had died overnight with the ongoing electrical problems at the Seaside House, and so her alarm hadn't gone off. She was going to be late for the first time since she'd started. She slowed down as she crossed the cobblestone street toward The Windmill, and adjusted the little pin on her shirt that said *Charlotte Keller, Pastry Chef*.

Something scuttled across the back of Charlotte's neck as the restaurant loomed in front of her. She stopped as a woman riding a bicycle carrying two young boys in a trailer passed her, returning her wave and smile. She pushed down the strange feeling, and opened the front door to the restaurant.

Or tried to. Charlotte frowned.

The door was locked.

Charlotte looked at her watch. A chill spread into her stomach.

She knocked on the glass door a few times and stepped back. And then she saw what that feeling had been. The lights were off inside the restaurant, and the blinds had been pulled and shuttered over the long glass windows.

Before Charlotte knew what she was doing, her fingers had already dialed Sylvie's number. Her heart seemed to beat irregularly as she waited. Nothing.

She called again. Nothing. Her stomach clenched. Thoughts were coming too slowly as she broke into a run.

Ten minutes later, she was at Sylvie's house. Somewhere out there, beyond the house, she heard the waves crashing against the shoreline of Decker Beach. Her temples were pounding as she knocked on the front door, hard.

Not two seconds later, the door swung open, and Charlotte's heart stopped. Sylvie stood there, her dark curls haphazard around her face, circles under her eyes. Her makeup was running as tears streaked down her face, her trembling hands holding a phone to her ear. She gripped Charlotte's wrist and pulled her inside.

Sylvie tore the phone from her face, let out a small choked sob, and redialed, squeezing her eyes shut. After a moment, she slammed the phone down on the small wooden table in the entrance, a crack in the screen spidering outward and sending little shards of glass scattering onto the floor.

And then Sylvie balled up her fists and screamed.

Charlotte took her by the shoulders and shook her. The words were thick in her throat. "*Sylvie*. Talk to me. What happened."

Sylvie shook her head and began to shake with sobs. Charlotte shook her again. "You need to tell me what happened!"

Sylvie ran a shaking hand through her hair. She looked small and frail, nothing like herself. Charlotte tried to take a breath but couldn't get her lungs to work. Sylvie shuddered, her words coming out in hitched gasps.

"It's gone, Charlotte," she choked out. "It's all gone."

A cold dread seeped into her skin. "What's gone, Sylvie? *What's gone?*"

Tears fell down her cheeks and onto the floor. "The money. All the money, Charlotte. Nick's still gone, and now *all the money from the restaurant is gone.*" She put a hand to her mouth and sobbed against it.

"I don't understand," Charlotte said slowly. The color was gone from Sylvie's face.

"I don't know what he did with it or where he is," she stammered. "But there's nothing left. I had to lock it up. We can't operate, there's nothing to pay anyone. *Every penny is gone.* Everything I ever worked for." She buried her face in her hands.

"The Windmill is done, Charlotte. It's over. It's all over."

RAMONA STRETCHED her arms over her head and leaned back against the swing, staring up at the sky and blinking hard. Her eyes were dry after poring through bookkeeping spreadsheets for most of the day. Afternoon sunlight dappled the porch of the

Seaside House where she'd been working and enjoying the fresh saltwater air and the view of the beautiful blue sea in front of her.

It was going to be a good night—Charlotte, Diane, Ella, and Mariah were all going to be at the Seaside House. Ramona smiled. She'd been surprised when Diane had suggested it. She'd been so distant since she'd first arrived in Marina Cove, and had kept whatever she was going through close to the vest, no matter how much Ramona tried to make her feel like she could open up.

She could see the pain in Diane's eyes over the last weeks, and it broke her heart. Maybe tonight was a first step. Ramona was looking forward to finding out.

The sound of approaching footsteps stirred Ramona from her thoughts. She leaned forward, and her eyebrows drew together.

It was Danny. He had a look in his eyes that sent a shiver down her spine.

Ramona set the laptop on a wicker side table and stood up. "Danny, is everything all right?"

He didn't answer, instead pulling Ramona into a hug. She breathed in his smell as he held her tight, for a little too long. "Danny," she said, pulling back. "What is it?"

Danny rubbed his eyes with the heels of his hands and shook his head. "I need to talk to you, Ramona."

Ramona's heart began beating faster. Nothing good ever started with that sentence. She looked at him and nodded.

He looked at her with a pained expression before exhaling and gazing out over the sea. The water shimmered with pale golden sunlight, and the scent of wildflowers fell over the light breeze. Ramona stepped toward him and reached for his hand. "Danny?"

He turned and looked into her eyes. "It's Caitlyn," he said. Ramona's chest tightened. Had he seen her in the park? Had Caitlyn said something? "I don't even know how to explain this," he said quietly, almost to himself.

"Start at the beginning," Ramona said, bristling. He was scaring her.

He held her gaze. "You know Caitlyn has been around more lately. She's sorted herself out, I guess. Doing really well, from the sound of it. And Lily." His voice caught for a split second. "Cait hasn't been a good mother to Lily in the past, but Lily is enamored with her. She's so young...it's impossible to explain things to her. But Lily...she's desperate for

Caitlyn's love. And Cait's been giving it lately. I don't totally understand what's going on with her. But something has changed."

Ramona shivered as she thought of the sneer Caitlyn had given her. That knowing smirk. The smirk that said that Ramona was the outsider, that Lily and Danny were hers. She was up to something, only Ramona didn't know exactly what that was.

Danny ran a hand through his hair. "Ramona," he said, "Lily came to me last night. I guess she and Caitlyn have gotten to talking. Lily...she wants to enroll in the school near where Caitlyn lives. They've already got all the paperwork together." He let out a breath. "Caitlyn lives in Providence."

Ramona tried to respond, but her mouth couldn't form the words. Danny watched her for a moment before stepping closer to her. "I spoke with Caitlyn. She swears it was Lily's idea. She said she didn't push it. Lily wants to be closer to her. And this is how she wants to do it."

Ramona shook her head once. "Caitlyn can't do that."

"I know. But this isn't something Caitlyn is even pushing. Lily has her heart set on it. For better or worse, Caitlyn is her mother. And she lives and works in Providence. Cait's not gonna move here.

She also knows that I mostly manage Haywood's remotely at this point." He closed his eyes. "What am I supposed to do, tell Lily no? That she can't be closer to her own mother? She's not even my biological child." He stared at Ramona, shaking his head. "I don't know what to do here, Ramona. It isn't so simple. It just isn't. If I say no, Lily will resent me forever. I don't know what to do."

Ramona forced herself to draw a breath. Caitlyn's sneering face over Danny's shoulder reverberated in her mind.

They stood there and looked at each other, the unspoken implications hanging heavily in the air between them. Ramona was tied to Marina Cove; it was her home. Her sisters, her mother, her work...it was all here. She was in the middle of restoring their family home, mired in a lawsuit, working as hard as she could to earn money with her clients who all lived in Marina Cove. Ramona had to stay here.

But Danny didn't have to live here to manage his store. And there was obviously no way he was going to stay while Lily moved to Providence to be with her mother.

Tears welled in her eyes as she met Danny's gaze. She thought of everything they'd been through, how they'd only just taken the first steps together. How fragile it all was. She thought of Lily, that sweet, precious girl she loved with every part of herself.

How for the first time ever, she'd started to feel like she had a little family of her own.

Ramona's heart cracked in two as it all clicked into place. She realized just how powerful Caitlyn was. How she could take everything away, in the blink of an eye.

CHARLOTTE COULD BARELY THINK STRAIGHT AS she stepped onto the golden sand at the edge of Keamy's lot. She paused to let Ollie catch up with her. After losing a short race against a yellow butterfly, he appeared at her side, looking up at her with grave concern in his eyes that was perfectly appropriate for what Charlotte was feeling. She laughed despite herself, and scratched his ears and looked back through the lot. She could just barely make out Christian's figure through the trees as he stood on the front porch of his tiny cabin. He raised a hand to wave to her. She returned it, pushing down the bile forming in her throat.

They'd just spent a long time talking about everything that had happened, Christian holding her as she cried. She'd thought she finally had things figured out, had turned a page in her life. Her job at The Windmill was her future. It represented a new chapter. Never in her life had she felt so happy with her work, with the direction her life was heading.

And now that was all over.

Fresh tears sprang to her eyes as Sylvie's face popped into her mind, the devastation etched across it, the terror. Sylvie was spending the night at her mother's house, not wanting to be in her home with the oppressive silence that reminded her that Nick was gone. Gone with all their money, with everything she had. Charlotte had offered to accompany her, but she'd said that she needed the night to try to process everything, to try to figure out her next moves.

Charlotte's feet carried her mindlessly in the direction of the Seaside House. Diane had asked them together tonight to make dinner. Just the girls. It was an unexpected surprise, but Charlotte was unable to tear her mind away from what had happened this morning. How wrong the restaurant had looked, the lights off and the blinds drawn.

That old sensation crept across her skin, the pins and needles, the tightness in her chest, the burning behind her eyes. She was panicking. Her lungs screamed for a full breath. Charlotte tried to inhale slowly, but her breathing kept hitching in her chest.

How had she found herself in such a mess?

She wiped tears from her eyes as she stepped through the sand, her legs heavy and dragging. She'd been going about everything all wrong. She had no money, she was barely scraping by even with her new job. And now that too was gone.

At The Windmill, she'd had a financial stake in the restaurant, a percentage of new earnings she helped bring in, however small, but it was something that could be scaled. The better the restaurant did, the better Charlotte did. And now it had been stripped away from her. She wasn't going to find that anywhere else, even if they did hire a pastry chef with only a few weeks' experience. It wouldn't be anywhere *near* enough money to get by. And she had no other marketable skills after spending most of her adult life as a stay-at-home mom. What was she going to do, go back to school at this point? With what money?

Charlotte had been naive, a daydreaming child, playing dress-up with the big kids. Her life was a disaster, and she'd been too optimistic and hopeful to really see it. She was sleeping on the freaking hardwood floor of a half-burned-out inn that showed no signs of reopening any time soon, and even when it did, they still had money tied up in the agreement they'd made with Patrick before they discovered his fraudulence. She was helping Ramona tackle her incredible debt and contend with the lawsuit she'd found herself in after losing her home.

Her family needed her help. And now she was out of options.

Her conversation with Christian rang in her ears. He'd been supportive of what she was going to do, like she'd known he would be. But she knew something was off. He was wary. He didn't like it. And she didn't blame him at all.

She replayed Sebastian's visit to her as she lifted her phone from her pocket and pressed the number.

Ring. Ring.

She thought about his proposed meeting with Tex. She imagined standing there next to Sebastian, wedding ring on her finger, holding his hand and laughing at his jokes, trying desperately not to think about Brielle wrapped in his arms. About him and Steph, together in her own home. Sebastian and Charlotte, the happy couple, aren't they so sweet, nothing to see here.

She thought of the money that would result. Money that Charlotte deserved for all the long years of support, for everything she'd done as the equal partner in their marriage before he'd gone and torpedoed it. All the money he lost as he slowly bankrupted Carter Enterprises...but Sebastian was smart. Brilliant, actually. It seemed there was light at the end of the tunnel.

Ring. Ring.

Charlotte didn't trust him, of course. She wasn't stupid.

She would just have to keep her wits about her. Not let things get too far out of control. She could always walk away.

She would be in control of the situation.

With each step, Charlotte felt she was walking into a dark tunnel. Her arms and legs were numb. Her chest was too tight.

Ring. Ring.

Charlotte took a long, shaking breath, and pushed down the voice in her head shouting at her to stop now, to hang up the phone.

That time was over. She was done with her pie-in-the-sky thinking. This was real life, with real stakes, real consequences, not some game she was playing where everyone had a great time and no one kept score. She needed to think about her future.

She wanted a good life with Christian, with her family. Someday, she wanted to build the dream house on Keamy's lot that she and Christian had always talked about when they were teenagers. Someday, she was going to want to retire, and be able to live comfortably. Tendrils of fear snaked through her body and wrapped themselves around her heart, squeezing so hard her chest burned with pain. She wondered what Mariah would think of her now.

What other choice did she have here?

Her skin went cold as Sebastian answered the phone. "Charlotte," he said as she gasped for breath, feeling the steady ground beneath her disappear completely.

Diane stepped onto the front porch of the inn, savoring the cool breeze washing over her skin. She still couldn't get used to how close the shoreline was to the Seaside House, even though she'd grown up here. All those years she'd spent in Los Angeles, and she'd made it to the beach only a handful of times. It had been such a hassle, all the traffic, all the crowds. But here, it was right at their doorstep. She drew in a lungful of crystal clean air and leaned against the railing, watching the beams of moonlight spread across the dark water.

Charlotte, Ramona, and Ella were in the kitchen, working on gathering all the ingredients for tacos and homemade salsa. Mariah had been with them, but had excused herself upstairs, saying she wasn't feeling well. Something had tugged at Diane's mind as Mariah climbed the ancient wooden staircase. Diane recognized something in her look. Something in her voice. She wondered what was going on. Maybe she could bring it up to Charlotte.

Diane sighed. She had been hoping to gather the Keller women together, to talk, to...well, she didn't really know. To bond, or something. It went against Diane's instincts to draw inward, but she was trying to change. She just had no idea how to go about it.

It became clear as they began preparing dinner that they were all going through something of their own. Diane's life had been a whirlwind lately, and she had no idea what her sisters or her mother were doing, what they were going through. The tone wasn't somber, exactly. It was more like the silence before a storm, the air thick with electricity, waiting. Waiting for something.

They were all still learning how to navigate things. It was going to take time. Diane wanted badly to tell them everything about Grant, about his brother. To tell them all she'd learned about Trevor, her decision to keep him out of her life for good. About Austin.

The screen door swung open, and Ramona walked out onto the porch. "Hey, Diane," she said quietly. "Just came to get a bit of fresh air. It's a little hot in there." She sat down on the wooden swing and let out a hard breath, looking out over the dark sea.

Diane's heart beat a little harder as she glanced at Ramona. Her baby sister. A memory ripped through her, little Ramona in her highchair, a yellow bib tucked underneath the thick folds of skin at her neck. Ella helping Diane scoop up her very first spoonful of baby food, sweet potatoes, and gently guiding them toward Ramona's mouth, open with delighted anticipation, her tiny eyes sparkling with amusement, the sound of her giggling the most beautiful and happy sound Diane had ever heard.

Diane crossed the porch and sat down next to

Ramona. Somewhere in there, her baby sister was still there, here, right here in front of her.

Maybe they could find what they'd lost. Diane hoped it wasn't too late.

A few minutes of comfortable silence passed between them before the screen door opened again. Charlotte and Ella both stepped onto the porch and sat down in the wicker chairs across from Diane and Ramona. Diane's stomach twisted as she saw the look in Charlotte's eyes. She'd been putting on a brave face tonight, but something had happened.

Her eyes met her mother's. There was something there too. Disappointment...sadness. Ella looked around at her children.

"Well...here we are," she said, breaking the silence. After a moment, they all laughed, before it dissolved back into a hush.

They looked around at each other knowingly. It was all new to them. So much had changed. It would take a little time. They were learning how to be with each other. How to be there for each other.

Ramona let out a breath and rested her head on Diane's shoulder. Tears pricked at the corners of her eyes. A simple thing, but Ramona had never done anything like that before. Diane leaned her head to rest against Ramona's, breathing in her hair, feeling the slow rise and fall of her chest. Ella took Charlotte's hand and gave it a soft squeeze as a glistening tear trickled down Charlotte's cheek.

The Keller women sat there for a long time. There would be time to talk about everything they were dealing with, everything that had been happening in their lives. Time to take those steps to open up, to be vulnerable, to face the darkness, together.

But for now, they just needed to be with each other. For now, that was enough.

DIANE CLICKED the bedroom door shut and quietly padded down the stairs so she wouldn't wake the others. Everyone in the Seaside House was fast asleep. Diane had no idea what time it was; she'd been checking her phone less often, enjoying the newfound peace brought by no longer being tethered to it twenty-four hours a day.

A pool of moonlight illuminated the ground floor as Diane deftly avoided the creaky hardwood, spent two full minutes inching open the front door that was always stuck, and slipped out into the night.

She smiled as her bare toes crunched into the

cool sand. It brought back memories of summertime nights of long ago, sneaking out into the night, bonfires and dancing under the starlight. She walked toward the shoreline, breathing in the salty air, and then eased into the chilly water up to her knees, shivering slightly.

She looked out over the sea, following the long shimmering trail of moonlight painted against the water's surface that extended to the horizon. After another long, deep breath, the tension between her shoulder blades released. Despite the cold water lapping against her, she felt warmth spreading through her.

Diane watched the water for a long time before turning and following the water's edge south, with no particular place in mind. She'd been lying on the hardwood floor of the Seaside House, replaying everything that had been happening since she'd come back to Marina Cove. Thinking of Grant, of her children. Of Trevor. Of Austin. As her thoughts began to tangle and knot, she decided to go for a walk to clear her mind rather than try to figure everything out all at once.

Time would take care of that for her, she decided. It was time to let go of the reins a little bit. See what happened.

After a while, she came upon a spotless stretch of white sand that curved inland, forming a small bay. Behind the sand, the leaves of a dense copse of oak and birch trees fluttered in the summer breeze. She once knew the name the locals had given the bay, but at some point time had erased the memory, like so much else.

Diane made her way toward the middle of the little cove and sat down, digging her toes deep into the sand and wrapping her arms around her knees. She noticed the long scar running from her knuckle to the crook of her arm. It had stopped hurting after she left Trevor's house, after she let go of the blame she'd directed toward herself for so many years. Diane ran her fingers over the faded line, smiling to herself.

She looked up, and her breath caught as her eyes wandered over the bay in front of her. The sky was clear, cloudless black, and billions of pinpoints of light shone down and reflected against the calm surface of the bay's water like a mirror.

It was like she was floating in pure starlight.

She watched the light, mesmerized, and thought of Kayla. Of the strong woman she'd become. Diane had taken her first steps in repairing their relationship. All she had to do now was keep walking the path. Kayla had made plans to drive back in a few weeks for a little weekend trip. A drive that Diane would not be monitoring from afar.

If something happened...well, Diane's fretting and monitoring and attempts to control it had never had a real effect, had they? They only gave Diane the appearance of control. It was another way Diane was going to let go of the reins, a little bit more each day. She looked down at her wrist, where the rubber band used to lie. The urge to snap it, to try to push away the fearful thoughts, to try to shove down the things she didn't want to think about...it was still there. But it was less intense.

In time, she knew, it would go away completely.

She could face the things she was afraid of, face that feeling of letting go, that feeling of freefall. After finally confronting her grief with Grant's brother, she'd sensed a palpable shift within her. She and Scott had met their pain head-on, sharing the burden, together. As they left the café, they made plans to meet up again on Grant's birthday.

She wasn't alone. She had support now.

It was a start.

Her thoughts turned to Jamie. Hopefully it wasn't too late. She was going to have to try to track him down. Try to explain things. To show him that she loved him, missed him terribly. She would do what she could, and that was really all there was, wasn't there? Learning what you could and couldn't control, and doing what you could to make every day a little bit better than the last. That was all that could be expected of anyone.

Which meant that at some point, she would have to figure out what she was going to do next. Right now, she had an empty house in Los Angeles, and she was unemployed. Something told her that her future didn't lie in helping to sell vegan bratwursts and popsicles and detergent anymore.

As far as the rest of her life, well...she didn't know what that might look like just yet.

And that was okay.

The sound of crunching sand tore her from her thoughts. She whipped her head around to find the source. Someone was approaching her across the sand.

She peered through the semi-darkness, a lungful of air escaping her as she recognized the familiar angle of his jaw, the dark hair that whipped in the wind.

"Diane," said Austin, his eyebrows raised. "I thought that was you. What are you doing here?"

Diane smiled. She hadn't realized her feet had

carried her right to the bay near his house. "I was just going for a midnight stroll. To clear my head."

He nodded. "Yeah, me too." His eyes ran over her face. After a moment, he looked away bashfully. Diane's heart beat a little faster. "Mind if I join you?" he asked tentatively.

She grinned and patted the sand next to her. He sat down, kicked off his shoes, and dug his toes into the sand. They watched the glittering water in silence for a long time, listening to the cool wind. Just existing for a little while. Diane's heart was in her throat as they turned to look at each other.

Heat rushed to her chest as their eyes met. She watched the starlight reflecting against the tiny gold threads streaked through hazel. His expression held a vulnerability, a rawness that sent shivers down her spine.

They'd been through so much. Their lives were inexplicably intertwined, destined to circle around each other, set into motion by a terrible accident they'd both spent a lifetime blaming themselves for. Tears rose to her eyes as she felt what he was feeling, because it was what was flooding throughout her own body. Time had marched on relentlessly as they'd done what they could to move on, to carry on as they walked separate paths over the long years, split by distance and time and pain. Her heart broke as his eyes brimmed with tears. They held their gaze for a long time, the gentle rolling of the water fading into the background, wind whipping at their hair, before Austin's mouth gently curved up into a small smile.

Diane's heart fluttered like a hummingbird as a grin spread across her lips. She turned to look over the water, fire blushing her cheeks, thoughts tearing through her mind.

She had loved Grant, truly loved him. Her grief would be a long and winding path, and she would never stop being heartbroken over what had happened. And at the same time, after three years, she was ready to move on. She was ready to see what would happen next.

She was tired of doing everything alone. Of being alone.

When she'd arrived in Marina Cove, she thought that person might be Trevor. He'd been the perfect drug that satisfied her desire to avoid the misery of her dovetailing life rather than dealing with it head-on. Satisfied it, but only temporarily, taking so much from her in the process.

But just because he hadn't been the right person

didn't mean that she hadn't been ready to find some-one. To maybe find love again.

Maybe the right person had been in front of her all along.

Diane trembled slightly as she stared out over the ocean. She could feel Austin next to her, could feel his heat, his warmth, the swelling rise and fall of his chest. She wondered idly what his mouth might feel like against hers, sending bright sparks popping and cracking throughout her body. Their shared silence pulled and stretched between them, Diane's heart pattering, her stomach in nervous knots.

And then, guided by something outside her awareness, their hands slowly met each other's. She caught a soft hitch in his breath. Their fingers gently interlocked, a perfect fit.

Streaks of electricity leaped across her skin, her senses seeming to sharpen, to come alive. Tears lit in her eyes as the sky burned with brilliant sparkling starlight, the wind sweeping like a hurricane and time skittering around them with reckless abandon. Diane felt their separate, intertwining paths become one. He squeezed her hand, an exhilarating charge rushing from his body into hers. Diane's stomach somersaulted as she returned the squeeze.

She stole a quick glance at Austin out of the

corner of her eye. Color tinged his cheeks as he met her eyes, and they both laughed nervously. She looked back out over the dark sea, her face hot, smiling to herself. She didn't know what was going to happen next. What would happen between them. But right now, her heart danced with excitement, with anticipation, with hope. It was something she hadn't felt for as long as she could remember.

Diane knew that the road ahead was going to be a long one. But as she sat there under the shimmering sky, hand in hand with Austin, she knew she wouldn't have to travel it alone.

EPILOGUE

Ella sighed as she closed out the cash register, rubbing her lower back with one hand. Standing for so long wasn't easy. She glanced out through the front windows. The sun was just beginning its march toward the horizon, painting the sky with beautiful brushstrokes of grapefruit and gold.

Her stomach clenched as she slowly surveyed the bookstore, which looked different in the low light. It was cleaner, sure, more organized, and a wall or two had been repainted, a couple pieces of furniture moved or replaced. But it still looked like the same old bookstore.

Ella thought she'd changed a lot more than she actually had.

It was a work in progress, but Leo seemed to have an excuse for delays each time she had a suggestion. He always relented, telling her over and over that she could change anything she liked, that he knew that change was necessary if he wanted to avoid having to sell the bookstore altogether...but no matter how much he told Ella he was ready to move on, from Martha or whatever was holding him back, it looked like he wasn't ready after all.

Ella walked around the front desk and through the stacks, savoring that beautiful aroma of aged paper. She passed the old blue couch, and as always, thought of Jack. For a moment she could almost hear his voice whispering to her.

She slowed as she approached the back office. Leo had been working in there for several hours. He'd given her an awkward wave when he arrived earlier, his face turning beet red as he then barreled his way through the bookstore in that hunched-over way of his, like he was fighting a storm. It was the first time she'd seen him since the dance.

Ella squared her shoulders, took a breath, and approached the door. It was half-open. She gently knocked and pushed it open at the same time.

Leo was sitting at the desk, his hair unruly, his

eyes red. At the sight of her, he jumped in his seat, his face flushing. He glanced down at a mess of papers in front of him and hastily piled them together and shoved them into the top desk drawer, his eyes skittering across the desk. Beads of sweat dappled his forehead.

Ella frowned. That feeling that he was hiding something brushed against the hairs on the back of her neck.

"Everything okay, Leo?" she asked in a quiet voice.

He ran both hands over his face. "Yes, yes. Sorry, Ella. You just startled me. I was just going through, ah, some paperwork. How can I help you?"

Jack ran through Ella's mind. How much he'd hidden from her. How little she'd known about what he was going through. Until one day, he was gone.

She raised her eyes to meet Leo's. His piercing blue eyes reflected the soft light above his desk. Her mind drifted to their dance, to the way he swept her off her feet, the look in his eyes, the pounding of his heart against hers as they held each other on the dance floor.

As he met her gaze, his eyes softened. There was pain in that expression. Silence stretched between them, Ella's pulse rising faster and faster. He opened his mouth to speak, but then after a moment, slowly closed it again.

There was something there, something between them. She wasn't imagining it. But he seemed to be going through something that he wasn't ready to share, and Ella couldn't make herself vulnerable for someone who wasn't ready to do the same, to open up to her, to be honest with her.

It just wasn't the right time. Maybe it never would be.

But Ella wasn't ready to give up just yet.

She let out a long, slow breath that she'd been holding. "I just wanted to say goodnight."

He nodded softly without breaking eye contact. "Goodnight, Ella. Thank you for all your help. Today...and with everything. I appreciate it more than I can tell you."

Their gazes held for just another moment. Ella knew that if she let go now, they might never find whatever was there between them again. Tears pricked the corners of her eyes as she felt the cold sting of loneliness.

No matter how much you wanted something, you couldn't force it. It wasn't the right way. If it was meant to happen...well. Ella would just have to be patient.

With Leo, and with herself.

She nodded and turned to leave, her throat constricting.

"Wait," Leo called to her. Ella froze for a moment. Something in his voice unsettled her. She stepped back into the office.

He looked haggard in the dim light. "Ella," he whispered.

"What is it, Leo?" she asked, her voice tight. The hair on her arms stood on end.

His bloodshot eyes were wide as he slowly shook his head from side to side. Tears pooled in his bright eyes.

"Ella, there's something I have to tell you," he said. "Something I should've told you a long time ago."

And then Leo began to cry.

THE STORY CONTINUES in book four of the Marina Cove series, *The Shifting Tides*.

Sign up for my newsletter, and you'll also receive

a free exclusive copy of *Summer Starlight*. This book isn't available anywhere else! You can join at sophiekenna.com/seaside.

Thank you so much for reading!

~Sophie

Made in the USA
Las Vegas, NV
23 December 2024

15270513R00256